# MAGIC MINUTES

THE TIME SERIES BOOK TWO

JENNIFER MILLIKIN

ISBN-13: 978-0-9967845-8-0
www.jennifermillikinwrites.com

# PROLOGUE
## NOAH

IT'S SAID THAT WHEN YOU'RE ABOUT TO DIE, YOUR WHOLE LIFE flashes before your eyes. There's no way for me to confirm this, because I'm not currently about to die—as far as I know, anyway—but I'm certain what I'm about to do will create one of the images I'll see before I kick the bucket.

"Noah," my brother says, his voice traveling through the thick wooden door. "You about ready?"

His question could be answered two different ways. Am I dressed? Is my hair combed? Have I tied my bowtie correctly? Do I look like a doofus but also maybe like James Bond in this monkey suit? Then yes, I'm ready.

Am I ready to walk out into that courtyard and create the image I'll probably see on my deathbed?

"Almost," I croak out.

"You nervous?" He pushes open the door and walks in without asking. Brody is shorter than me by two inches, and I've never let him forget it. He insists he's better looking because his chin is square, and his cheekbones are chiseled —just like the shirtless men on the covers of the romance novels his wife reads. I told him Alyssa is looking at the rippled abs on her bookshelf, not the pretty faces.

"A little." Maybe I shouldn't be nervous, but I am. Mostly because I can't stop picturing *her*.

Brody slaps me on the back, the thick black fabric muffling the sound. "I was nervous too. It's normal." He grins his wide, toothy, confident Sutton smile. As if everything has always gone his way, and everything will continue to be grand for him. He married his college sweetheart, and has two kids. Nothing like me. My own lips waver in my second-born, opposite of the first son, Sutton smile.

Brody bends at the waist, falling back onto the small tan couch inside the room I've been given to get ready. From his pocket, he pulls a small plastic bag with five gummy bears.

"Want to relax a little?" He pops one into his mouth and holds out the bag.

"No." I frown at him. "I'd like to be fully present today."

"Suit yourself." He shrugs and throws another one into his mouth. After stuffing the bag back into his pocket, he stands and heads for the door. Before he walks out, he tosses me a last glance. "Noah?"

"Yeah?"

"You made the right choice." The door shuts softly behind him.

Choice? Did I ever really have a choice?

In a few minutes, I'm going to take a trip down the aisle, but the walk down memory lane is too alluring. The memories are easy to conjure, perhaps because they're never far away.

So readily she comes to me, her copper hair alive when sun streaks across it, shades of deep red and burnt orange, like the glow of a dying fire. Her smile, the way it tugged on the constellations of freckles that dotted her nose and beneath her eyes.

Just like on that day, her face twists my heart.

As though I'm dying right now, I see everything in slow motion. Every moment of Ember, drawn out to allow for careful examination. Everything that led me to this day, to this spot. I think, I see, and I wonder.

What if I hadn't stopped when I saw her? What if I let her quirky, electric personality keep me from leaving? What if, on the day I met her, I'd kept my eyes closed instead of letting her open them?

Were those choices I made? Or inevitable plot points in Fate's never-ending story?

Without a knock or warning, the door to my dressing room flies open again. Brody walks in and opens his arms, a question on his face.

I turn back to the full-length mirror and adjust my bow-tie one last time. "Sorry. I'm thinking a lot. About—"

Brody shakes his head, and my words die on my lips.

"You got this man." He says it with strength. His smile is confident, the grin of a man who believes what he's about to say. "Ain't nothing like the real thing."

A smile tugs at one corner of my mouth, and for the first time since I stepped foot in this small room, my nerves disappear.

That woman out there... She's the real thing.

# 1

## NOAH

*Seven years earlier*

I didn't come to the lake for this.

Running without a purpose. That's why I came here. And I would've kept on running too, except for the violent splashes and thrashing arms.

"Hey!" I stand on the shore and yell, panic edging my voice. I pull off my shoes and toss them aside, walking in a few feet. Water splashes the tops of my calves. I pause, waiting to see if the person will stop when she hears me. I'm desperately hoping she's just goofing off.

The movement doesn't stop.

I know it's a girl because of all the hair. It floats on the surface of the water, and when she comes up again, it's slicked halfway down her head. It's red, like a flame.

The water is on fire.

"Hey," I yell again. No response. Fine. I jog in a few more feet and dive under the surface. It's not all that deep here, and there are no waves. I could stand, but it's faster to swim.

My eyes stay open in the fresh water. I'm not sure how long it takes me to reach her. Twenty, maybe thirty seconds? I'm a fast swimmer, and my lung capacity is larger than most.

Her body arches above the water again, just a foot away from me. Reaching out, my arm wraps around her waist and tugs her to my side. With one arm, I keep her locked against me and above the surface; with the other, I tow us through the water. It's slow going, not to mention cold, and it doesn't help that the girl is still struggling. She's twisting and pushing. She's probably scared. Maybe she still thinks she's fighting for her life.

My one-armed strokes are enough to get us to a place where I can stand. The muddy bottom wedges between my toes. Trudging toward the shore, I glance down at the girl I'm towing along. Her body has gone slack, and she's looking at me. Her lips are taut and her eyebrows are pulled together. She's pissed?

"What?" I say sharply, but I'm panting, so it doesn't come out as strongly as I'd like. I can play ninety minutes of soccer with hardly a break, but this *rescuing someone from a lake* thing is harder than it looks.

She doesn't respond. When the water is only to my knees, I let her go. It laps to the middle of her thighs, but I figure she's okay in that depth.

Her arms cross her chest, and she stares at me. Her mouth is still a straight line, and her eyes are bright. Full of something. I don't know what.

The longer she stares, the more my stomach starts to feel weird. She's not just staring... she's evaluating. And for the first time in my life, I'm afraid I'm not measuring up.

"I wasn't drowning," she says, as though it's no big deal. She starts for the shore.

"Looked like it to me." I follow. My voice isn't as calm as hers. The wind picks up, and my wet T-shirt clings to my skin. She's wearing a dress, bluer than the water that surrounds us, and it clings to her. "What were you doing out there if you weren't drowning?"

If anybody's keeping score, let it be known I don't believe the girl.

"Wait." A horrible thought slams into me. "Were you... drowning on purpose?" I can't bring myself to ask her if she was trying to commit suicide.

"No," she answers quickly, looking back at me. "I'm not suicidal," she says softly. "I was dancing."

She resumes trudging through the water, and again I follow. In no time my long strides easily overtake hers.

"Dancing?" I ask.

"Ever heard of it?"

"Nope. Never."

She laughs, and I'm struck by the feeling that I know her from somewhere. She's around my age, I think. It's possible she goes to my high school.

Once on shore, she heads for a cluster of rocks and sits down on the largest, flattest one. Her head dips back, face lifted to the sun, and she stretches out.

"No soccer practice today?" she asks, eyes still closed.

So, she does go to my high school.

"Practice finished up a while ago." My mind races to figure out who she is. I walk closer, looking harder at her under the safety of her closed gaze, as though proximity will increase recognition.

She's beautiful in an unconventional way. If the red hair weren't enough of a differentiator, she wears a tiny diamond in her right nostril. How many girls in my class wear a nose ring? I catch sight of her left ear and count. Seven earrings.

Why only seven? Why not eight? And why aren't there any earrings in her right ear? Does one nose ring equal seven earrings, so that now the left and right sides of her body are balanced?

Despite the excessive earrings, she looks better than any half-drowned possibly suicidal person has a right to. The blue fabric drapes against her creamy skin, and the shocking red hair fans out around her. Her chest rises and falls with her breath, and my eyes are drawn to her collarbone. I've never noticed that part of a girl before. On her, it's captivating.

"Don't you have a girlfriend?" She's got one eye cocked open, and her hand lifts to shield it from the sun.

"Sort of," I say. My unease has more to do with the fact that she knows me, yet I have no idea who she is, and way less to do with the fact that my break-up with Kelsey is still secret, and I've just lied to this girl.

"How do you dance in water?" I ask, before she can ask me to explain my *sort of* relationship status.

"The same way you dance on land." She gives me a perplexed look, like I'm the one who needs help.

"Sure," I say, nodding. I turn, heading to the shoes I threw off before running into the water.

"You don't believe me?" The wind takes her voice and throws it, but I catch what she's asked. With goosebumps covering my arms, I spin around.

"Not really."

Rising gracefully from the boulder, she comes toward me. Her lithe gait reminds me of a goddess. The sun has dried some of her hair, and it falls around her face in waves.

"Put your hands above your head," she instructs.

"You can't be serious."

"I am."

I sigh and look at the lake. It's so calm now.

Raising my hands, I look back at the girl whose name I still don't know.

She nods her approval and lifts her own arms. "Now," she says, "close your eyes and think of your favorite song." As I watch she closes her eyes, and in seconds her hips are swaying. A smile plays on her lips, and she turns in place, until she's facing me again. She looks free. And happy.

Her eyes narrow after she opens them and looks at me. "You didn't do it."

"I...uh...I meant to." I can't confess I was too busy watching her. "I don't know how to dance by myself."

She stares at me again, and again the feeling of being evaluated comes over me. She holds out a hand. "Dance with me?"

I take her open palm and curl my fingers around hers. She steps into me, bringing with her a rush of nerves. Her other hand comes to rest on the back of my neck, and it's her, not me, who makes us move.

It's slow, so slow, and there's nothing to move to. No beat, no timing, no constraints. Nothing to tell us when to start. Nothing to tell us when to stop. She lays her head against my chest, and when I look down at the shock of red, I feel nothing short of wonder. It's a color I've never been this close to.

"I know you don't know who I am," she says against my chest, as we sway together.

I opt for silence. Nothing I say will make it better.

"I'm not mad," she says, with her head still on my chest. "I wouldn't expect you to know me."

Suddenly, I wish I did. She's everything I want to be, and everything I don't have the guts to admit I am. She is all the things.

At some point, she decides our dance is finished. When she steps away from me, I fight the urge to pull her back in. Then, when she picks up her sandals and walks away, I want to ask her to come back.

She pauses just before stepping onto the trail and looks back at me. Tree branches hang down around her, some low enough to brush her shoulders. She looks like she stepped from a fairy tale. "My name is Ember." Then she turns around, and in a few seconds I can't see her anymore.

I want to chase her, take her hand in mine, and tell her I'll never hear music the same way again.

---

"NOAH, WHERE HAVE YOU BEEN?"

My mother stands in the foyer, hands on her hips, her shrewd gaze taking me in. She's not the kind of warm, loving mother I've seen on TV, or like my best friend Tripp's mom. My mom is no-nonsense. Harsh. I tell myself she means well. In my head, I come up with excuses. *She works hard. It's not easy running the vineyard. Raising two boys who want nothing to do with the family business is probably frustrating.*

"Hi, Mom." I come closer, skimming her cheek with a kiss. For some reason this evening I'm feeling softer toward her. Maybe I'll blame it on Ember. "Sorry to worry you. I went for a run by the lake."

"And you're wet because?"

Oops. My fingers touch the side of my shorts, testing to see just how wet I still am. Wet enough to not say I dumped my water bottle on my head after my run.

"I jumped in quickly, to cool off."

She clears her throat and takes a step back. "Dinner is on the stove. Gretchen made zoodles." She throws her eyes upward, a half roll. I hold back my laugh. The half eye-roll is a Johanna Sutton signature look.

"Zoodles?" I ask, glancing apprehensively in the direction of the kitchen.

She twitters her hand in the air. "Your father. You know how he is."

"Right," I say slowly. I've never understood my mother's antagonism toward my father's willingness to try new things. She likes constancy, and he wants to raze a section of field and plant hybrid grapes.

She gestures to the next room. "Go get dinner. I have emails to return."

We go in opposite directions, but her pace is much faster than mine. Her heels make loud clicking sounds against the floor.

In the kitchen, Gretchen prepares a plate for me. Her wide frame takes up nearly the entire front of the oven. She's worked for us for so long, she's practically a member of the family. As a small child I loved burying my face in the front of her apron. There was so much of her to hug, and she always smelled like brownies.

"You're eating late today." She sets the plate on the counter beside the stove and reaches for the ladle. I eye the pile of pale noodles with suspicion. Some of them are green on one side.

"Don't make such a face, Noah. They're not that bad. Mr. Derek requested them." She laughs to herself. "He saw them in a magazine."

There's no point in telling Gretchen she doesn't have to call my dad *Mr*. She ignores me every time.

When my plate is ready she hands it to me. I stifle my automatic revulsion at whatever these fake noodles are and smile my thanks. At least there's tomato sauce on top. "If you made it, I'm sure it's delicious."

She winks and gently pushes me out to the dining room. "Your dad asked me to send you in when you arrived."

Rounding the corner, I walk through the open doorway into the dining room. "Hi, Dad." I step up to the long oak table. The best word to describe my dad is *jolly*. But not like Santa. More like...joyful. His personality can fill a room. He's happy, and makes people laugh. He's a third-generation Sutton, and loves the vineyard with all his heart. Brody and I joke that he loves those grapes more than us. Everyone adores my dad. From the vendors who supply the restaurant adjacent to the vineyard welcome center, to the groups he leads on the daily tour, and all the way out to the cleaning staff.

He looks up from the hardback spread open on the table next to his empty plate. "Noah, there you are." His large hand pushes aside the book. I can't see the title, but I'm interested to know what book is that huge. "Late tonight."

"Yeah." I take my place on his right.

"Kelsey?"

"Uh, no." My eyes flicker down to my plate. My first thought is that the dinner looks like Christmas, but the red sauce reminds me of all the red hair that was nestled against my chest an hour ago.

"Not Kelsey?" His salt-and-pepper eyebrows are on his forehead. "Someone else?"

I push the noodles around and shake my head. I don't want to talk about Kelsey. "I went for a run after practice. I need to increase my cardiovascular stamina."

He nods slowly. "It's getting pretty far along in the school year." He steeples his fingers and rests his chin between the index and middle ones.

My chest puffs out. Heat fills me.

"It's what I want, Dad." It's only ever been soccer for me. I live it, I breath it, I dream it. I have to play it in college, or else... I don't know. The alternative is inconceivable.

"I know, son, but it might be time for you to pick your gaze up from the ball and start looking around." His face is fixed in a concerned stare, the skin between his eyebrows cinched together.

I want to tell him if I kept my gaze on the ball I wouldn't score as many goals as I do, but I keep the comment to myself. Besides, I've heard him say it enough times that I could've said it myself the second he opened his mouth. He's been saying the same thing since the fall when Tripp was picked up by Stanford. But how can I give up on my dream now? And how can he expect me to?

I get where he's coming from. His parents died in a freak boating accident when he was my age. There was no time for college, no time for him to goof off and go to frat parties. On the day they died, he became the owner of Sutton Vineyard, Sutton Wine, and the whole Sutton brand. My determination to play professional soccer doesn't help my dad keep Sutton Wines in the family.

He frowns and sits back in his seat, crossing one ankle over a knee. "I'm not saying anything we haven't talked about before, but I think it bears repeating. The clock is ticking."

He's saying one thing, but all I hear is that I'm not good enough to play on the college level. I know my left foot needs work. I can't score from all angles.

Sullenly I shove a bite of noodles into my mouth. They're okay, a little soft, and they drip sauce, but they're not awful. Honestly, I don't know if I'd even recognize if it tasted bad. The taste in my mouth is already sour.

"And Brody?" I ask because it's my best defense. My

brother is a loner, a guy who sometimes likes to go off the grid. He's not following in Dad's footsteps, he's not a protégé. He's so laid-back he might as well be lying down. He only went to college because my mother made it clear she would kill him if he didn't go. If I believed in the whole birth-order-determines-personality idea, I'd say God switched us by accident.

My father eyes me with the same shrewd attention he gives a withering grape on an otherwise healthy vine. "What about Brody?"

"He's the one half-assing his way through college." Deflect. Always a good strategy when the heat is on me. Plus, Brody's not here to defend himself. If he were, he'd spout some baloney about how he's finding himself.

"We're talking about you. Not Brody."

I sigh around my next mouthful and lean back in my seat.

"I want you to think about what *could* be next for you. Just *in case*." He pushes his chair back from the table and uncrosses his ankle from his knee. "My job is to prepare you for outcomes you may not see yourself. Your job is to act surly and certain I don't know what I'm talking about." He tries to hide a smile. "You're excelling right now."

In another part of the house my mom calls for my dad. He stands and claps me on my back. "Try not to put so much pressure on yourself, Noah. Everything has a way of working itself out." He walks from the room, calling, "Coming, Johanna."

I look down at my plate. A majority of the fake noodles are still piled there, soaked in red sauce. All I can see is a spray of red hair, arms circling the air, and the face of a person who knows much more than I do. I can tell by looking at her that she's not being suffocated by questions with no answers.

If anybody's drowning, it's me.

———

"Come on, Noah," Coach Hutchinson yells, his irritation evident. He has a right to be annoyed. I wasn't paying attention, and I missed the pass.

"You gonna do that in the game?" Coach yells again.

I shake my head, embarrassed. "No, Sir."

To make up for it, I spend the next forty-five minutes giving this practice my all. I'm not the most accurate shot, but my footwork is better than everybody's but Tripp's. The guy has magic feet. Stanford claimed him as soon as they were allowed to.

I follow Tripp to his house after practice. On Wednesday nights his mom makes fried chicken and mashed potatoes. I haven't eaten at home on a Wednesday since I got my driver's license two years ago.

I stand to help Tripp clear the table. "Thanks for dinner, Mrs. B."

Tripp mimics me in a high-pitched voice, and I slug him in the arm. We finish the kitchen and are almost to Tripp's room when he asks where my head was at practice today.

"Nowhere, man." I take my physics homework from my backpack and set it on his desk. "Just a missed pass, that's all."

Tripp falls back on his bed and winds his hands around the back of his head. He looks up at the ceiling, where an almost naked woman spraying herself with a hose stares back at him. *Trash*, my mother would announce with a curled lip if I ever tried to put a poster like that up in my room.

"You were probably dreaming about the ass you get from Kelsey." Tripp says it in a lazy way, like if he says it off-handedly, I'll divulge. Baiting me for details about my sex life is his second-favorite pastime.

I pick up the soccer ball on Tripp's desk and throw it at him. It catches him in the stomach, and he grunts.

"Relax, man," he says, setting the ball on the nightstand. It rolls off, bounces twice on the floor, and comes to a stop against my foot. Reflexively, my toes extend toward it.

"You know I don't talk about Kelsey like that." He doesn't need the reminder. I've never given even a morsel of information, despite his repeated attempts.

It's not like I don't have anything to tell him. Six months of dating Kelsey made for more than enough stories. She has a bit of wild in her, hidden behind the cheer uniform and sweet smile.

"One of these days you might." Tripp laughs.

"Why are you so interested?"

He sits up and grabs his backpack from the floor beside his bed. "If she would've seen me first, she'd be dating me." He takes his homework from his bag and sets it on the bed.

Tripp's said this enough times that I'm over letting it bother me. And, to be fair, he's right. If Tripp had been tasked with showing her to class on her first day of school, she'd probably be my best friend's girlfriend right now. Instead of my ex.

I'm still waiting on Kelsey to break the news to everyone. She wasn't at school today, and I know she doesn't want me telling people why we broke up. Keeping quiet about the true state of my relationship, I raise my middle finger at the best friend I've had since I was seven. He laughs.

We start on our homework, but just like at practice this afternoon, I'm only partially present.

The same face scatters my thoughts again, her gaze strong and mysterious, daring me to be attracted to her. The memory is so vivid, I can nearly feel the thin fabric of her dress, her body heat seeping through. My fingers curl into fists, the pencil gripped awkwardly in my right hand, until I've generated enough warmth to make the memory even more real.

## 2

### EMBER

I HATE THESE STAIRS.

All sixty of them.

And not because there are sixty, but because they're the narrow kind. With their very presence, they dare a person to fall. I'm embarrassed to admit the number of nightmares I've had about them. Realistic ones. With grotesque, limb-cracking endings.

After climbing the obscene number of steps, I stay rooted in front of the door to our small apartment and listen to my mother and sister's argument seep through. This makes tonight their forty-seventh argument about college and my sister's refusal to go. I sigh quietly, count to fifteen, and make my grand entrance just in time to hear my mother inform my sister she's allowing her *condition* to stunt her growth. My sister responds by slamming our door. I say *our* because my sister and I share a room. Not that I'll be getting in there anytime soon.

My guess is that Sky is now hiding in the dark, trying to breathe through the tightening of her chest. My sister's panic attacks can occur at any time, but they often happen following a fight with my mother. They also happen in crowded places, and when she thinks people are looking at her.

My sister is named Sky because her eyes are blue. I'm named Ember for the most obvious reason ever.

My mother must have a thing for colors. When Sky laments her name, I remind her she could have been Sapphire or Cerulean. Then again, I could have been Terra cotta or Maroon, so we should really just find peace with where we landed.

"Hi, Mom." I walk into the kitchen.

Her back is to me, and she's digging through her collection of plastic cups until she finds the one she wants. *Surf City Bar.* On it is a picture of a shark in shorts carrying a surfboard. It's her favorite. I think it's cute she collects these little souvenir cups from random places.

"Hey, hon," she says, turning on the tap and filling her glass. "Sorry you had to come home to that."

I shrug. It's typical. My mom and Sky don't get along much these days. Mom has been pushing Sky to work through her anxiety and go to college. Sky doesn't want to. That's the gist of it.

My mom is right. It has been two years since Sky graduated high school.

This year, I'm the one graduating. I have only two months left, and there has been almost no talk of my college aspirations. No anxiety, no racing heart, no fear of public situations, and I'm left to figure things out on my own. Which I have. Unbeknownst to everyone, I applied to six high-ranking colleges. I've been saving money for years, starting with my first baby-sitting job at twelve. College applications don't come cheap. I've never told my mom, but to be fair, she hasn't asked. Her focus is on Sky, on getting her well, on helping her create a happy life for herself.

It's always the squeaky wheel that gets the grease.

Mom turns around, resting her backside against the sink. She sips from her cup and looks at me with defeat. "Do you want to try talking to her?"

"Sure, Mom." I would rather not, but I feel bad for my mom. Coming home from work and walking in to fight with Sky is probably the last thing she wants.

Together we walk from the kitchen. She goes to the couch and reaches for the remote, while I make the short walk down the hall.

"Sky?" I say with a cautious knock on our bedroom door. Behind me I hear the TV turn on, the sounds of the evening news filtering through our apartment.

The door opens six inches, and Sky peers out. She spends less than a second looking at me, then cranes her neck out to make sure our mom isn't close by, using me as bait to lure her out.

"Why can't she turn that junk down?" Sky mutters, ushering me in and quickly closing the door.

My mother loves the news. Turning it on is the first thing she does when she walks in from work. Actually, no, that's not true. First she washes her hands, and when I say *wash*, I mean she scrubs them. She even uses a little brush to get under her nails. I'm not sure if she's washing off the germs she has picked up being in other peoples' homes all day, or if she's trying to wash off the fact that she's a cleaning lady.

I don't think there's anything disgraceful about her job. But she does.

To me, she's a contributing member of society.

To her, it's embarrassing.

I found a book once, its unlined pages filled with her

flowy script, and a second—sometimes illegible—chunky text. Some pages were poems, some were letters, but both people wrote flowery words of love. My mom and this person were going to spend their lives together, they were both certain of it.

Whoever the man was who wrote those things to my mother, he wasn't my father. My dad left soon after I was born, and from what my mother says, it was the nicest thing he ever could've done for us. She doesn't talk much about him, only to say he had a penchant for making bad choices.

The words in that book, the larger-than-life promises, came from a man my mother refuses to talk about. A few months ago our building's fire alarm went off in the middle of the night, and as we hurried from the apartment, my mother had the book clutched to her chest.

When the tenants trudged back to their apartments after the false alarm, I watched my mother lift the cover to her face and briefly hold it against her cheek.

I don't think I ever want that for myself. To be so hung up on someone I can't move on. To let the past keep me in its clutches. I also don't want to be in the clutches of what's gripping Sky right now. With her hand over her heart, she draws in a gulp of air. Her slow exhale rattles out of her.

"Are you okay?" I flip on the light and go sit beside her on my bed. I don't know why she chooses my bed whenever this happens, but she does it without fail.

"Getting there," she says, placing her free hand on mine.

I stay with her, listening to her draw in a breath. I hold her hand, breathe with her, and do the only thing I know to do to help her.

"I met someone." Met? Such a passive word for what happened when he dragged me from the lake. He *demolished* my senses. *Fractured* my sanity. I was *shattered* by his stoicism, and the desire for excitement that run through him like an undercurrent.

Her head snaps up. Surprised eyes search my face for the possibility of a joke.

"For real?"

"Um hmm." I dig my big toe into the purple cloud-shaped rug that lies between our twin beds.

"Well, come on. Tell me more." She turns so she's facing me, one leg up on the bed. Her face doesn't look stricken anymore, the way it did when she let me in.

"He was nice. Really nice." Another lame word. *Hypnotizing. Soul-infiltrating. Agonizingly beautiful.* We've gone to school together for almost four years, so I already knew he was gorgeous. He became beautiful when he thought he was rescuing me. When I saw his need to understand my swim, subsequent dance, and his curiosity and desire to experience it too. When he shed the skin of unflappable soccer god, and looked at me like I held the key to his whole life, he stopped being merely gorgeous.

His face when he thought I needed saving... Determined, persistent. In that moment, I was the most important thing in the world to him. A stranger mattered enough to dive into a lake fully dressed.

It's hard to explain why I got in the lake. Mostly just to do it. To experience the chilly water, my limbs dancing despite the temperature. I heard that cold water is invigorating, so I thought, *why not?*

Turns out, the person who made that claim about cold water is right. I was full of energy after being in the lake. Full enough that I asked Noah Sutton to dance with me. Even knowing he has a girlfriend. It didn't mean anything. Yet in that moment, the way he was looking at me as if he didn't believe a person could move their body without hearing music, it seemed like I owed it to him to show him how unimportant real music could be. After all, he did think he was saving me from drowning. The least I could do was remove some of his blinders.

"I need more than nice," Sky complains. "Flannel socks are nice. So is the check grandma sends on my birthday. Give me more." She's animated now, no longer frightened of the feeling in her chest.

"He was at the lake. I went there to…"

I don't want to lie, but I also don't want to anger Sky. She hates it when I follow through on my wild ideas. *Just like Mom*, she says, with disapproval she doesn't attempt to conceal. Sky see's Mom's sense of adventure as irresponsible. She doesn't like it when Mom brings home cake for dinner, or saves boxes because maybe we could cover them with washi tape and make a magazine holder. Sky believes in roles, and to her, our mother is not fulfilling hers.

"I went there to be alone for a while. Meditate. Be one with nature. That crunchy stuff." I smile when I say it. *Crunchy* is her favorite word when it comes to describing me, even though I tell her she's wrong. I wash my hair, and I don't make my own shoes out of cardboard and rope.

She barks a laugh, and tells me to stop stalling.

I settle back, my palms on the bed behind me. "There was a guy there jogging. I recognized him, of course." I say *of course* because who wouldn't know who Noah Sutton is?

He's a legend at Northmount. With thick hair the color of straw, and wide shoulders that seem to stretch into forever, he walks the halls of our high school as if they were made for him to step foot there. The girls whisper about him, the guys boast about his abilities on the soccer field. The only person people talk more about is Tripp Benson. He's a carbon copy of Noah, except he has white-blond hair and no desire to do well in school. The girls fall all over him, too, and he rules the soccer field.

None of this is information I've learned firsthand. It's amazing what you can glean when you don't talk to anybody.

"It was Noah Sutton. He didn't know who I was, of course." This *of course* is because I go out of my way to stay hidden. Paired with the fact that we've never had a class together, this means I've pretty much been transparent to him.

Sky groans, her hands on her eyes. She shakes her head. "Why him, Ember?"

"What are you talking about?" The image of Noah standing on the shore, water droplets from the bottom of his soaked shorts making polka-dots in the sand, sticks to my mind. I want to protect it from my sister's dubiousness, from whatever she thinks she has to be skeptical about.

Her eyes are on me, her hands placed on the bed between us. "We're talking about Brody Sutton's little brother, right?"

"I think so," I say slowly. The name sounds vaguely familiar.

"Hopefully Noah is nothing like his brother." She shakes her head, as though I've just made the most grievous of errors.

I shrug. "Doesn't matter anyhow. Noah has a girlfriend." Perky, bouncy, golden-girl Kelsey. She sits three seats away from me in English. Physically, she's a perfect match for Noah. They look better together than Ken and Barbie.

Relief settles over Sky's face.

"You don't have to look so happy," I grumble.

"Sorry. It's just that it's better this way. The first guy you actually like can't be someone who's taken."

I think what she meant to say was that the first guy I like can't be Noah Sutton.

"I know," I say. I know I can't like a guy who already has a girlfriend. And I know I shouldn't like a guy like Noah. He's too... typical. Affluent family, big man on campus, soccer stud. But still, I can't get Noah's kindness and gentle disposition out of my mind. He was so different than what I had assumed he would be.

It's the look in his eyes when we danced. That's what's plaguing me. For a guy who's *common,* his eyes betrayed that his letterman jacket and perfect teeth shouldn't be his defining characteristics. I wonder if Kelsey knows that?

"I'm just looking out for you, Ember. You know that, right?" Sky taps my forearm.

I nod.

"Thanks for helping me out today." With her finger she traces the abstract print of my comforter.

Sky hates her panic attacks. She lives in fear of having one in public. She experiences so much anxiety about having one that I wonder if it creates them.

"Mom is doing the same thing," I say. "Looking out for you, I mean."

Sky gives me a reproachful look. I decide not to tell her she looks like Mom when she does that.

"I thought volunteering at the library would get her off my back," Sky says.

Volunteering was my idea. It got Sky out of the apartment for ten hours a week. If it weren't for that, Sky would stay in our room with her used laptop, working as a medical biller, and hiding out from the world.

"So did I," I admit. "But can you think more about what she's saying?"

"We can't afford it, Ember."

"So?" I challenge her because she needs it.

Sky is a rule-follower, a person who's perfectly content to stay within the parameters she has set for herself. She needs me to tell her to step outside them. My message is the same as my mother's, but she won't listen to Mom.

Sky loves our Mom. I know that. The problem is that she doesn't understand our mother's life choices. Mom's pile of failed pyramid-scheme businesses infuriates Sky. Her choice to break up with Andy, the man she dated for three years, instead of saying *yes* when he proposed, bewildered Sky. With a steady income and a house that would have given us our own rooms, Andy seemed like someone who could stop my mother from having to clean other peoples' toilets.

But, she said no. We weren't told why, either. All she said was, *you know when it's wrong, and you know when it's right.*

I think I know why, and it's romantic and tragic. She must still love the poet.

Maybe they couldn't be together.

Maybe they fought as much as they loved.

Maybe they were doomed from the beginning.

## 3

### EMBER

I'VE SEEN NOAH THREE TIMES SINCE THE DAY AT THE LAKE. Three times in two weeks. I've thought of him at least 1,892 times. Give or take a few.

He was far away, and surrounded by people each time I saw him in person. Does he know he does that? Draw people to him that way? His kindness seems too good to be true. Maybe that's one of the reasons people gravitate to him. They're getting a closer look, trying to figure out if someone can be both handsome and kind.

I can answer that question.

*Yes.*

He's cocky, too, but I can't tell if it's real or for show.

"Ember, aisle five is ready for restocking." Griff, who I call Gruff because he growls most of his words, points in the direction of my next task. "Boxes are waiting for you."

I walk the length of the long checkout counter and step out in front of the candy display. "You know where to find me, Gruff."

He shakes his head, and ambles over to help someone who's walked up to the photo counter. I watch him go, wondering when the last time was that he could look down and see his feet? Judging by all the junk I've seen him consume in the break room, my guess is that it's been a while.

Like Gruff said, there are two boxes waiting for me at the end of aisle five. On my knees, I open them, then pull out the first five deodorant sticks and load them on the shelf. I'm still involved in the mind-numbing work when I see three people pass by and stand at the end of the aisle.

"Shut up, you guys." A female voice says, but she's laughing as she says it. "It's not, like, that big of a deal."

More giggling. Words spoken in a low tone. I scoop another handful of deodorant and line them up on the shelf.

"We just kissed," the same person says. If she's trying to whisper, she's doing a terrible job. "Okay, maybe we did a little more than kiss, but you guys would never tell, right?"

The other girls pledge their devotion and loyalty in a volume that matches the first girl's. I roll my eyes and keep doing my job.

"This doesn't mean I'm not devastated, you know? We dated for *months*. I, like, don't even want to go to school. I don't want everyone to know yet. Especially not with prom so close."

*Is this real?* I'm close to pinching myself right now. Maybe it would wake me from the most ridiculous dream ever.

"Excuse me."

I turn to the person speaking and try not to gape when I see who it is.

"I just need to grab this," the girl says, reaching over and plucking one of the deodorants I stocked. My gaze follows her hand. *Kelsey Moss uses cucumber melon scented deodorant.* As if that is what's important about all this.

"Thanks," she says, skirting me and my boxes. Her friends follow her down the aisle and disappear from my view.

I sit back on my heels, my hand lifting to cup my mouth. The news, and what's possible because of it, sinks into me.

*Kelsey Moss.*

Noah's girlfriend. Or, ex-girlfriend. I think.

It had been her talking, right?

I'm certain it was. Mostly.

Or do I just want it to be her?

Crap.

I finish my stocking while their conversation plays through my mind. Even in replay, I can't figure out which of the three girls was speaking. It couldn't have been Kelsey. It just...couldn't. Nobody would be crazy enough to cheat on Noah Sutton. Seeing her was a reminder I desperately needed. He has a girlfriend. End of story.

With a heavy sigh, I carry the empty boxes to the back. There's no way to know it was definitely Kelsey talking. Thanks to my wishful thinking, there is only one thing I know for sure.

My name has been added to the long list of girls who have a crush on Noah Sutton.

I'm common.

It's the last thing I want to be.

---

Sky's the one who should be doing this, but she's too busy making life harder for herself.

*Self-sabotage.* I read about it online. If Sky doesn't try

harder to get scholarships so she can go to college, she never has to face the fear of having a panic attack in a class full of people. She can continue to work from home, and argue routinely with our mother.

I've come to Northmount High School's library today in hope of someday soon being free from my mother and Sky's locked horns.

The library is impressive. Stacks upon stacks of books, rows upon rows of computers, couches and chairs dotting the landscape. Inspirational posters touting quotes about perseverance and hard work decorate the walls. I'm hunkered down in front of a computer as far as possible from the door. I suppose it doesn't matter how well-hidden I am, because I'm the only one in here. There were five of us, studiously ignoring one another, but now they've all left. *And then there was one*.

Though I came here for Sky, I did need to finish my history paper. I accomplished that task first, now I'm working on the main reason I came. If Sky won't go out and find the scholarships, then I'll do it for her. It isn't hard, and it doesn't take long. She easily could do this herself, but there's no sense in me telling her that.

I hit a button on the screen and hear the sounds of the printer across the room waking up. I get up and grab the paper, but when I take it off the tray I lose my grip and it floats to the ground. Bending to pick it up, I notice a pair of shoes walking into my line of sight, and not just any shoes.

Black, orange, and yellow striped cleats.

They come closer, and I'm frozen in my huddled position.

Paper crinkling in my hand, I look up to the person who's now standing in front of me. Slowly my breath leaks out. My stomach flips, nerves twirling and jumping about.

"Hey," Noah says, lips curling around the word. He brushes back a piece of hair that has fallen into his eyes. I track the movement, taking note of his damp and disheveled hair. I almost laugh when the disobedient hair falls back to nearly the exact place it was just moved from.

I straighten. "Hi." My voice is too soft. So different from the way it sounded when he first pulled me from the water. I was mad he'd interrupted me. That was before I realized he'd thought he was saving me. Before I saw the uncertainty on a face that had only ever looked certain.

We're quiet. I move the bracelets on my wrist up my forearm until they are stuck in the thicker circumference of my arm. Noah looks down at the ground and then back up at me. Three times.

*Since when is the king of Northmount nervous?* He plays in front of packed stadiums. By now his nerves should be numbed by screaming fans and bright lights.

He tilts his head to the side and grins. "You come here often?"

I can't help it. I laugh.

"I expected way better from you."

He pretends to be hurt. "What do you mean? Why?"

"Gee, I don't know. Because you have plenty of practice delivering pickup lines."

The muscles in his face shift, he blinks twice, and I wonder if I could stuff my foot in my mouth any further. The hurt in his expression isn't pretend anymore.

*Way to go.*

"I'm sorry." My apology rushes out, the words tripping over each other. "I didn't mean it like that."

"I'm not a player." His voice grows deeper when he says it, full of conviction, as if he's willing me to believe him.

"That's not what I was saying."

He raises his eyebrows.

I lift my hands. "Okay, it kind of was. But I didn't really mean it. Not in a bad way."

He pulls a strand of hair from my shoulder, looking at it. "I like the color of your hair. It's special. Unique. Like you."

At this I get angry.

I yank my hair from his hand, ignoring the pain in my scalp.

His eyebrows draw together, the confusion in them clear.

"You have a girlfriend," I hiss.

He opens his mouth to speak just as a vibrating sound comes from his pocket. Sighing, he pulls out his phone. "It's my coach. He asked me to run here to give a message to Ms. Crenshaw. He wants to know what's taking me so long."

Noah takes two steps away from me. I hate those two steps.

Even though he has a girlfriend, I hate those two steps.

Even though he's a Sutton and not the kind of guy I should like, I hate those two steps.

"Ember," he says, eyes burning as brightly as my name. "Meet me tomorrow. After school?"

I'm stunned, and it ties up my tongue until all I can say is "Uh..."

"The lake... That can't be it for us." He shakes his head quickly. Another step back. I hate that one just as much. "There's more to us, Ember. When I'm with you, it feels like..." He trails off, a faint pink appearing on his cheeks. "You feel it too. I know you do. There's no way you couldn't."

I swallow hard.

"Five o'clock. At the same spot at the lake. Okay?"

He looks so hopeful that I say yes.

His grin is worth the lie.

I watch him jog out the front door, then trudge back to the computer and shut it down. On my way out I pass Ms. Crenshaw. She waves at me, and the stack of books held against her body by her left arm wobbles.

Sky better nominate me for sister-of-the-year after all of this. I deserve a medal. Possibly a plaque.

One sheet of scholarship opportunities. The price? Me lying to the only boy who's ever taken my heart and put it somewhere below my knees.

Sky had better go to college.

# 4

## NOAH

I stopped by the library today after school, just to see if she was there. She wasn't. Disappointed, I hustled to practice.

I knew I was going to see her at the lake in a couple hours. I just... I don't know. I guess I wanted to see her sooner than that.

I managed to focus during practice, but my stomach has been twisted in knots since I stepped under the spray in the locker room shower. I'm the first person cleaned and dressed today, and I nod at Tripp as I sling my bag over my shoulder and walk out to my car.

Tripp will probably chalk up my odd behavior to me telling him about my breakup with Kelsey. I'll let him think that was it. How can I explain to him about Ember? I barely understand it myself. How could one person, *one encounter*, hit me with the force of a freight train?

My fingers tap the steering wheel the entire drive to the lake. When I get there, I park and climb from my car, following the path through the trees. Last night's rain soaked the aspens and cottonwoods. My shoes press into the ground with each step, imprinting it with the design of my tread. I step from the trees and onto the sand, looking first to the rock where she sat. She's not there, so I turn my gaze to the lake, making certain she didn't decide to dance in the water again. The water is still, the only movement the brilliant prisms of light glittering on the surface.

I go to her rock and sit down to wait.

I wait, and I wait, and then I wait some more.

Pulling out my phone, I decide to see if I have any detective skills. I tap the Facebook icon on the screen and type in her name. I don't know her last name, but how many people can there be who are named Ember?

Turns out, a lot.

Scrolling through the tiny pictures, I search for her, and try not to look at the time on the top of the screen.

After a few minutes and no reward for my efforts, I shove the phone in my pocket and gaze out at the lake. Ember is twenty minutes late. Will she be a no-show? I've never been stood up before. To distract myself, I go over what happened last Monday. The day before Ember came dancing into my life. I think I would've rather not known about Kelsey. Her cheating on me stung more than her breaking up with me.

Looking back on it, I'm happy Kelsey did what she did. She didn't have to cheat, but I'm glad she broke up with me. If I'm being honest, her cheating makes it easier to think about Ember as much as I want to. Without it, I might feel guilty for spending so much time thinking of someone with red hair, when I'm supposed to be mourning the demise of a certain blonde. And what would've happened if I'd met Ember, but Kelsey hadn't confessed what she'd done? I would want Ember no matter what, because magic doesn't happen often. Thankfully things will never have to get that messy.

A very small part of me wants to thank Kelsey. I could return one of her teary voicemails, cut through her *I'm sorry's* and say *thank you*. Kelsey made getting to know Ember an option for me. It's an opportunity I want to have.

Assuming she shows up. Yesterday in the library she was shocked to see me, and then she was happy. She wore a skirt that reached all the way to the ground and a tank top with a feather printed on the front. Her ear was lined with all those shiny earrings, and I wondered again how I've been missing her all these years.

Fishing my phone from my pocket, I check the time. Five forty-seven.

She's not coming.

The realization sinks me, pushing my shoulders down and vaporizing the elated air I came here on. I climb off the rock, trudge back through the sand, and cross the moist forest floor, twigs snapping beneath me.

My phone vibrates in my hand, and for a thoughtless second, I think somehow she got my number. Maybe her detective skills are better than mine.

It's not her.

My mother wants me to bring home pain reliever. She has a headache. I toss the phone on my passenger seat and rub my own head, as though I'm the one with the headache.

All the way to the drugstore, I replay the first time I met Ember. I go back over the blue of her eyes, with those three brown dots in the left one. Even her eye color is extraordinary.

I want to find her. I want to ask her why she didn't show.

More than anything, I really want to kiss her.

HEADACHE MEDICINE IN HAND, I HEAD UP FRONT TO THE cashier. I'm almost there when I see it.

Red hair, tied in a loose braid. The person it belongs to grabs it from her back and lays it over one shoulder. She's sitting on her knees so I can only see her back, which is covered in a bright yellow vest. I sneak around into the next aisle and walk its length, coming out and rounding the end. I stop ten feet away from her.

"You either forgot to meet me or you lost track of time." I hear my arrogance. Blame it on my wounded ego.

Ember's head flies up from the open box in front of her. Her eyes are wide. Her lips twist, and a small smile breaks through. She stays where she is, and since it's awkward for me to be standing above her, I walk closer and sink down so we're eye to eye. Peering into the box, I see random junk. A water gun. Stickers. One of those paddles with the little rubber ball attached to it by a string.

"Neither of those things happened." She pulls out a handful of toys.

Crap. She no-showed on purpose.

"You said you'd meet me," I remind her. "I was there. At five."

She sighs, threading the last of the small children's toys around the metal rod they hang on. She stands, and I stand with her.

"I know."

"Why didn't you come?"

I feel like an idiot. Can't I just take it on the chin and move on? I'm single now. I should be enjoying that. The problem is that I don't want anyone else. Ember arrived in my life suddenly, splashing and flailing, asking me to dance without music, and now all I want is to get to know her. I want to understand why I felt lighter and happier in the few minutes I spent in her presence. My parents' insistence that I learn to love the family business, and my stress over playing soccer in college, disappeared.

She opens her mouth, but a large, bearded man comes around the corner and barks her name. I jump when he does it, but Ember doesn't flinch.

"Check-out," he says, stiffly throwing a thumb behind him.

Ember's lips tug at the corners as if she wants to laugh. I don't know why. I want to slug the guy for talking to her like that. She turns and walks to the front of the store. Her braid slides off her shoulder and onto her back. The copper shade looks garish against the yellow vest.

Holding the bottle I came in here for, I join the others in line. When it's my turn, she rings up the medicine and places it in the plastic bag. She recites the total, and I panic. I can't leave now. I don't have her number. I don't even know her last name.

Quickly I grab a bag of some kind of candy from the display below the counter. I toss it onto the surface, and blurt out the most important thing I have to say to her, because I'm not sure when I'll get a chance to again. "Kelsey and I broke up."

Her eyes widen a fraction as she scans the barcode and recites my new total.

I need more time.

Without looking, I grab at something else and toss it down. "She was cheating on me." I don't want her to think I broke up with Kelsey for her. That might scare her off, and it's becoming clear she's not tripping over herself to date me.

She nods but now a smile tugs at one corner of her mouth.

"Come on," the guy behind me mutters. I ignore him.

To make sure I get more than a second with her, I grab everything my hands can carry and dump it onto the counter. Her shoulders shake with her laughter as she scans the candy and various last-minute items. Chapstick. A pair of nail clippers. I don't know what else.

"Let's try it again, okay?" I say. "Tomorrow? Same place and time?" My heart does a ridiculous dance when I see her lips say *yes*. I slip my mom's credit card through the machine so Ember can get back to her job.

She flashes me a shy smile as I turn to go.

I'm happy the whole way home. I don't think she'll stand me up again. Maybe if I'd told her about Kelsey when I saw her yesterday at the library, she would have met me today. The more I think about it, the more I like the fact that Ember didn't show. She thought I was still in a relationship. Like any decent person, she wasn't going to pursue something with someone who wasn't available. It's makes me like her even more.

I park in the garage and head into the house, feeling more prepared to face my parents than I have in weeks. The bag with the medicine smacks my thigh as I walk to my mom's office to give her the Tylenol.

The bag is far heavier than it should be, but I'm feeling lighter than air.

## 5

## NOAH

"WHAT ARE YOU DOING HOME, NOAH? NO PRACTICE TODAY?"
My mom pulls open the pantry door and steps in. It's good
to see that medicine worked for her yesterday. When I went
to her office last night to hand her the pills she had her head
down on her desk, and one arm draped over her head.

"It's Friday." I lean a forearm against the counter and
wait for her to come back out.

"Noah?" she calls, her voice muffled. "Come help me."

I walk in behind her, and she loads me up with ingredi-
ents. "What are you doing?" I ask, bewildered. I'm holding
flour, salt, and three bottles of seasonings I can't read the
name of because they're facing away from me.

"Cooking. What does it look like I'm doing?"

I bite back my response. When was the last time I saw
my mother cook anything?

"Do you want help?" I have some time before I leave to
meet Ember. She promised not to show me up today, and
I'm really hoping she keeps that promise.

She leans a hand on the marble countertop and pushes

her hair from her eyes with her other one. "I'd like to say no to that, but unfortunately I think I do need some help. My talents don't lie in the kitchen."

Leaning over, I glance over the recipe she has printed out. *Shepherd's Pie.* We divide and conquer. She tells me my job is to brown the ground beef, while she focuses on the dough.

"How are you, Noah?" she asks.

It's an odd question to be asking your son, isn't it? She sees me every day. Shouldn't she have an idea of how I'm doing?

"Fine. Why?"

"I talked to Laurel today." Hesitant eyes meet mine.

*She thinks I'm heartbroken.*

Now I understand her question.

"She told you about Kelsey and me?" I pick up the bag of frozen mixed vegetables and pour them into a different pan.

Kelsey's mom and my mom are close friends. They meet for spin every morning. It's a form of exercise I don't understand. Why ride a bike to nowhere? I like to run, to kick the ball. I want every individual pass, kick, and dribble to be focused on that one thing—scoring a goal.

"She said Kelsey was upset this whole past week. I looked like a fool asking her why." She gives me a reproachful look.

"Sorry," I mutter, stirring the meat.

"Why haven't you told me before now?"

I shrug. "No reason. I guess I just didn't think to."

Mom wipes her hands on a kitchen towel and stares at me. "Aren't you upset?"

"Sure," I lie. More of a fib, really. Lies imply a degree of malice. Fibs protect. Sometimes, anyway.

The hamburger meat is brownish gray now, all the pink cooked out. I set down the wooden spoon I've been using to stir and step back from the stove. "I'm going to take off."

If I hadn't looked her way, I wouldn't have seen the hurt that flitted across my mom's face. But I did, and now I feel bad. Just not enough to keep me here.

"Save me some?"

"Of course." She nods as she adds the cooked veggies into the pan with the meat. "For someone who was broken up with recently, you seem a little too happy." She eyes me for a moment, then turns her attention to folding the mixture.

My hand runs through my hair as I wait for her to ask the question. When she's finished folding, she knocks the spoon against the rim of the pan. Utensil poised in mid-air, she turns to me. "Was there someone else? Were you cheating on Kelsey?" Her face is calm, no judgment furrowing her brows or challenging gleam in her eyes.

I screw up my face, the very opposite of her stoic expression. "That's a terrible question to ask. Do you think I would do that?"

"If you did, I would need to know. So I can be ahead of it. Manage the damage. Laurel will be furious if she finds out." She turns back to the stove, lifting the pan and turning down the burner. The orange flame changes from yellow to orange to blue as it dwindles, and then it disappears.

My mother's lavender silk blouse is protected by an apron as she pours the meat and veggie mixture into a pie plate. In this exact moment she looks like a classy home-maker, but I'm not letting this once-in-a-decade scratch-cooking routine fool me. She's a shark.

"I didn't cheat, Mom." I can't throw Kelsey under the

bus. She didn't tell her mother what really happened, and I won't be the one to say it. "Sometimes things just don't work out. You've been with dad forever, so maybe you've forgotten that."

When she turns around, she is less poised. A moment ago, she was unmoved by the possibility of me cheating on Kelsey, maybe even callous about it, but that has been replaced by some emotion I can't name.

"I've been married to your father for twenty-two years, but my memory stretches back a bit further." She slams her hands into baking mitts and slides the pie into the oven.

"Sorry, Mom, I didn't mean—"

"It's fine." She waves off my apology. "I'm fine. You should go to wherever it is you're going."

For a second I consider telling her about Ember. How just the thought of her makes my heart race like it wants to burst from my chest and run a marathon. How the only other time I've been this excited was when I was a freshman and saw my name on the roster for varsity soccer. That was the day I stopped being known only as Brody Sutton's little brother. Finally I was making a name for myself.

If my mom had a modicum of understanding, if she weren't so embroiled in living a life free from emotion and love, maybe I would tell her about the girl I stumbled upon.

"Bye, Mom." I reach out for her, but she's facing away from me now. Her back is rigid, her shoulders stiff, and she says goodbye to the air instead of me.

I feel bad leaving like this, but I have somewhere to be. By the time I'm halfway to the lake, thoughts of my mom and the kitchen conversation drift away. Images of Ember fill my brain, and excitement sweeps my body until I'm pulsing with adrenaline. It's the same feeling that comes over me when I'm preparing to take the field, a stadium filled with cheering students and parents surrounding me.

Like yesterday, I come upon an empty parking lot. According to the clock on my dash, I'm five minutes late.

My heart heavy, my adrenaline decreasing at a steady rate, I climb from my car. On uncertain legs I walk the trail I blazed yesterday afternoon. She won't stand me up a second time, will she? I get closer to the lake and see red. It's stark against the colors of the landscape. I think it's officially my favorite color.

I make it through the trees and onto the sand. Ember grins when she sees me.

"You came," she says, glancing at her watch. Her chest heaves with her relief.

I walk to where she sits on the smooth, flat rock, legs dangling off the side.

"I would never no-show. That would be rude."

She laughs, head thrown back, and I know in this very moment, I will always see this image when I think of happiness.

"You're beautiful." I should be embarrassed to be that forward. Aren't I supposed to keep all my thoughts and feelings to myself? I'm in front of her now, and I can't hide from what I said. The words float between us, growing bigger and wider by the second, like block lettering in an advertisement.

Ember doesn't shy away from my compliment. She doesn't demure, say something about how it's her new make-up, or try to brush it off. She tilts her head up and smiles, soaking in my compliment, unabashed and unafraid.

I've never been so attracted to anybody in my whole life.

Without thinking, without knowing what I'm doing, I

reach out and capture a lock of her hair. It slides through my fingers, copper against cream, softer than silk. This time she doesn't snatch it away.

"I think you might be obsessed with my hair." She twists her lips as she says it.

"This shade of red is my new favorite color," I confess, holding the hair out between us. "What would you do if I smelled your hair right now?" I ask, emboldened by nothing more than the beautiful girl in front of me.

Ember laughs again. "I'd run, screaming in fear."

"Would you?"

She shakes her head, her hair falling from my grasp. "No. Though I didn't take you for a hair-smeller."

"What does that mean?"

"You look like someone who's more likely to drape his letterman jacket across my shoulders than smell my hair."

"Maybe I have some freak in me after all."

Ember's lips purse together as she watches me with eyes that wait for me to realize what I've said.

*Oh, shit.*

"I didn't mean it like that," I say, the words tumbling from my lips.

Ember tips her head and studies me. "How did you mean it?"

What is it about that gaze that rips me in two? She studies me like I'm a brand-new subject. AP Noah.

"Um, just that, you know, maybe I'm not so normal after all."

"Normal is a relative term."

I nod, not sure what to say. Ember seems wise. Too wise for her age, which makes me realize I don't know exactly how old she is, or which grade she's in. And I still don't know her last name. I haven't asked around school about her, because the last thing I need is a churning rumor mill.

She laughs when I ask her age. I figure this is the safest question, because her age could help me guess her grade.

"I feel stupid asking." I'm trying to come across as goofy, but really I'm embarrassed.

"That's okay with me." Ember places her palms behind her and leans back on them.

The rock she's sitting on is large enough for two, so I sit beside her. Glancing up at her, I reach down for a small rock and run it through my fingers. "You're okay with me feeling stupid?" The sun's glare makes my eyes water, and I blink away the moisture.

"Yes," she answers quickly. "I've been in school with you for three-and-a-half years." She points to her head. "My hair could be a beacon in the dark, and you have no clue who I am."

"But you still came," I say, a burst of breath puffing out as I hurl the rock at the water. It bounces one, two, three times before disappearing beneath the surface.

"I couldn't pass up the chance to see if Noah Sutton was as dreamy as he's seemed all these years." She places prayer hands across her cheek and rolls her eyes upward, pretending to swoon.

My eyes go upward too, but it's because I'm rolling them.

Ember drops the act and turns to face me, pulling her legs up into her chest. "I already know the Noah Sutton I've seen at school. I'm here because I want to know who you are when you're not kicking a soccer ball, or parading around campus." She untucks her legs and crisscrosses them on the small section of rock between us. Leaning forward, she lightly touches my temple. "I want to know who you are in here." Her hand falls to my chest. "And in here."

My pulse quickens. She can't possibly know, and yet she's zeroed in on my secret. I've never told anybody, and the words, teetering on the brink in that space between my lips, still won't come out. Instead, I say something just as true, and it takes me by surprise.

"I don't think I know who I am yet." Did I know that about myself before I said it?

"I don't think any of us do, Noah."

"You seem to know more than most people our age."

Her face shifts into a reluctant, sad smile. "Different experiences teach us different things."

She looks at her watch, the smile slipping away. "I need to go."

"But we've only been here for a little while. Can't you stay?" I try my lower lip pout and pleading eyes. It always works with Gretchen. She gives me extra chocolate silk pie when I bring out the puppy dog eyes.

"I have to work."

"This late?" I glance up at the sky. It's already turning dark pink and purple.

"I close every Friday night." She says it matter-of-factly, no regret at being unable to attend parties or go to the movies. Things I do on Friday nights.

I lean in to her, so that only six inches separates our faces. "You know I'm going to have to kiss you before you go."

Ember's hand finds my arm, it's warmth seeping through the thin cotton shirt I'm wearing. "I'd be angry if you didn't," she whispers.

And then Ember blows my mind.

She takes every experience I've had with girls and tosses it right on its naïve head.

Closing the distance, *she* kisses *me*. Not with a small,

tentative peck either. No, this is an all-out, balls to the wall, hands tangling in hair kind of kiss. One that has me rising and falling, gasping for air, and then taking it from her. Just as suddenly as she started it, she pulls back.

"I'm not done," I complain, my eyes tracing her reddened cheeks. I'm certain they're flushed from the kiss, not from embarrassment. She doesn't seem to embarrass at all.

She laughs and gets up from the rock.

"Next time," she says. "I can't be late for work."

"Next time," I echo, standing too. "Can I take you to a movie tomorrow night?"

"I'm baby-sitting until five."

I fall into step beside her. "You're a hard worker." We reach the path where I first spotted her in the lake. She shrugs but stays quiet. Did I say something wrong? "It's admirable," I add quickly, pulling her hand into mine, and when she leans her head on my upper arm, I feel the relief drip from me.

We step from the trees and into the parking lot, and I wish she didn't have to leave. I want to take her somewhere and ask her questions, starting with *where the hell have you been hiding yourself?* I can't imagine I was ever in proximity to her and didn't know it. The way I react to her, the automatic interest, how could any of that have slipped by me? How has she been slipping by me for the last three and a half years?

"There's my ride." She points to a bike leaning against a tree on the far side of the parking lot.

"You're going to bike all the way to work?" That's crazy. It's way too far, especially with the sun going down.

"It's three-point-four miles from here. I checked."

"Wouldn't a car be faster?"

"Yes," she says, lifting her head slowly and bringing it

back down in one drawn-out nod, "a car would be faster." She levels me with her gaze, and my heart lands with a heavy thud in my abdomen.

"Can we reverse to twenty seconds ago, before I asked the presumptuous question that made me look like a privileged ass?" I rub the back of my neck with my free hand.

"Aren't you privileged?" Her eyes have laser-beam focus. Her voice doesn't convey any jealousy or indignation. She's merely asking a question and seeking an honest answer.

"Yes, I am. Am I also an ass?"

She holds up a hand, tipping it left to right. "A little, but you do it with finesse. You make it cute, not so...ass-y."

"Ass-y?"

"It's a word. I just made it one."

She looks adorable right now, with the breeze moving the baby hairs around her face and the smattering of freckles across her cheeks. I can't help what I'm about to do.

This time, *I* kiss *her*. It's easier now, without the rock to dictate how we can move. I pull her against me until I can feel her heart pounding on my chest. The lines of her body melt into mine when she throws her arms around my neck and kisses me as if I'm going off to war. That's the only way I can think to describe it.

Ember kisses the same way she accepts a compliment. Freely and without reservation. She puts her whole self into it.

I could stand here and kiss her until every star in the sky makes an appearance, but I know she needs to leave. "Let me drive you to work," I plead, dragging my mouth from hers.

She agrees, and I jog to her bike. It has to go in my trunk at a weird angle, but it fits. We get in and she looks back at her bike.

"I thought soccer *moms* drove SUV's. Not soccer *players,*" she teases, turning around to face front. Reaching across the center console, she lightly pinches my forearm. I give her a dirty look as I start the car and put it in drive.

"Black Beauty is not a *mom car*." I try to give her the stern look Gretchen sometimes gives me, but it falls apart when my gaze lands on hers.

"You named your mom-car after a horse?"

I can't help it. I laugh so hard I nearly miss the turn onto the main road.

"You're impossible," I say, reaching over to rest my hand on her thigh.

"You're ass-y." She replies, setting her hand on mine.

In minutes we're in front of her work. I pull her bike from the back of my car while she digs through her purse.

"Here." She scribbles onto a small piece of paper and hands it to me. "Text me tomorrow and tell me what time you'll be picking me up."

I agree and pull Ember in for a quick, chaste kiss. Before I let her go, I run a thumb from her lips to her ear. She leans into my touch and grins, then turns to leave. Like a lovesick idiot, I stand there, smiling, and watch her wheel her bike to the rack.

She turns around and cups her hands to her mouth. "Dane," she calls, giving me a final wave as she sails through the automatic doors.

*What?*

Oh. Her last name. I shake my head at the absurdity of all this. At Ember and me. At this incredible girl who was there all along. I'm chuckling to myself and not paying attention. I'm so wrapped up in my thoughts that I don't notice my mother's car parked two spaces down until I'm in the driver's seat.

Our eyes meet through our windows. I feel the guilt on my face, but it's her expression that doesn't make sense. Her hand is across her heart, and her face looks stunned.

I back out first, and my mother follows.

When we get home, she says nothing. She pretends as if she didn't see me in the parking lot. In a high-pitched voice she tells me there are leftovers for me in the fridge, and that my father will be working late tonight. When I go to the fridge, I see a whole lot more than leftovers. The entire shepherd's pie sits in its glass pie plate, untouched.

My mother has disappeared, it seems, so I dig out a massive slice and warm it in the microwave. Sitting down by myself at the dining room table, I count eleven empty seats.

Why do we have a massive table? I can't remember a time when it was full. The only person who comes for dinner is my grandmother, and it's clear my mother invites her over out of obligation. Every moment with her is painful. She criticizes every move we make, usually focusing on Mom. She's ninety-one and healthier than anyone that old should be. Secretly, I think she's just too mean to die.

Aside from that royal pain in the ass, nobody else comes for dinner. So why all the chairs?

My dinner, although delicious, is lonely. It makes me miss my brother. If he were here, he'd make a joke about Mom being a better cook than Gretchen, and then he'd sneak me some beer from the second fridge in the garage.

Pushing my plate away, I unfold my legs from under my seat and lean back. The only light on is the one above my head. The rest of the room is under shadow.

If Ember were here, she'd light up the whole room. Not just with her red hair, but her whole personality. I like the way she teases me. *Ass-y*. What is it about that made up word that makes me smile?

Right now Ember is at work, wearing that terrible yellow vest and ringing up people's purchases. And I'm here, in this big house, with only my thoughts for company.

Something tells me Ember never has to eat dinner alone.

## 6

### EMBER

I DON'T DO SNEAKY WELL. FOR ME, HONESTY IS PREFERABLE, even when it hurts. I'd rather hear *I don't like you* than *it's not you, it's me*. But every other Saturday, after I cash my check from the drugstore, I sneak into my mother's room and open the top drawer of her nightstand.

Today just happens to be the day of my bi-weekly sneak. A few minutes ago my mom and Sky left to run errands, giving me plenty of time to get in and out of her room. When I saw her car back out from the space and drive away, I came in here.

Drawer open, I remove a small stack of white envelopes and lay them out on her bed. *Groceries. Rent. Sky college. Ember college. Gas. Spending money.*

Reaching around to the back pocket of my jeans, I pull out a small wad of cash and unfold it.

The largest amount goes into the rent envelope. Groceries and gas gets less. Next is spending money. I don't touch the college envelopes. It's sweet of my mom, and it makes me love her even more, but realistically there will never be enough money in those envelopes to pay for us to go to college. It'll be scholarships and loans for us. If Sky ever goes at all.

My college situation is a mess. Yes, I applied. Yes, I've received acceptance letters from all but one. I'd jump at the chance to go to every one of them, but it's not in the cards for me. At least, not right away. Most of them are out of state. Sky still needs help. I applied knowing I wasn't going to go. I wanted the validation of an acceptance letter. *You're good enough to be here.* And I got it. Five times. Jury's still out on the sixth one.

"Ember?" Sky yells from the living room.

I jump at the sound of my name and scramble to gather the envelopes. My fingers shake as I toss them in and attempt to gently close the drawer.

"Yeah?" I yell, then walk out. Sky stands in the kitchen, her eyes moving quickly from countertop to table, then around one more time.

"I need Mom's car charger." She looks at me as I come in. "Why were you in Mom's room?"

"Uhhh..." I don't lie well either. It kind of goes hand-in-hand with the sneaky thing I don't like doing. "I was looking through her stuff. I have a date tonight." Both of those things are true, so technically I didn't lie.

"You have a date tonight?" It's not Sky asking me this question. It's my mom, who's standing in the open apartment door.

"Yep." I grin. I can't help it.

"And he's coming here to pick you up?" Her eyes sweep our home, picking out the faults.

"I'll clean up before he arrives." I could clean for ten years and it wouldn't put thread back into the couch cushions or remove water rings from the coffee table, but my words seem to appease her.

"Here's your charger, Mom." Sky passes me on her way to the door, the white string dangling from her outstretched hand.

"Don't forget, you're babysitting at eleven." Mom leans on the door handle, opening the door wider so Sky can walk through.

"I won't. See you both at five."

She blows me a kiss and closes the door. I count to ninety, then go to peer out the window and make sure her car is gone. It is, so I hurry back into her room and open the drawer. She keeps the envelopes in a tidy stack, and they're always in the same order. When everything is straightened properly, I shut the drawer and leave her room.

Unless she believes in some kind of money fairy, she must know it's me padding the envelopes every two weeks. Still, I'd rather she not tell me she knows.

Some things are better left unsaid.

---

"WYATT, COME HERE." I FEIGN RIGHT AND LEAP LEFT.

The Ficus tree Wyatt is hiding behind tips as he leans onto the edge of the woven basket it sits in. Wyatt has turned his body into a pogo stick, and the Ficus is going to either fall on him, or fall on the ground. Apparently, the boy thinks what I'm doing is funny, and his screeching laughter bounces off the walls of the small living room. His eyes are the size of Frisbees, and he jumps up and down repeatedly.

*I swear on all that is holy I will never have a child who acts like this.*

Lurching forward, I grab the other side of the basket just before it tips all the way over. Wyatt cackles and runs to his room.

And me?

I slump down onto the floor and lean my head against the couch. Two minutes of rest before I have to stand on tiptoe and feel along the top of the door for the nail. No doubt Wyatt has locked himself in his room. It's one of his many tricks.

The bright spot in all this is what's on the schedule tonight. Not even the behavior of a tyrannical three-year-old can take away from my excitement about seeing Noah again. A real date. No lake, no school library, and no drugstore.

At the sound of Wyatt's wail, I rush toward his room. He opens his door as I approach, his face scrunched up and tears flowing.

"I bonked my head," he says, lips quivering. His arms are open, so I scoop him up and hold him close.

His little body settles into me, and I smile into his hair. Wyatt is as mercurial as they come.

When his mother gets home at five, she looks as exhausted as I feel.

"Three more hours until bedtime," she says with a laugh, handing me some cash. I don't count it. Her Saturday lunch shift at the restaurant around the corner isn't a big money maker, and sometimes she can't afford to pay me my hourly rate. I come back every Saturday because she needs the help, and Wyatt is good birth control. Not that I need any, because that's what someone who actually has sex would need, but it's a joke I make to Sky.

On the short walk back to my apartment, a text message pops up on my screen from an unknown number.

*Can I pick you up at six?*

A grin stretches my cheeks. I write my address and pause, wondering if I should say something else. Something cute. I can't think of anything and, thanks to the three dots, now he knows I'm over-thinking my response. I shake my head and hit send.

Noah arrives at exactly six o'clock. He's wearing jeans, a T-shirt, and an expensive looking hoodie that's zipped up halfway. I know because I watched from my bedroom window as he got out of his car.

My mom is on my heels as I go to the door. I frown and swat at her. She jumps backs and laughs nervously. I think she's more excited for my date than I am.

I open the door, and there he is. "Noah. Hi."

He grins at me but doesn't say anything. We stare at each other for a few moments before my mom's hand snakes past me. Her *hello* is loud in my ear.

"Mrs. Dane, it's nice to meet you."

"Call me Maddie. Would you like to come in?" She steps back, pulling my hand so I'm forced to step back too.

"Noah and I have a movie to get to, Mom." I incline my head to the world outside our door. "We should probably get going."

"The movie doesn't start for a while," Noah chimes in, his gaze on me. "I was going to take you to grab some dinner first, but we can visit for a few minutes."

I back up all the way, and Noah steps in. My mom leads him to the couch and offers him a glass of water.

I'm not embarrassed about what little we have. Not at all. I love that my mom works hard to provide for us. I don't waste one second of my life wishing for more. I have everything I need to be happy. The rest is material. But I do wonder what Noah is seeing. I know what his eyes are taking in, but how is he processing it?

I sit beside him as my mom places a glass of water on a coaster on the table. It's hard not to laugh, considering the coaster is right beside a place where the wood is swollen from a spill from some unknown time, maybe even from a previous owner.

"Thank you, Maddie."

Mom sits in the butter yellow recliner adjacent to the sofa. "Noah, tell me a little about yourself."

Noah wipes his palms on his denim-covered thighs. "I'm a senior, like Ember." He glances quickly at me. "I play on the soccer team. I'd like to get on a college team, but..." He pauses, shakes his head, and one side of his lips curl up. It's not a smile though. Just disappointment. "I'm not sure that will happen."

Mom nods. "Are you good?"

"At soccer?" Noah ducks his head. "Yes," he answers in a quiet voice, rubbing the back of his neck with one hand.

Mom smiles. "Don't be embarrassed to say you're good at something. There is nothing wrong with that."

Noah casts his gaze on me. The look of disappointment is gone, and now a smile pulls at his lips.

"Is there something funny I'm not aware of?" I ask.

"Nope. Just thinking of something."

"Well," my mom says, rising. "I'll let you two get on with your night. It was nice to meet you, Noah."

"You as well." Noah stands and reaches out for a second handshake, but my mom takes him by surprise with a hug.

"I'm a hugger." She steps back and shrugs. "It's a disease for which there is no cure."

Noah grins at her. I get up as he walks around the coffee table. Mom grabs my elbow from behind and leans into my ear. "Last name?" she asks in a whisper.

Oh, duh. Concerned parent, and all that.

"Sutton," I whisper back without looking at her. "Bye."

We walk out, and behind me I hear the lock slide into

place. Noah's hand slips in mine, and we take our time going down the treacherous stairs to the ground level.

After we get buckled into his car, he turns to me. "Your mom is...warm."

"Warm?"

"You'll understand when you meet my mom."

"She's...cold?"

"She doesn't like to show emotion, and she doesn't like when others show it. She likes to be strong all the time. Stoic, my dad calls her. He loves her, though. That counts for something, right?"

"I guess so. Tell me about your dad."

"He runs Sutton Vineyards. He loves it." Noah's mouth turns down as he says it.

"Why does that make you frown?"

Noah is quiet as he turns out of the apartment complex and onto the street. He taps the fingers of his free hand against his lips.

"It's what I'll probably end up doing."

"You didn't answer my question." I arch an eyebrow and cock my head to the side.

"If I work for the family business, it means my soccer career is over. It means it never even started." His whole body deflates, like he's melting into the driver's seat.

My heart twists at the sight of his vulnerability. "You're scared?" My voice is soft. I can't imagine what it must feel like to have a passion with a stop sign. As though reaching a certain time in life signifies the ending of a dedication and devotion that has ruled all your years until that point.

Noah lifts his shoulders and drops them quickly. "I guess so. I've never told anybody that."

I place a hand on his upper arm, wanting more than

anything to be able to wipe the look of fear from his face. "Everything will be okay."

"Do you know that for certain?" The hope in his voice tells me he wants me to answer in the affirmative.

I can't help the sad feeling that comes over me. For a guy with a seemingly solid future, he's very unsettled. "No. But things have a way of working out."

"I like your apartment." His subject change is anything but subtle.

I move my hand back from his arm. "You only saw the living room." Not that he needed that pointed out to him.

"I know. But I like it. It felt...home-ish."

"Now who's the one making up words?"

Noah tips back his head and laughs. He takes my hands from where they lay intertwined on my lap, slips his fingers through mine, and gives me a squeeze.

"Ass-y and home-ish." He barks a laugh. "We're quite a pair."

"We could switch the words around, and it would be ass-ish and homey." Though homey isn't a word that could ever be used to describe Noah.

"You're ass-ish," he says, his eyebrows wiggling.

I scrunch my nose. "False."

"Your ass looks pretty good to me."

I feign shock. "Are you admitting to having checked out my hiney?"

Noah glances at me, his eyebrows about an inch above where they normally are. "Did you just say hiney?"

"Yes."

"The only other person I've heard use that word is my housekeeper, Gretchen." Noah's eyes grow wide as soon as he's finished saying his housekeeper's name. "I'm so sorry. I didn't think—"

I hold up my free hand. "Stop. I don't care. You can tell me that you have seven hundred and eighty-two pairs of shoes and I wouldn't care. I mean, I would suggest you give ninety-two percent of them to charity, but other than that, I don't care."

Noah pulls into a space in front of a little Italian restaurant and cuts the engine.

"I feel like a fool." He pushes back his hair and turns his body so he's facing me.

We need a re-do. That's what my mom calls it when one of us says something we don't mean, usually when we're hangry. We start the scene or conversation over, and it's like the prior one never existed. Placing my hand in the space between us, I smile. "Hi, my name is Ember Dane."

Noah squints and his eyebrows scrunch together.

My outstretched hand shakes the air, and Noah gets the idea. He places his hand in mine and says, "Noah Sutton."

"It's nice to meet you Noah. Aren't you glad we live in a Utopian society where money doesn't matter? Where all that matters is how kind we are to one another?" Our hands fall to rest on the console, but I'm not finished talking. "Noah, I don't come from money, but that doesn't mean you should be embarrassed that you do. It's okay with me if you talk about Gretchen. You can tell me about your gardener too, if you have one. Money is nice to have, but it doesn't dictate how happy we are. What brings you joy, Noah?"

"Soccer. Running on the field, and feeling my legs burn. After I've been playing for a long time my breath feels thicker, like it's working harder to come out. And—"

He tears his gaze from me and out to somewhere on the street.

"Go on," I urge.

"I like the games," he continues hesitantly. "The crowd.

Their enthusiasm. Bleachers full of people yelling my name." He looks back at me, worry in his features. "Is that shallow?"

"Not at all. There's nothing wrong with being recognized for your passion."

"If only Stanford would recognize me." He shakes his head. "It's too late now though. They've already made their choice."

"It's still spring." I don't understand, but that's not surprising. I don't watch sports, and I have no idea how recruiting goes.

"The guys they want on their team next fall were picked at the beginning of this school year." Sadness isn't even the right word to describe what he looks like he's feeling. Maybe heartbreak? "This season is it for me. I'll start telling people I *used* to play in high school. Then time will go on and it will change to *I played growing up*."

His eyes swim with emotion, hopelessness and anguish brushing the surface. And when I see that, I understand. He's mourning a dream. From the moment I looked into Noah's eyes, I knew there was more to him than a letter jacket and the most perfect hair on the planet.

"I'm so sorry." Our hands are still wrapped around each other, so I pull one free to rub his arm.

"You make it better." Releasing my hand, he uses both of his to cup my face. "You're magic."

He leans in and softly brushes his lips on my cheek. I feel the hot breath of his gentle sigh, and the dragging of his lips across my skin. Before he can reach my lips, I've turned toward him, meeting him. I feel his smile, and then his need. Grateful, hungry kisses, and I feel like I'm floating.

When he pulls back, I miss his touch. My core is warm

and my limbs feel like they're charged with electricity. I want more, even though I've never had *more*.

"Wow." He clears his throat, but his lips are curled into a satisfied smile. "I don't know about you, but I just worked up an appetite."

A deep breath slides through me, slowing my heart rate to a less frenzied pace. I reach for my purse, hook it around my shoulder, and point a warning finger at Noah. "Don't be scared off by how many ravioli's I can eat. I chased a crazy toddler around for six hours today." I can eat a ton of ravioli even when I've done nothing but be a couch potato all day, too.

"Let's get you fed then."

We walk across the parking lot, and he pulls me close to his side. Dipping his lips to my ear, he whispers "Soccer isn't the only thing that brings me joy."

"No?" I grin up at him.

"Nope."

He pulls me in again, just before we reach the entrance. His kiss tastes like everything I want. Devotion and yearning, love and lust. The gotta-have-it-or-I'll-die feeling I read about in romance novels. And magic. Before Noah, I didn't realize magic had a taste. But now I know it does. It tastes like longing. Fascination. Magnetism. A blend where flavor meets feeling, swirling and mixing until they combine into one powerful experience.

# 7

# NOAH

"Are we ever going to meet this secret girlfriend of yours?" My mom gives me a look.

"Wait, what?" Brody pauses, a bowl of sautéed green beans held in mid-air. I swipe them and add some to the empty spot next to my roasted chicken.

"You have a girlfriend?" Brody roughly grabs for the dish, and a few green beans fly onto the table. "Didn't you and Kelsey break up two seconds ago?"

"We broke up three weeks ago, but you'd know that if you came around more."

Brody tucks into his plate instead of responding. I know he's irritated I haven't filled him in, but I've been spending every minute with Ember that I possibly can. It has been two very glorious weeks since we went on our first date.

"Well, Noah?" Mom has her dark eyes zeroed in on me.

It's not that I don't want my family to get to know Ember. It's more that Ember is important and all-consuming. She has absorbed every part of me. With her quiet under-standing and infectious personality, she slipped into my soul. I've seen her every night since our first date. Even on the nights she works. Those nights might be my favorite, because she only has fifteen minutes between her shift ending and when her mom wants her home. On those nights, she kisses me with something she called *reckless abandon*. I laughed when she said it, and she told me the phrase is cliché, but she finally understood what it felt like.

In a short time, Ember has become my world. I've been keeping her to myself because I don't want to share her. It's that simple.

"Soon," I mutter, looking down at my plate. *Never*, I want to say, even though I know that's impossible.

"This weekend." My mom gives me a pointed look. "Saturday dinner. Got it?"

I nod. My stomach knots. My mother loved Kelsey, but she might not feel that way if she knew Kelsey cheated.

Ember and Kelsey couldn't be more different. Which pretty much guarantees my mom won't like her.

*Fuck.*

I lean over my plate and eat quickly, then leave the table as soon as I can manage. I need some air.

I should have known Brody would head straight for me. So much for being alone.

"What are you doing out here?" His voice reaches me before he does. I'm glad it did, too, otherwise I might have pissed myself.

It's quiet out here, and dark. I'm only a quarter mile from the house, but it's far enough that the outside lights don't penetrate the space. The vineyards are in the distance. The grass is overdue for a cut, and the wind makes faint whistling sounds as it zooms through it. On the right side of the property is a line of massive trees, their bare branches outlined in the moonlight. In the light of day I can see the trees have new green leaves that haven't fully unfurled. Over the years I've spent a lot of time out here at night, and I've never been sure whether to call it eery or peaceful.

Brody slides besides me onto the top of the picnic table.

"Kind of creepy out here at night." He surveys the scene as he leans sideways and digs into his jacket pocket. After pulling out two beers, he hands one to me. "What's up, little brother?"

For a moment the only noise is the sound of tops popping.

I shrug and take a drink. My dad's beer is way better than the crap my friends have at house parties.

"I'm not Mom." Brody nudges me. "You can talk to me about your girl."

My mind swirls with thoughts, but none of them make it into a coherent sentence and out of my mouth. How am I supposed to tell my big brother that it's taken me only two and a half weeks to fall harder for Ember than I ever did for Kelsey? He said it himself at dinner. *Didn't you and Kelsey break up two seconds ago?*

"Okay, I'll talk instead." Brody sets his can down between us and props his elbows on his knees. Chin resting on an open palm, he looks out at the dark vastness before us. "I met someone too. Alyssa."

I look at him, surprised. Brody doesn't do serious. He never has. And I mean never, even though plenty determined girls have tried to change his mind. I'll never forget the day he stood in my room and told me the cardinal rule of girls: Tell them what they want to hear. He followed it up with: And always please them first. My fourteen-year-old brain wanted to explode.

"Do you like her?" It's a stupid question, but I'm not sure what to say.

"I love her."

I nod, trying not to show my shock. "That's great. You should bring her to dinner on Saturday. Take a little heat off me."

Brody barks a laugh. "No way. Saturday is all about you. And it's too bad I won't be there to see it. LA trip." He lifts his hands and shrugs quickly.

I groan, rolling my neck in a circle and rubbing the back of it with one hand.

"Now it's your turn. Talk," Brody orders in his superior, I'm-the-older-brother voice.

Given what he said at dinner, I figure it best to start by explaining what happened with Kelsey. "It was some guy she met in Cancun on spring break. Unoriginal, I know," I add when Brody raises his eyebrows. "She could've done better than that, right?"

Brody chuckles, and I can't believe I can even make a joke of it now.

"Mom doesn't know Kelsey cheated, and I want to keep it that way."

"You don't owe Kelsey that."

"I know, but I don't need to smear her name."

Brody eyes me suspiciously. "You're being really zen about your girlfriend of six months cheating on you."

"Ex-girlfriend," I clarify.

Brody waves his hand dismissively. "Enough with Kelsey. Let's get to the good stuff. Who is your new girl?"

I halt. The words were flowing a minute ago, and now they're jumbled in my head again.

"Stop thinking. Just say it. I can tell it's serious."

Running a thumb over my lip, I think of this afternoon with Ember, before I had to be home for dinner. She'd stayed at the library and read articles on the internet while I was at soccer practice. When I finished, she met me at my car and I drove her home. That was all the time we had.

In the car she confessed to having applied to six different colleges, just to see if she'd get in. She got in to five so far, all out of state. The last one is the same place I'm still waiting on. *Stanford.*

"You're going to see a sixth letter of acceptance," I'd stated confidently. Inside, I wanted to cry. How had I not thought that far ahead? Mere months separate us from fall. The possibility of us going to different colleges just doesn't seem real.

Thinking about our conversation upsets me, so I open my mouth and tell Brody everything. Even about the lake and how I met her. He laughs hysterically when I tell him how annoyed she looked when I pulled her out.

"Here I was, thinking I was some knight in shining armor on a white horse, and she gave me this look that screamed *beat it.*" I laugh too, and shake my head, remembering Ember in that soaking wet blue dress and the irritation in her eyes.

"Where is she going to college?" Brody asks.

"Well..." I pause, thinking of what Ember told me in my car this afternoon. "She's been accepted at five places, but they're out of state and a little out of her price range." Technically, she said she'd never be able to afford anything but community college, and even then she'll need financial assistance.

He gives me a bewildered look. "So why doesn't she go somewhere in-state?"

*Oh.* This is how Ember must feel when I thoughtlessly assume she can do something without considering the money it takes to do it.

"Her family isn't well-off."

"Gotcha. Sorry." He claps my back. "What are you doing about college?"

"Still waiting on Stanford. I'll try-out for a walk-on if they don't recruit me." I shrug. I hate that idea. I know it's my ego talking, but I can't stand the idea of not being sought out. I don't mind working hard, but being chosen is the best feeling in the world.

"Would Ember be able to go to Stanford? Scholarships, financial aid, all that?"

"Maybe. I'm not sure. It's an awkward subject."

He nods and falls quiet. I wish I could snap my fingers and make everything work out for us. Until talking to her this afternoon I hadn't even thought about us going to different colleges... Or her not going at all. I've been too busy falling in love with her to dip my toe in the pool of reality. The idea of not being with her makes me sick inside.

"Ember's better than the rest, Brody." My voice sobers when I admit this.

Brody shakes his head. "Not better than Alyssa."

He reaches out a fisted hand and I pound it. We sit back and finish our beers in silence.

Maybe Stanford not picking me up is a blessing after all. Maybe Ember and I can be one of those couples who stay together forever. I can take over the vineyard. We can get married, and at our wedding people will talk about how we were high school sweethearts. We'll have kids, grow old, and I'll have her breakfast ready before she wakes up in the morning, and we'll do old people things, like garden and golf.

Yeah.

YEAH.

Fuck you, Stanford.

I don't need you.

I have Ember Dane.

And we're meant to be.

---

Turns out, Ember doesn't share my hesitance about Saturday night dinner.

"That sounds great." She smiles and nods happily, stretching out on her twin bed in her small room. I look over at her sister's bed. I made a fool of myself when Ember brought me in here tonight and I asked why she had two beds in her room. Ember laughed and kissed me, pulling back once to mouth the word *privileged*.

I laughed too, and then resumed kissing her. My lips on hers has quickly become one of my favorite pastimes. It ranks somewhere close to soccer. Hell, it may even surpass it.

Ember was the one who pulled away first, gasping for breath. She giggled and placed a hand over her heart. That's when I told her about my mom's dinner invite, and her eyes lit up in excitement.

"You should come early. I'll show you around the property." I'll have to get a crash-course from my dad first. He'll probably die of shock that I'm showing interest.

"I've never been to a vineyard before." Her voice is dreamy.

From my back I roll to my side, pushing up onto an elbow and peering down at her.

"Are you dating me for my vineyard?" I wiggle my eyebrows.

"Ding ding ding!" She pokes my chest as she says each word. "We have a winner!"

Dipping my head, my lips suspended millimeters above hers, I whisper "I'll take my prize now."

Ember doesn't wait for me to lower my lips. She lifts up, and with a hand cupping the back of my neck, pulls me down with her.

I love this about her. Willing, wanting, and not at all embarrassed by it.

I kiss her until my lungs nearly burst. She kisses me until her cheeks are scarlet and her body trembles. My hand moves down to the hem of her shirt, and I feel her sharp intake of breath when I grab a fistful of fabric and lift it. I make my way down her torso, kissing her exposed neck and collarbone as I go.

My goal is to start at the belly button and make my way up to her breasts. Every time we kiss she presses them against me, and it's been killing me not to be able to touch them and taste them. This is the first time we've been alone, and the first time we've been horizontal. It's like her body is a display window of confections, and I'm a kid with a fistful of money, just waiting to be let in.

I lift her shirt higher, but I'm distracted before the fabric can ascend her breasts. On Ember's right side and extending across her ribcage, is a tattoo.

"When did you get this?" My fingers trace the exploding dandelion, following the little pieces that float onto her ribs. It's mesmerizing...and sexy.

Ember props herself on her elbows and looks down at me. Over the swell of her breasts I spy her face, eyes hooded and pink lips parted.

Lowering my head, I kiss her tattoo, then trail my tongue over it, leaving goosebumps in my wake. What is it about her having a tattoo that is making me want to ravage her?

"Last September," Ember pants, lying back down. Her hand runs through my hair. "On my eighteenth birthday."

"I like it," I say, my words muffled by her warm skin.

I know my plan was to explore her breasts, but my hand seems to have a mind of its own. It's trails down, over the flatness of her stomach, and dips beneath the waistband of her sweats. Skimming along the smooth skin between her hip points, my hand rides her rapid breathing like a wave.

She's sweeter than frosting, spicier than gingerbread, and every cell in my body is screaming at me to devour her.

My hand drifts lower, lower, lower.

*Go slowly.* It's our first time together, and I want to cherish it.

I bring my mouth to hers and kiss her deeply, drinking in the girl who splashed her way into my life, and proceeded to soak my whole being.

Heat radiates from between her legs, searing the palm I have held an inch above her.

I can't take it anymore.

I can't take the tip of her nose running up and down my neck. The arch of her back and the soft, mewling sounds she makes when I kiss her.

"Look at me," I say, and her eyes slowly open. I want to watch her face the first time I touch her.

My open palm drops a heavy inch. Moisture and warmth coats the underside of my hand the second I touch her.

Her eyes widen, and not in a good way. The muscles at the top of her inner thighs tense against my hand.

"I'm sorry," she says, squeezing her eyes shut. "I'm stupid, I'm sorry."

"No, no, it's okay." I pull my hand away and surreptitiously wipe it on my jeans. She wouldn't have seen me even if I'd waved it in the air in front of her, because now she has a forearm thrown over her eyes.

"Are you all right?" I tug at her fingers, making her arms flop down. Her eyes open, peering at me through copper lashes. In them I see embarrassment and frustration, but also relief.

"It's just..." She tries to push herself up, and I moved aside quickly to give her space. I'd give her anything right now. She's not the only one feeling embarrassed. *Did I misread her signals? Was I pushing her to a place she didn't want to go?* The thoughts nearly crush me.

When Ember's upright, she folds her legs beneath herself and bites at her bottom lip. Red blossoms onto her cheeks as she opens her mouth. "I've never done that before. I've never done *anything* before."

Her words sink in. "So you're a—"

"Yes," she answers. "And obviously you're not," the words rush from her mouth, and when she realizes what she's said, she slaps a hand over her lips. "I'm sorry, I didn't mean it like that."

Then Ember does something I didn't imagine my strong, fierce, and bold girlfriend could do. Tears dribble over the lower rims of her eyes and glide down her face. I pull her against me, and she cries softly against my chest.

I don't tell her, but I'm crying on the inside too. I wish I were as inexperienced as she is. I wish I could give her my first time.

She lets me soothe her only for a minute. When she sits up, she wipes at her cheeks, and her eyes are bright and wide. "I thought I was ready. I'm kind of sick of being a virgin, you know?"

"Don't worry. You'll know when you're ready." A dark thought crosses my mind, and possession snakes through me, curling my insides. "I want to be your first, though, Ember." The thought of someone else being inside her, earning a place in her memory as her first time, makes me see red. And I'm not a violent person.

Ember slices through my internal outrage with peals of laughter.

"What?"

"You," she says, and offers no more.

"Me, what?"

"You're being possessive. I kind of like it. Of course you'll be my first, unless you're planning to break up with me tomorrow. Then no deal."

"Ember. Mine." I pound my chest with a fist and growl the words. "Ember belong to Noah."

I grunt, and she laughs again. I grunt two more times, she calls me a caveman, and I knock her back onto the bed. Through trial and error, I've learned the only place she's ticklish are her thighs, so I squeeze the tops of them, making her howl with laughter. Between her loud laughter and my prehistoric grunting, we don't hear anyone come home until the bedroom door flies open and her mom and sister are standing there, staring at us.

Ember laughs even harder at their faces, but I sober quickly, thinking of what they could have walked in on instead.

Later, when I'm in bed, trying hard not to think about Ember's body and her physical readiness *again*, my phone pings with a text from her.

*I can't imagine anyone else but you being my first. I want that memory.*

Lifting my chin to the ceiling, I mouth two words.

*Thank you.*

8

---

**EMBER**

If the way I'm feeling right now is any indication, I'm not as confident and self-accepting as I think I am.

I like these pants. Made of stone colored linen, they cinch at my waist. A stretch of the same fabric wraps around my waist and ties into a pretty bow, the remaining fabric hanging down to my upper thigh. My fitted tank top is white, and I chose it for two reasons. One, white looks great against my hair color. Two, it's my favorite color. The color of innocence, light, and goodness. And virginity. *Something I almost lost a couple nights ago.*

The words *keep going* had been right there, dangling off the tip of my tongue as I trailed it over his bobbing Adam's apple, but I didn't say them. I know what I want. I knew it then, too, but something stopped me. Maybe it was the hugeness of the choice that made me put on the brakes? Right now, meeting his family feels as overwhelming as nearly handing out my v-card.

"What do you think?" I ask my mom, walking into her line of sight and blocking the television. Sky sits beside her on the sofa, her head tipped back and her mouth open. She makes soft sleeping sounds with every exhale.

I turn in a circle and stretch my arms out, so I look like a revolving T. I've added three beaded bracelets to my right wrist—one black, one gray, and one lemon yellow. I like yellow with white. It's happy.

"Nose ring?" Mom asks in a quiet voice, setting her knitting project down in the middle of a row and looking up at me. There's hope in her eyes, and as much as I hate to dash it, I have to.

Poking the tiny fake diamond with my pointer finger, I shake my head. "It's me. It's who I am."

She sighs. I've heard that sigh so many times, including last September when I came home with the tattoo Noah thinks is beyond sexy. "Fine, fine," she mutters, holding up her hands.

Nodding to Sky, I ask my mom if she has plans tonight.

She glances at the sleeping person beside her, and her lips twist into a half smile. "This is it."

Suddenly I wish I were staying here with them. I could change into my pajamas and take my position on my mother's left side. We'd turn on a cheesy 80's movie, and giggle about how bad it is.

"I got my outfit at Bradley's Exchange," I blurt out. My eyes fall to the floor, to where my toes peek out from the tan wedges I borrowed from my mom's closet. I'm not embarrassed to be admitting this to her. I'm mortified that I care where I got my outfit. *I don't care about those things, right?* I think the nerves have me feeling other things that don't fall in line with my beliefs.

It doesn't matter how much money Noah's family has. Kindness can't be bought. I've believed that ever since fourth grade when I saw some older popular girls bully someone in gym class. Those girls all came from money, but their behavior was cheap. Brand-name clothes eventually go out of style, but decency never will.

"Never mind," I add quickly. "Forget I said that."

Mom beams. "That's my girl." She pulls her knitting from her lap and sets it beside her. The scarf she's making Sky unrolls and nearly reaches the floor. She'll make my scarf next. Every year she makes Sky's first. Don't ask me why she starts in the spring. It's not like they take that long. It's also not very cold here, but on the days when it's cold enough to wear a scarf, I find myself thankful to have one.

Mom stands, holding open her arms. I allow her to fold me into her scent. She smells of tropical-flower shampoo and lemon-scented cleaner.

"I feel like I'm releasing you into the lion's den, Ember."

I make a face and step back. "Why?"

She shakes her head and rubs her fingers over her tired eyes. "No reason. Don't worry about it. I'm just a silly mom nervous for you, that's all."

I laugh and step back. Noah will be here any minute to pick me up. "Everything will be fine," I assure her. Not that I believe it.

"Wake me up when you get home, okay?" She looks over at Sky, who hasn't moved an inch even though we've been talking a few feet from her. "Just looking at her makes me tired."

I smile and say nothing of the ten hours of manual labor my mom put in today.

"Mom, I—" I'm cut off by a knock at the front door.

"Knock 'em dead, honey." She smiles at me mischievously. "Slay." She's trying to keep a straight face but she can't. The giggle breaks through.

"Slay?" I ask, throwing the word behind me as I open the

door for Noah. There is nothing worse than a parent using popular slang in an awkward way.

"Slay?" he repeats, laughing. "Did we slay our outfits?" He's in a white dress shirt and tan slacks. Oddly similar to mine.

Leaning his head in the door, he waves at my mom.

"I think we slaughtered them. No originality at all." I blow my mom a kiss and close the door behind me.

"Couples who stay together for a long time start to look alike." Noah takes my hand as we walk down the stairs.

"Three weeks, though? What will we look like when we're old and wrinkled? Twins?" I scrunch my nose at the thought.

Noah pauses on the bottom step. He plants his feet and turns to where I stand on the second step. "Speaking of old and wrinkled"—he snakes his arms around my waist and pulls me flush against him—"my grandmother is coming for dinner tonight."

"So?" My fingers lightly stroke the back of his neck and trail through his hair. I love touching him like this. It's intimate. Comfortable. A month ago, I would never, ever have said I'd be in this position at all, let alone with Noah Sutton. "I'm great with old people," I tell him. It's true, they love me. I talk with them in the drugstore all the time. Last week a sweet old woman couldn't find her purse, and I located it next to the condoms. For real. Nestled right there between *ribbed for her pleasure* and *magnum-size* boxes. I couldn't make up a story like that if I tried.

The apprehension seeps from Noah's wary eyes. "She's not a normal, sweet old lady. She's awful."

I frown.

"I'm serious, Ember, and I'm afraid I'm tossing you into a shark's tank. An ancient, ill-tempered, white-haired shark."

"You're being dramatic."

"I'm not, and I wouldn't blame you if you faked an illness to get out of tonight."

My hands fall away from Noah's neck, and I cross my arms. It's awkward, because of how close he's standing, but I keep them there. "I am not faking an illness, but I am starting to think maybe you don't want to introduce me because of *me* and not *her*."

Noah rolls his eyes. "I couldn't be prouder of my girlfriend."

"Girlfriend?" I'm smiling. I've never been anyone's girlfriend before.

Noah unfolds my arms and steps in to kiss me. "Do you have a problem with labels?" he asks against my lips.

I've never thought about it before, but now that I think about it... No, I don't.

"Nope." I kiss him lightly. He kisses me back, then smiles as he steps away.

I laugh and jump down the two steps, forgetting for a moment that I'm wearing wedges. I land safely and tug Noah's arm until he follows me to his car.

"Are you sure you're ready?" He eyes me as he shifts into reverse.

I nod. Bring on the predators.

I'm not scared.

Lions, sharks, and rich families, oh my.

---

WELL, CRAP. I WAS WARNED.

Noah said shark, but I was picturing one of the more benign sharks. Like the kind I've seen on Shark Week. Maybe Sand Tigers, with their ferocious sharp teeth that have never tasted human flesh. Or Whale Sharks, which survive solely on zooplankton. Gentle giants.

The shark in front of me is a well-honed killing machine. Without any type of conscience, I'm certain. Those wrinkles don't fool me. She's shrewd enough to know better, wizened enough to feign being senile. *The sweet spot.*

I was nervous to meet his mother, but I shouldn't have been. Johanna is nothing compared to his grandmother. Where Johanna is quiet and watchful, Mrs. Rosenthal is outspoken. And racist. And xenophobic. Noah warned me just before we walked into his house. I feel bad for her. What a crappy way for a person to spend her days.

Noah's dad is the total opposite. Derek is friendly and kind—and carrying the entire dinner conversation.

"Ember, have you applied to any colleges?" He looks genuinely interested.

"I have." I pause to wipe the corners of my mouth with a napkin before replacing it on my lap. "Six, actually." Halfway through rattling off the list, Mrs. Rosenthal interrupts me.

"You'll have to go on scholarship, I'm sure."

Johanna's sharp intake of breath is the only sound at the table. Derek and Noah wear different expressions of shock. Bulging eyes, open mouths. Mrs. Rosenthal's head bobbles on her neck, and she takes a tiny bite of food.

"Probably," I nod. "I imagine I'll also have to take out student loans, and work my way through school. It may take me longer than four years."

It's hard to keep a straight face, but I manage it. She's not pleased to hear about my station in her twisted world, and I've just sunk in the dagger a little further.

Johanna changes the subject, and Noah's grandmother

has very little to say after that. She may have even nodded off once while Derek was telling me about the vineyard.

After dinner Noah asks me to take a walk with him. Johanna tells her mother it's time to go back to the independent living facility. On their way out the door, I hear Mrs. Rosenthal gripe loudly about my hair color. "It's just so red," she squawks. "Like her—"

They're out the door before I can hear the last word. It doesn't matter anyway. I don't need to hear the disparaging remark.

Noah's cheeks are the color of my hair. "I am so sorry," he murmurs.

I shrug. "Doesn't bother me. I like my hair."

We step onto the dark back porch and Noah pulls me into his arms.

"For the record, I love your hair."

"Thanks."

"And there's nothing wrong with getting scholarships and student loans. I can't believe she said that." I feel him shake his head. "Actually, I can, but how did she even think to say something like that? She doesn't even know you."

I chuckle against him. "I almost told her I was going to become a circus clown and start a homemade soap-making business, but I didn't want to give her a heart attack."

"I wish you had."

"Noah!"

He turns to the backyard and grabs my hand. We head down the steps and into the grass.

"Come on," he says, the moonlight shining down on his face as he looks back at me. "I want to show you a spot I like to go to be alone."

He leads me away from the house. I look out, taking in as much as the landscape as I can in the darkness. My eyes adjust quickly, and I see acres of grass and, beyond that, vineyards. It's so vast, it's dizzying. If I'd grown up here in all this space, it would've been hard to convince me to come inside.

"Here," Noah says, helping me up onto a wooden picnic table. "This is my spot. It's quiet out here. Problems don't exist when you're sitting on this table." He slides his arm around my back, and I curl into him.

The night is quiet, and so are we. Noah's fingers brush my hands, bumping over my knuckles. He flips my hand over and traces designs on my palm with his fingertip.

At the sound of an owl, I startle and watch it leave its perch in a tree. "I didn't even know it was there," I whisper. The owl flies until it disappears from our view.

Noah takes a deep breath, and my head rises and falls against his chest.

"What?" I ask.

"Thank you for putting up with my grandma tonight. And my mom."

"They weren't that bad." I'm stretching it a bit, and we both know it.

Noah laughs softly, and my head bumps along with it.

"I don't think your mother likes me." I bite my lip. Noah told me she was cold, but it's more than that. A feeling in my gut that hasn't let up since she first cast a glance at me.

"She doesn't like anybody."

"Did she like Kelsey?" Noah's silence is all the answer I need. I groan and look up at him.

"Stop, stop, please." He pushes his hair away from his forehead. "My mom knows Kelsey's mom. They're friends. My mom doesn't know your mom."

I laugh, just a short sound. "Can you imagine our moms being friends?"

Noah grunts. "Not in a million years." He leans back until he's lying on the table. "Come here." He motions with his hand.

I lie down on my side and put my head on his chest, right onto the warm spot it was in before.

"Don't worry about anything but us, okay?"

"Okay," I agree, my voice small. Normally I wouldn't care who likes me, but this is different.

"We're magic, Ember. Say it with me."

I look up at him. The tree towers behind him, it's long branches drooping down. The moonlight filters through the leaves, casting iridescent arcs that dance over us.

"We're magic," I whisper.

And I believe it too.

## 9

## NOAH

THREE DAYS DOESN'T SEEM THAT LONG A TIME TO IGNORE someone. But, according to my dad, who's using his firm voice and standing in my bedroom doorway right now, any time spent ignoring my mother is too long.

"She wasn't nice to Ember, Dad." Why am I telling him this? He has eyes, he was there.

He sighs and looks over his shoulder, then steps inside and shuts the door. Coming to a seat in my desk chair, he looks at a picture of Ember that I leaned up against a soccer trophy. She hates the picture, but I love it. I took it last week with my phone, when the wind was so strong it made her hair swirl around her. She laughed and closed her eyes, just as I captured the moment. I had printed it out that night.

"What happened last Saturday night wasn't your mom's fault. She can't control her mother's mouth any better than you can control hers."

"It wasn't just grandma. I mean, yeah, she sucked." I sink down onto my bed. "But Mom didn't even try to get to know Ember."

Dad tips his head back until it's supported by the back of my chair. "She doesn't mean it," he says to the ceiling.

"She could at least try. I know she liked Kelsey, and Ember's not anything like Kelsey, but she makes me happy. Can't that be enough for Mom?" I punch the pillow beside me.

"I'll talk to her." He looks down and then back up to me. "You want to kick the ball around with me?" He props his foot on top of a red-and-blue soccer ball lying on the floor beside my desk chair.

"Only if you promise not to start wheezing again." My taunt prompts him to slip his toes under the ball and bounce it up into the air. Using the inside of his left foot he gives it a small kick and looks at me with challenge on his face.

I jump off the bed and steal the ball away, kicking it from my room. "Let's go, old man."

"Are you going to stop ignoring your mother?" he calls after me. Still doing his dad/husband duty, I guess.

"Yes," I respond, even though I still think my mother deserves to be in the doghouse.

Ember doesn't seem to mind my mother's behavior. She's more concerned about people at school finding out we're together. I don't give a shit what people think about us, but Ember does. That surprised me, because I thought Ember lived in a special land where people at our school didn't exist. She doesn't seem to care about anybody there, and she never participates in anything. When I asked her yesterday, she explained that she has made it this far by being drama free, and she'd like it to stay that way.

I get it. But I have a small plan that will let me kiss her at least once during the school day. If she won't let me openly show affection to her at school, I'll just have to sneak it.

MY IDEA IS UNORIGINAL, BUT IT'S ALL I HAVE. I NEVER SEE Ember at school. We don't have the same lunch hour, no classes together, and she's not in any extracurriculars.

My breath whooshes out of me when I see her come around the corner of the english building. I saw her last night, kissed her until our lips were numb, and then missed her the second she left my car and went upstairs to her apartment.

Now she's coming to me, walking in that graceful way she has, as if she's floating and thinking of something peaceful.

"Hey, you," she says in a thick voice, sliding her arms around my neck. "Good idea."

I texted her two hours ago, right before school, and asked her to meet me ten minutes after third period began. I chose third period because I know Kelsey will be across campus in a math class. No chance of her leaving class for any reason and spotting us.

"I come up with good ideas from time to time." My hands wrap around her waist, and I tug until she's flush against me.

She breathes deeply, her chest filling and pressing into me. Leaning my head into her, I groan into her ear. Ember does things to me that I don't understand. She steals my breath and fills me all at the same time, makes my head spin and kidnaps my thoughts. She smells like sunflowers and citrus, and it gives me the very best high, one I never want to come down from.

My lips hover a millimeter from hers, and I let them hang there. Her lips turn up in a playful grin.

"I can resist longer than you can," she says playfully.

The competitor in me awakens. "I doubt that."

"Try me," she whispers, her breath tickling my lips. I nearly lose it right there, but my love for sport stops me.

I start at her wrist, trailing my finger along it, then up the sensitive skin on the inside of her arm. She's wearing a tank top, and when I reach her shoulder, I slide my finger beneath the strap and let it slide down the curve and onto the swell of her chest. Her quiver makes me want to stop, drag her into my car, drive to her empty apartment, and take her places she's never been before.

"Mmmm," she moans softly, pressing harder into me.

"What the fuck?"

Our heads turn as one.

Hands on hips, mouth open wide, eyes gleaming with shock and the pleasure of a juicy secret, is Tana Blockhill.

*Kelsey's best friend.* Loose term, of course. Kelsey calls Tana a bitch behind her back.

Tana laughs. A deep, throaty, *I-can't-believe-it-but-I'm-happy-I-know-it* sound.

Four seconds ago, Ember was moaning from enjoyment, but the sound she's making now is frustrated and fearful.

Tana walks closer. Her sneer reminds me of a jungle cat, the way it pulls up on one side and bares only a few teeth.

"You've moved on quickly," she says, gaze fixed on me. She flicks her eyes to Ember, who has taken two steps back from our embrace. "With fire crotch."

I flick my hand out, gesturing behind Tana. "Run along. Go tell Kelsey what you saw. We both know it's the first thing you're going to do."

"She deserves to know," Tana hisses. Her gaze shifts from me to Ember and back again.

"You know we broke up, Tana. Go do something better with your time." I grab Ember by the hand and pull her until we're around the side of the building. I try to tug her into my arms, but she resists.

"I've made it almost all of high school without drama." Her eyes flash. She's angry.

"I'm sorry. I didn't mean to bring this on us." Reaching out, I run a finger along her cheekbone. Her mouth runs in a straight, pissed off line, but her skin warms beneath my touch. "Are you opposed to skipping?" I ask.

She doesn't seem like the rule-following type. Ember does whatever she feels inclined to do. With her, it doesn't seem like there's much forethought.

She slowly shakes her head.

"Then let's get out of here," I say, encouraged when I see her bite her bottom lip and nod excitedly.

I pull her past the science building towards the gym. "There's an exit over here. Nobody uses it, and it's not visible from any of the classrooms over there."

"Do you skip often?"

"Not usually during the season. When it's warm, Tripp likes to lie out by his pool, and I tag along. We don't have a pool." I shrug. "Plus, Tripp's cousin has good weed, and he invites him over."

"Noah!"

I look back and nearly laugh at her shocked face. "You're the one with the tattoo," I remind her.

"So?"

"That's kind of bad-ass."

"You could get a tattoo. You're eighteen."

"My mother would disown me. She hates them." *Crap.* "I didn't mean it—"

"Shut up." Ember says it good-naturedly, her free hand waving around in front of her. "I don't care. Add it to the list of things she doesn't like about me, which isn't very long, and yet..." She shakes her head, the messy red bun on top of her hair tilting.

"I don't get it either." We get to the exit and slip through undetected. My car is in the first row of the parking lot, just fifty feet away.

On the way to my house we stop at a drive-through and grab lunch.

"My mom left this morning," I tell Ember, when her mouth is full of fries. "She had to go see a restaurant chain who's considering carrying Sutton wine."

Ember's eyes grow big as she swallows. "And your dad?" Her voice is high-pitched.

"In his office at the welcome center." I'm trying not to sound like it's a big deal, but *it's a big deal*. We came close that time at her apartment, and every time I kiss her I think I'm near combustion. I know it's important for her, and even though it's not my first time, it's important to me, too.

"But that doesn't mean anything, Ember." I take my hand from the wheel and rest it on her knee. "We can just watch a movie, chill out, or whatever. No pressure, okay?" I wish I could spend more time watching her instead of the road. I love to watch her think. Her expressions change quickly as she flits among emotions.

"What if, maybe, I mean, um..." She clears her throat. I look over for just a second and see her square her shoulders. "What if I want to do more than watch a movie?"

I hit the gas and our heads fly back. She laughs, yelling my name.

Taking my foot off the pedal, I laugh. "Kidding, but if Black Beauty had rocket boosters, I would've already enabled them."

She smiles and feeds me a few fries.

"Are you trying to shut me up?" I ask, but it comes out garbled because my mouth is full.

"Basically." She shoots me a sassy look.

I'm trying to stay calm and not focus on the fact that she wants to do *more* than watch a movie, but it's hard. Pun intended. It's a good thing she has started feeding me the hamburger I ordered. I need the distraction.

We pull up to my house, and just as I said, it's empty. Dad's car is down at the vineyard with him, and mom's car is parked at the airport. On Tuesday's, Gretchen prepares a make-ahead meal and takes Wednesday's off. We are really, truly, alone.

"Movie?" I ask Ember after we throw our trash away in the kitchen and grab drinks.

"Sure," she answers. Her voice is small.

We head upstairs to my room, and I grab the remote and lie on my bed. Ember folds herself into a seat beside me, but her body is stiff, like a puppet.

"Sometimes I think about getting a tattoo," I say as I flip through channels looking for something good.

"Yeah?" Her voice sounds a little better now. She's intrigued. "Of what?"

There's nothing good on, and I'm not interested in picking a movie, so I turn off the TV and roll onto my side so I can face her. "How do I choose?"

She slides down until she's on her back, then props herself up on her elbows. Twisting her lips like she's thinking, she turns to me. "You have to search yourself. Your soul. A tattoo lasts forever, or it's supposed to, so whatever you choose has to be forever too."

"Can I choose you? I'll get your face tattooed across my whole back. Life-size."

She tips her head back and rolls her eyes at the ceiling. "Be serious. What's important to you?"

"My family, soccer, you." I don't have to search myself to know that.

"Are there any credo's you live by? Any symbols that represent your personal philosophy?"

I close my eyes and think. And I come up with...nothing. Absolutely nothing. I nod at her stretched-out abdomen. "What does yours stand for?" Maybe knowing her reasons will get my creative juices flowing.

"Our humanness. Explosion and regrowth. A dandelion explodes like a volcano, but in a much sweeter, more peaceful way. Before it does, it's whole and soft, and when it explodes, its seeds float out and can land anywhere. Wherever the seeds land, a new dandelion can grow. It makes me think of the human condition. How fragile we all are, but also how capable we are of getting up and going on."

Her face softens and pinks when she finishes speaking.

"Don't be embarrassed. That's deeper and more thoughtful than anything I could ever think. I'm a dumb jock." I'm smiling to show her I'm joking, but there isn't much joke to my words. I've lived and breathed soccer, and that left no time for reading or learning about much else.

Ember's lips draw together, but she stays quiet.

"What?" I know she has something to say.

"You're so far from a dumb jock, and as someone who formerly thought maybe you were one, let me be the first to tell you that's not true."

Narrowed eyes is my best response. She laughs at them and shrugs, as if she can't help her former assumptions. "Do you have a Sharpie?"

"Top drawer," I answer, inclining my head to my desk.

Ember gets up, going to it. She pauses to frown at the

picture of her, and then digs through my drawer until she finds the navy-blue marker. She keeps her eyes on me as she comes back to the bed, her eyebrows wiggling.

My mouth suddenly feels like it's stuffed with cotton. "What are you planning?"

She sinks down onto the bed and folds her legs under herself. "I'm going to give you a tattoo."

Hmm... That I can handle. It's marker. It will come off eventually.

I sit up and take off my shirt, then lie back down. "Across my ribs, like yours."

She uncaps the marker and bends down. Steadying herself on the bed with her left hand, and with her right hand poised an inch above my body, she grins. "Are you ready?"

"Do I get to choose?" I've propped myself up on my elbows, like she was before she got this wild idea, and I'm looking down at her. She looks so beautiful right now with her sparkling, excited eyes and flushed cheeks.

"I'd like to, if you don't mind."

I can't deny this girl. I can't say no to her hopeful face. Not when she's licking her lips like she's doing now, and then sinking her teeth into the bottom one, like she's doing *right fucking now*.

"Go ahead," I say as I gesture to the middle of my body.

She beams. *So worth it. I don't care if she draws Rainbow Brite on me.*

Lying back on my pillow, I look up to the ceiling as the tip of the marker hits my skin. It feels moist. She's intent on her work, and I'm not about to talk to her in case it distracts her and she messes up. Instead, I think of ways to keep this tattoo a secret from my teammates until it washes off. It's going to be hard, considering we shower after practice.

A few minutes later she sits up, and I hear the marker's cap snap back into place. She leans back down and blows warm breath on my skin, drying it. Funny how her warmth causes goosebumps to rise on me. "Done," she announces, moving away.

Trying to look down at your ribs is a lot harder than it sounds. From what I can see, it looks like upside down letters.

"Tell me about it." I've lowered my head as far as it will go and still can't understand what it says.

"Sit up," she instructs, pulling my hands until I'm seated. Her fingers graze the space beneath the letters. "It says shmily."

"Shmily?" My nose crinkles. I don't mean for it to, but it does. "Does that have a special meaning?"

She grins, tapping the center of her open palm on the marker in time with her rapid head nods.

When she doesn't say anything, I ask "Are you going to tell me what it means?"

"Noooo." Her voice is soft, her lips curling with her amusement.

"Are you kidding me?" A medium-size child could probably fit their fist in my mouth right now, that's how far it's open.

"I'll tell you. Someday. Just not now. But I promise, it's not bad."

This girl is crazy. Ember is joyful and funny, weird and incredible, challenging and unexpected.

"Now"—she turns, tossing the marker to the floor, where it lands with a soft thud—"I don't know about you, but I didn't cut class just to fulfill my dreams of being a tattoo artist." The slightly upturned corners of her lips and her shimmering eyes make her look playful.

"No?" My body feels hot already, as if her words started a fire that was an inferno from the onset.

"Nope."

I grab her shoulders and push her down, pinning her with mine. Her arms wrap around my neck, and she nips my earlobe.

"I'm ready," she whispers.

I am too. More than I've ever been. To the point where I know any other experience before this is about to turn to vapor. Because Ember is magic.

She's wearing a dress, and when I push it up I find that the tops of her thighs are freckled. When my finger traces the dots, it's as if I'm connecting them. This time, when I touch her, she doesn't stop me.

Kissing Ember, touching her smooth skin, listening to the soft sounds she makes, is like a collision of everything overwhelming at once. All I can think about is that one word I've been using to describe her since the moment I pulled her from that lake.

*Magic.*

What's not magic is hearing my dad's voice when I'm sliding a second finger into Ember. Sweet, innocent Ember, who has never done this before. She's squirming beneath me and digging her fingers into my skin, probably leaving marks and giving my teammates a second reason to tease me.

Thank the flipping lord my dad knocked first. Ember's limbs are frozen, her eyes fearful.

"It's okay," I mouth. I don't know that for certain, but it seems like the right thing to say.

"Noah, the school called and said you left during third period and didn't return." Even through the wooden door I can hear his irritation. "You and Ember need to go back to school, and don't do this again."

How the hell did he know? Coughing, I call out, "Okay, Dad." His footsteps are loud as he walks away.

Ember reaches down and pushes my hand until it's outside of her. Her red face combines with her copper hair and makes her look like the flame atop a torch.

"I have an idea," I say quickly.

"Is it as good as the one to kiss outside third period?" She tries to narrow her eyes but the expression falls short. She's still too worked up to look disapproving.

"Better." I place a kiss on her forehead and tug on her dress. She lifts her hips and I pull it down and smooth it out. "I need you to get off work the third weekend in April. And you need to make a new friend and stay the night at her house that weekend."

"But that's—"

"Prom?"

She nods.

"Did you want to go?"

Her wrinkled nose is my answer.

"Don't worry about that."

By some stroke of luck, she doesn't press the issue.

We tread quietly down the stairs and through the living room. When we get out front I notice my dad's car is already gone. Again I wonder how he knew exactly what I was up to.

The question rattles me. Especially considering what I have planned for the third weekend in April.

## 10
---
## EMBER

I GET IT.

I can see why all this is happening.

Jealousy.

Open hostility.

Curiosity and its best friend, *awareness*.

People are aware of me now. The periphery. That's where I was B.N.

*Before Noah.*

But A.N.?

I'm in the middle of it all, an unwilling and reluctant participant.

Kelsey hates me. She's made it clear, and her group of fake friends have supported her en masse. It's been two weeks since Tana saw Noah and me together and blabbed.

Every day since, Noah and I have arrived at school together. We knew there was no way Tana would keep her mouth shut, so I figured it wouldn't hurt to let Noah drive me instead of riding my bike every day. The whispers started the minute I climbed out of Black Beauty, and they haven't stopped.

That was the first day Kelsey began staring at me through slitted eyes in English, her version of shooting electrical bolts at me, but today she's stepped up her game.

I glance down at the sheet of torn paper she dropped on my desk when she passed me on her way to her own seat.

*SLUT!*

I roll my eyes and crumple it into a ball, then flick it off my desk.

*Common.* Kelsey's response is common. Everything about her is common. None of this surprises me.

After school, Kelsey and her top three best friends of the day corner me at my locker.

"What makes you think you can date Noah?" Kelsey stands at the locker beside mine, her hand on her hip. Her head bobbles with the attitude in her voice.

"Do you actually want an answer to that?" I ask without looking at her. I put my books in the locker and slam it, turning to face her.

"Yes, that's why I asked it." She's snarling. It's not a good look.

"Because it's a free country. Because we were both single. Because I wanted to."

"You're not the right girl for him."

"Neither were you. That's probably why you cheated on him."

Fear creeps into her eyes. She wants her indiscretion to stay a secret, and that's fine by me. I have no desire to watch her skeletons run around.

I move, leaning close enough that I can see where her mascara is clumped. "Kelsey, you don't have to be upset by me and Noah," I say in a quiet voice. "Maybe you think you're supposed to be, and so you are, but you don't *have* to be."

"What are you talking about?" Her tone is snippy, but she looks confused.

"Exactly what I just said." Reaching down, I grab my book bag by its strap and sling it across my body. Sidestepping Kelsey and her crew, I leave the locker bay behind.

Noah is standing next to his car, waiting for me. When he sees me, he runs his hand across the hair on the top of his head, where it's the thickest. Today it's unruly, sticking up all over the place, but in a way that looks like he meant for it to happen.

"I thought maybe you'd ditched me," he says when I reach him. His arms encircle me, and he plants a long kiss on my lips. "I missed you," he says when he comes up for air.

"You've been texting me all day," I remind him, but I understand what he means. We haven't seen each other since this morning.

We climb into his car, and he turns it on. "Where to?" We usually have until four-thirty, when soccer practice starts. We get something to eat, a smoothie or a frozen yogurt, and make-out in his car in the parking lot of my apartment, milking the clock until he has to race to make it to practice on time.

I groan at his question. It reminds me where I'm supposed to be headed. "I have to work. Gruff left me a voicemail, asking me to come in early. Edna doesn't feel well. Something about her hip being sore." Edna is the retired nurse who had to come out of retirement. She lectures me endlessly about saving money, so I don't end up like her.

Noah looks disappointed, but he grabs my hand and brings it to his lips. He kisses all my knuckles. "We have this weekend to look forward to," he murmurs against them.

"About that—"

"No way."

"Noah." I'm trying to sound stern.

"Ember." He's doing it too. He starts driving, and I'd bet the money I put in my mom's envelopes last weekend that he's hoping I'll drop it. No can do. Once this experience passes by, it's gone. There won't be a second chance.

"It's senior prom. Not that I care about that, but you do." I shift in my seat as I try to reason with him. "You're nominated, remember?" The announcement was made in homeroom two days ago. People stared at me when his name was called, because the girls' names were called first, and I was obviously missing from the list. They were probably waiting for me to burst into tears or run from the room. "Isn't it a requirement that you be there?"

He coughs. "I have malaria."

"You do not, and I don't think malaria makes you cough."

"Typhoid fever."

"Noah, be serious."

"Scurvy."

I laugh at the last one. I can't help it.

"Ember, I'm serious. I'm not going to prom. It's not important to me. They can crown the squirrels who live in my backyard for all I care."

"You're crazy," I say through my laughter.

"Yes, I am. And this weekend, it's just going to be us."

We're almost to my work, and I wish we weren't. I don't want to be apart from him.

"Are you going to tell me where we're going?"

"Are you going to tell me what 'shmily' means?"

"No."

"Then, no." He draws pinched fingers across his lips, zipping them.

I throw up my hands. I want to know where we're going. How am I supposed to know what to take?

Noah answers the question I haven't asked. "Just bring couple changes of clothes, a bathing suit, maybe a sweatshirt, and whatever girly stuff you need." His eyebrows draw together, and he motions at my hair and face, as if I'm a lifeform he knows nothing of.

He parks as close to the entrance of my work as he can, undoes his seatbelt, and leans toward me, resting his forehead against mine. "See you at nine?"

"Like always," I say. I work four nights a week, and each night, Noah insists on picking me up. He doesn't want me riding my bike at night, despite the fact that I did it for two years before meeting him.

"Good luck at practice." I retrieve my bag from the backseat and kiss him lightly.

His smile is uneasy. "Thanks." The word is filled with melancholy. Of all days, I wish I could be with him until the clock demands he leave me. Two more practices, three more soccer matches, and the season will be over.

He looks sad and lost. Wistful. As if he's preparing to say goodbye.

I squeeze his hand. "Try not to anticipate the end. It'll take away from the experience you're having now."

"How did you get so wise?" he asks, his head cocked to the side.

"I read that on a fortune cookie."

His eyebrows lift. "Really?"

"No."

He chuckles. "Ember, I..." His mouth clamps shut, he pauses, then he opens it again. "This weekend will be fun."

Quickly I kiss him and open the door. I climb out and close it, and through the window Noah has rolled down, I say, "It should be great. I'm going to have a great time during my sleepover at my new best friend Kelsey's house."

Smiling at Noah's laughing face, I walk into the building to find sweet old Edna.

---

I WENT TO FOOTBALL GAMES WITH SKY BEFORE SHE graduated from Northmount. She loved them, but not me. I didn't understand why anybody would want to ram their heads into one another, or chase a ball, but I liked the energy of the crowd. All those people, rooting for a common cause. It was inspiring to be around.

This is different. Noah's soccer match makes those football games look like they were Pop Warner.

Pandemonium surrounds me as screaming, bleacher-stomping fans hold posters to support their favorite players. I tried to be surreptitious about it, but I've since given up and started blatantly craning my neck to read all the signs.

*We flip for Tripp.* The cheerleaders hold these signs. They're down near the front, a few rows away from me, and ten feet over. Through observation, I learned soccer doesn't have cheerleaders, and my confusion about why they're in the stands has been cleared up.

Looking behind me, I spot a group of girls holding a giant sign that reads *Sutton can press my button.* My eyes go wide and I try not to show my unease. I keep looking around, and the feeling passes. Signs with his last name are everywhere. One is in the hands of two girls who look like they're twelve, but are probably older. Others are held up by girls I recognize from classes. Even Elsie Sweetzer, class president, hoists a sign above her head.

Memories of lying in Noah's bed run through my mind. Sutton was certainly pressing some buttons, until his dad spoke through the door and I nearly had a heart attack. Before that happened, other things were taking place. Good things. Things I didn't want to stop.

Suddenly my chest feels hot, and the tops of my thighs start the now-familiar ache. To distract myself I run a palm over my face and pinch my lower lip. It works.

"Hey, Ember."

I look up. The too-bright stadium lights blind me momentarily, and I blink until my eyes adjust and I see Noah's dad standing above me.

"Hi," my voice squeaks.

"Mind if I join you?" Derek points to the empty space beside me. "Noah's mother and Brody are on their way, and I was going to sit alone until I saw you over here."

"Of course." I scoot over. "Nobody likes to sit alone."

"Except you," Derek points out with a playful chortle.

My laugh sounds nervous. "Oh, well. Yes, I guess so."

"Excited for the game?" Derek reaches into the pocket of his jacket and pulls out a bag of candy. He offers some to me, and I accept. We're chewing the sweet, fruity candy when he asks about my parents.

I give him the short version. Not that there's really a long one. I just skip the editorializing.

"And your mom's name is...?"

"Maddie."

"Got it," he says, looking off into the distance. He stares for so long that I wonder if maybe he's forgotten I'm here.

"Well, anyway," he finally says, snapping back from wherever he just went, "you ready to cheer on Noah?"

Glancing around at all the signage and clothing bearing Northmount's name, I confess that I feel ill-prepared.

"You're in luck." He winks at me. Reaching into a bag he brought in with him, he produces a large, rolled-up piece of paper. "You'll have to help me hold it, because it keeps rolling in on itself. You up for the task?"

I nod, helping him unroll it. *#1 Go Sutton! #1*

When the team takes the field, the stands erupt in ear-splitting screams. *How did I not know soccer was this big of a deal?*

Noah runs out, his eyes on the crowd. He sees his dad first, and then me. He smiles at the sign held above our heads, and I can only shrug, but I'm smiling. I love cheering on Noah.

———

WHEN I GET HOME THAT NIGHT, MY MOM IS ALREADY ASLEEP. Sky is not. She's lying on her bed, listening to music on her iPod. She sits up when I come in and pulls out her earbuds.

"How was it?" she asks, swinging her legs beneath her and settling down on them.

"Fun." It's hard to admit it, but I had a good time.

Even afterward, when Noah's parents asked me to get a bite to eat with them, it was enjoyable. Derek was friendly and never mentioned catching Noah and me together, and Brody was nice too. Affable and funny. He even suggested Noah and I double-date with him and his girlfriend, Alyssa. Mrs. Sutton was still stiff, but she tried. She asked me how my week was. The question felt odd, but I answered it. I told her about Edna, which in retrospect was probably as boring as getting a play-by-play about the hardening of concrete. I was flustered and couldn't stop thinking about what had almost gone down under her roof, so I rambled.

"Just fun?" Sky says. "That's it?"

"Pretty much." I pull my shirt over my head and toss it into the corner where we throw our clothes. "How was your day?" I reach for an oversize T-shirt and pull it on. When I look back at Sky, she's toying with a loose string on her nightshirt.

"What?" I ask, plopping down on her bed and scooting until my back is against the wall.

She meets my eyes, and her cheeks are scarlet. "There was a new person at work today. Ryder. Isn't that such a cute name for a guy? *Ryder*. He was nice, too, and they asked me to train him."

"That sounds like it could be interesting," I say, careful to keep my voice happy but not too happy. Too much, and she'll become anxious that she came off wrong and embarrassed herself. Too little, and she'll think she's not good enough.

"He has blondish-brown hair, and a crooked smile. There's a scar next to his left ear. I didn't ask how he got it." Sky runs her fingers over her bent knees.

"I'm glad you met someone you like. Maybe soon you can all go to a work happy hour and get to know him better." *Careful, careful.*

"Ember, please." Sky's voice has changed from excited to disdainful. "I live with my mother. In a room I share with my high-school-age sister." Her worried eyes lift. "No offense."

"None taken."

"Ryder's not going to be interested in me." Her voice is tiny. I wish I could take it away from her, and make her feel big and strong.

"Have you thought any more about those college scholarships I found for you?" I ask, thinking maybe this is my chance to help her.

"Yes," she whispers. She swings her legs out from under her and scoots until she's beside me with her back against the wall. "I'm scared though. What if I have a"—she looks around anxiously, as if the walls have ears—"you know what?"

"Period stain on the day you wear white?"

Sky rolls her eyes. "No."

"Montezuma's Revenge?"

"Gross!"

"Spontaneous and foul-smelling—"

Sky screeches in protest. "Can we please stop playing this game?" But she's laughing. That was my goal.

I turn to her, sister to sister, my soul link. "Will you please consider it?"

"I will if you will," she challenges, huffing. "Where are all those acceptance letters of yours? Shouldn't they be pouring in? You applied to enough places."

I know exactly where they are. In a place nobody will find them.

"You know how colleges like to drag it out," I say. "Like announcing the winners on those cooking contests on TV."

"Want to watch one? You know they're always on late at night."

I should tell her no. I have to get my overnight bag ready for tomorrow. Noah is picking me up around the corner from the apartment complex at ten, and Wyatt's mom found a different baby-sitter for the afternoon. Everything is set and ready to go.

Based on the nerves in my stomach, I'm not likely to sleep tonight.

"Sure," I say, knowing I shouldn't. I can't help it though, I want to be with my sister.

Leaving our room, we cuddle up on the couch until we notice Mom walk out for a glass of water. Her eyes settle on us and she smiles, joining us instead of going back to bed. Instantly, the guilt of the lie I haven't told yet begins to sink in.

Just not enough for me to change my mind.

Whatever Noah has planned for us this weekend, I'm game.

## 11
---

# NOAH

LAST NIGHT, WHEN I WAS CERTAIN EVERYONE IN MY HOUSE WAS asleep, I snuck into my dad's office. Quietly, I opened the center desk drawer and slipped the key I found there into my pocket. Then I crept out to my car and put my overnight bag in the trunk of Black Beauty.

I'm ready for this.

Time alone with Ember.

No practice for me, no work for her, no parents expecting us. Twenty-four uninterrupted hours with Ember.

"Hey, Mom." I walk into the kitchen where she's sitting at the breakfast nook, coffee cup in hand. The smile on my face is sure to tip her off to something, so I stick my head in the fridge and try to stop grinning. After grabbing an apple and stuffing it in my mouth like a pig at a luau, I back out of the fridge.

"Do you have plans today?" She tears her eyes from the iPad lying on the table in front of her. This is her Saturday morning ritual. Maybe one day I'll drink coffee and read the news, too. It sounds very adult. For now, I'll pass.

I munch the rest of my bite and swallow. "Going to

Tripp's."

"What are you two doing today? Certainly not pampering for prom." She sits back in her chair and pulls one bent leg into herself. "Guys have it so easy. Just a haircut and formal clothes."

"Yeah, so easy," I echo. I completely forgot prom is today. To make this charade look believable, I'm going to have to bring my suit with me when I leave.

"I'm assuming you're taking Ember tonight?"

"Ember's not going. She's not interested."

My mom frowns, then tries to fix her face. "That's...atypical."

I nearly laugh. *Atypical*. I have a strong feeling she was about to say *weird*.

"Laurel said Kelsey told her you were dating someone. She was asking me about the new girl in your life."

Leaning back against the sink, I sigh with annoyance. "So?"

"Why are you on the defense when it comes to Ember?"

"Why are you on the offense when it comes to Ember?"

"I'm not," she says, her voice hard. "It's just..." She shakes her head. "Never mind."

I turn around and leave the kitchen. My anger at my mom leaves me like a slow leak while I get my stuff ready to look like I'm going to Tripp's. By the time I'm walking out the door, I've forgotten about our hostility.

"Tripp," I say into the phone as I pull out of the long driveway and onto a bigger street.

"Why are you calling so early?" His voice sounds like gravel.

"What time did you get home last night?"

"This morning," he corrects, "and I don't know. There was sun when I went to sleep. Just be happy you didn't go out. Be happy you have sweet little Ember to keep your ass in line."

Oh, I am. Happier than Tripp could ever know.

"Listen, I'm not going to prom tonight, and I need—"

"What? Why not? This is senior prom, man, and you're nominated."

"So are you. Just cover for me, okay? I'm at your house today, and I'm staying there tonight."

Tripp starts making the high-pitched sounds of a girl climaxing. I think he's been watching too much porn, because in real life it doesn't sound like that.

"Grow the fuck up, Tripp."

"Don't get testy. I'm just fucking around. I'll cover for you, and I'll accept your crown, too."

"You can keep it."

"Gee, thanks, it's what I've always wanted."

Hanging up, I continue to drive. We could banter for hours, so it's better to cut it off now before I get to Ember's.

When I get to her apartment complex I keep going, turn the corner, and pull into the parking lot of a Vietnamese restaurant. Ember stands up from the curb when she sees me. I lean over and open the door for her.

"Hey, you," she says, climbing in. When she leans over to kiss me, her scent fills my nostrils.

"I like how you do that," I say, pulling out of the parking lot.

"Do what?"

"Kiss me first. You don't wait to be kissed." To Ember, this probably seems ridiculous. Why wait to have something you want if it's available and right in front of you? But that's not the way most people work, at least not in my experience. They are shy, unconfident, want to be wanted, or afraid of rejection. Not Ember. She's comfortable in her own skin. It's not that she doesn't fear rejection. It's more that she doesn't fear going through the experience. She embraces it all. The shine, and the sting.

"Now can you tell me where we're going?" She looks up at me through her lashes.

Taking advantage of the red light we're stopped at I reach for her, winding my hands into her hair and rubbing my thumbs over the silkiness.

"Shmily?" I ask. She moves her head slowly one way, then the other.

The light turns green, and I release her. I want to keep her in my hands, but soon enough we'll have all the time in the world.

"Settle in then, because I'm not telling if you won't," I reply. "We'll be there in an hour and a half."

---

"NOAH, WHAT IS THIS PLACE?" EMBER LEANS FORWARD AND peers through my windshield. I watch her eyes as we travel slowly down the sloping street. Her gaze swings from home to home as we pass them by, and when I slip the car into the driveway of my parents' beach house, her eye widen. White siding and a gray-blue roof with too many black-paned windows to count stare back at us. It's not ostentatious, but it's impressive. Grass grows in abundance, surrounding the house except for the driveway. I roll down our windows, allowing the roaring sounds of the Pacific ocean to fill the car. The churning water is just a short walk from the back door and over the sand dune.

I pull into the garage and kill the engine. "This is my parents' second home."

"Umm...yeah. Okay. Totally normal." Her laugh is a bit

unsteady.

"Let's go," I say before I can think too much about her comment. She's overwhelmed by the place, that's all.

I hold the door for her as we walk into the mudroom. I'm happy the house is warm because it's chilly and overcast outside. Northern California beaches are nothing like their Southern counterparts. They are chilly, often foggy, and never overcrowded.

After depositing our bags on the kitchen counter, I grab her by the waist and spin her to face me.

"Do you want a tour?"

"Not really," she says. "What I really want is to get changed and go"—she points out past the windowed wall to the glittering ocean—"out there."

"Your wish is my command, my lady."

"I'll keep that in mind," she smarts, giving me a playful look.

Digging through her bag, she pulls out black leggings and a sweatshirt, and does the best thing I've ever seen in my eighteen years. She peels off her T-shirt and pushes down her cut-offs. Her bra and underwear land on top of the heap at her feet.

She laughs at my astonished face, and all I can think is *I love this girl*. Not because she's naked in front of me, though that's nice too. Really flipping nice.

She's bold and brave, audacious but tender. Kind.

"I love you," I yell out. I don't care anymore. I don't have to wait a certain number of months. I don't even have to worry that I'm too young to love. Ember takes all that worry away.

"Shmily," she says. Her grin fills her face.

"What?"

It's becoming hard to focus. She's still naked, and even

though I've seen parts of her naked, it was never the whole. The whole is beyond words. It's taking every ounce of self-discipline I have not to bound over to her right now, lift her, and set her on the counter. The only thing stopping me is knowing it will be her first time.

"Shmily." She pulls on her leggings, tugging them up over the curves of her hips and letting go with a snap. I'm sad to see her sweatshirt go on, but feel better when I realize she's not wearing a bra anymore.

She walks to me and lifts my shirt. Her fingers butterfly over the faint outline of the word. I tried not to wash it off but it was difficult. "See How Much I Love You. Shmily."

I say it over in my head, slowly. "It's an acronym."

Ember taps the tip of her nose.

So, she said it first. Weeks ago.

Of course she did. She felt it, and that was all there was to it. No worries over convention.

"You better believe I'm going to show you how much I love you. Later." I drop my shorts too. Two can play this game. Ember's trying to keep her mouth from dropping in her shock. I may have seen her parts, but she hasn't seen mine. I feel a surge of pride and ownership knowing my body will be the first one she touches. Is it crazy of me to also want it to be the last?

She gulps, raising her eyes up to meet mine. I can't help my smirk. Watching her reaction is too good.

"Beach?" she asks, the word drawn out.

"Sure." I pull on my trunks and lead the way outside. I stop to grab two beach blankets from a plastic trunk beside the white wooden gate. Ember eyes the blankets, unsure. "It's only April," I remind her. "Once we get down there, you'll want these." Pushing on the gate, I step through the opening and lead her onto the narrow sandy walkway.

We stay on the beach for hours. Ember watches the waves for a long time, alternating between talking and growing quiet. I lie back on the blanket and tug on the other blanket wrapped around her shoulders. She let's me pull her down into me, and we kiss until we're out of breath. When the bright sky grows dull, and then duller still, we sit up in time to watch the sun dip below the horizon.

Ember announces her hunger the way a starving man might. "Food," she tells me, hanging on my arm. "Need food. Now." She pretends to swoon.

"Come on. Let's get changed and get you fed. We'll have to go somewhere. There isn't any food at the house." Taking her by the hand, we head back up with our beach blankets thrown over our shoulders.

Ember knew better than to change in front of me this time; instead, she went to the bathroom to get herself ready.

*The next time I see her naked, all bets are off.*

Quickly, I send a message to Tripp and thank him for covering for me tonight. Later on, I'll text my mom and tell her I'm staying the night at Tripp's. While Ember's in the bathroom, I change and grab my phone to search the internet for a good place for us to go eat.

---

I won't admit to rushing through my shrimp paella, but *I might have* rushed through the shrimp paella.

"Do you have somewhere to be?" Ember asks. She tilts her head to the side, her eyes big and wide. She's feigning innocence.

"Yes, I do. There's an unexplored place I need to investigate." I wiggle my eyebrows.

She sputters on her bite of Oaxacan sea bass.

Slow isn't the word I would use to describe how Ember's eating now. Let me put it this way—the tortoise could lap her.

I drum my fingers on the table and watch.

She laughs.

Finally, the server clears our plates.

"Is that our prom dinner?" she asks.

"I thought you didn't care about prom?"

Her eyes become worried. "I don't. I just hope you don't either."

"I'm where I want to be."

She beams and I'm certain I'll never see a sight so beautiful. We're quiet on the short drive back to the beach house. Ember's hands are wedged between her rigid knees.

"Nervous?" I ask, pressing the button for the garage. I look at her while it opens. The darkened car makes it hard for me to decipher her expression.

She tucks a strand behind her ear and nods.

I pull into the garage and cut the engine. She starts to climb out, but turns around when I speak. "We don't have to do anything, okay? That's not why I brought you here."

"Why did you, then?"

"So I could get more time with you. We're always running off to practice or work, and we hardly see each other at school. I want more than that."

She smiles. "Would you like to know why I came here with you?"

"Why?" My stomach feels a little sick now. I have no idea what she's about to say. With Ember, it could be anything.

"To have sex with you." Her admission is simple and pierces through all the pretense. I love it. I love her.

Prayer hands lifted, I mouth *thank you* to the roof of the car.

She laughs and gets out.

Inside, I get to work. Fire in the fireplace. Thankfully it's a gas fireplace and I only have to press a button. If it were wood-burning we'd be out of luck.

Chilled white wine poured. The fact that my parents keep the place stocked with Sutton wine works in my favor.

Should I turn on music? Would that be too much? Trying too hard? Maybe I should stop overthinking. No music.

"I feel so fancy," Ember jokes in a silly voice when I hand the wine to her.

We sit on the couch and sip. Ember stares into the fire but doesn't say anything. I'd be worried, except this is how she operates. She doesn't need to express her every thought or concern, she trusts her feelings enough not to need input from others.

When my wine is finished and Ember's is half-empty, she takes both glasses and sets them on the side table.

"There." She points at the gray-and-white rug in front of the fireplace.

I get up and push the coffee table off the rug. "Anything else?" I ask. Her take-charge attitude is cute, and it's making the front of my pants grow tighter.

She stands and steps to the center of the rug. Light from the fire dances on her hair. She looks more beautiful than any sight I've ever seen, and my chest swells when I think of what she's about to give me.

"We have you, me, space, and quiet. You know what that means?" Her lips quiver with mirth.

I close the few feet separating us and reach for her, pulling her in. "What?" I ask into her hair. The fire has already warmed one side of her body.

She leans back and giggles. "Tonight, Sutton, you can press my button."

I throw my head back and laugh, and she reaches me on tiptoe to press a kiss to my neck.

Then, I do just that.

With my hand, I lead her to the ending she was so close to a few weeks ago. When she comes back down from the high, I sit up to roll on a condom. She sits up, too, and asks me to teach her how to do it. When she rolls it up successfully, she claps for herself, and I laugh. I don't think I've ever laughed during sex before.

Ember lets out a long, slow exhale when I'm finally all the way inside her. I've gone slowly, allowing her to adjust to each inch.

"This is my first time," I tell her, pushing a stray hair from her face.

"No, it's not." Her voice is raspy. I've started moving above her, and she's clinging to my shoulders.

"I've never been with anybody I loved." I can't believe how different it is.

It's better than I've ever had it. Ember makes it better.

*Magic* makes it better.

I've always considered myself a straight line. Maybe a few right angles thrown in, but still, I'm two straight lines meeting at a harsh point.

Ember is all curves. Maybe it's not even as simple as that. She's a spirograph. Dramatic curves, convex and concave, deep dips and high heights.

Each time I kiss her, I feel her longing. My heart calls to hers. My right angles want her wavy, meandering curves.

We're different, and that's good.

We're the same, and that's good.

I want her forever, and that is unbelievably good.

## 12

### EMBER

People don't *fall* in love.

Well, maybe some do, but not us. Noah and I didn't fall. We crashed, and in the collision, the pieces of me and the fragments of him scattered.

Mixed.

Coalesced.

He's asleep beside me, one arm tucked under his head like a child, the other across my chest. The bed we slept in is monstrous, but we stayed in the center in a tangle of limbs. My soreness didn't stop me from waking him in the middle of the night. That time, however, when he climbed on top of me, I wrapped my legs around his backside, and it felt even better than the first time.

Last night I asked Noah to leave the drapes where they were, pulled all the way back and revealing the moonlit ocean. Endless swaths of darkness with no way to separate sea from sky, but there were stars. They looked close enough to touch. That was my last thought before I slipped into sleep. Now the sun pours in, and the ocean waves crash against the shore just as they did yesterday, and the day before that, and all the other days before that.

What's different now is me.

Not just because of the sex. Obviously that's huge, but it's more than that. A silent promise, attached to the admission of love. It's like I'm no longer only Ember. Now there is Noah, injected into my life. As if crashing together has made us responsible for one another's hearts.

The knowledge of it makes my chest feel tight and full, like the contents are too much for me to contain, and at any moment, I could explode. My fingers trail over the dandelion on my exposed ribcage.

"I like waking up this way." A sleepy, muffled voice comes from beside me.

Noah peeks at me with one eye open. He struggles to open the second, then blinks a few times. "Who wanted those curtains left open? Terrible idea."

I poke his chest, and he grunts like a fighter who was just punched.

"I thought you were in soccer, not drama club." I poke him again. This time he knows it's coming and flexes his muscles. My stomach growls, and I drop a hand onto the bare skin. "Where should we get breakfast?"

Noah grins and pushes messy hair away from his face. "Well, I don't know about you, but I already know what's on the menu." He grins and disappears under the covers.

The day has only just begun, but already I'm certain it's going to be the best day of my life.

---

"Do we have to go?" I'm pretending to drag my feet. Except, I'm really not pretending. I'm actually doing it, and

Noah is behind me, gently coaxing me through the mudroom and toward his car.

"We don't have a choice. Our parents are only going to think we're staying at our friends' houses for so long. We have to show up sometime."

I pout and stuff another donut in my mouth. After the most exceptional experience of my life, Noah took me to get breakfast at Bertrand's Bakery, home of the world's best strawberry donut. They make that claim in paint on their store window, and they aren't lying. I took two for the road.

"Fine, fine," I sing, my mouth full, pausing at the open garage door to watch a girl go by on a beach cruiser bike. The curves of metal and pretty white paint put my rickety ten-speed to shame.

"Ready?" Noah comes up behind me and touches my back.

I watch the bike until it disappears. "Yeah." I follow him to the open passenger door. How much money would it take to buy a bike like that? Way more than I have, probably.

We both get in and buckle up. Noah backs out and points the car toward home. He extends an open mouth to me, but his eyes stay on the road.

"Here." I fill his mouth with the rest of my donut. The mouthful is too much, and crumbs tumble into his lap. He swipes them onto the floorboard and asks me a question I never saw coming.

I open my mouth, but there are no words ready. I'm silent because I'm stunned.

"Would you mind?" he repeats.

I'm grappling with the answer. He wants to know if I care that he plans to follow me to whatever college I decide on. How can I tell him that college isn't in the cards for me? Not yet, anyway. I applied to all those places, but there's no way I can go. How easily I can picture the stark white envelope, *college* written in my mother's loopy handwriting. It's well-intentioned, but it's also practically *empty*.

I can't take on tens of thousands of dollars in school loans, assuming I could even qualify. Scholarships don't want a girl like me. I'm not special, not according to them anyway. I haven't lost a limb, or developed a cutting-edge method for providing clean water to third world countries. I'm a low-income girl from Northern California without a discernible talent of any kind.

"I can't go out-of-state, Noah," I say, swallowing a big drink of orange juice and setting it back into the cup holder between us.

"Why? You told that horrible old lady I'm related to—"

I give him a look and interrupt him. "Your grandmother."

He waves one hand. "Yeah, her. You told *my grandmother* that you could do it with scholarships and a job. Is that not true?"

"Noah," I start, but I pause. How can I say this to him? He already knows I don't have the means to go to any college of my choosing, but he knows it the same way we all know about the Berlin Wall. Yeah, it existed, but it doesn't affect us personally.

"Ember, whatever you're going to say, don't. We're going to go to college together, and do all the things college boyfriends and girlfriends do. Whatever that is. Meet between classes, go to parties, and football games. It kind of sounds like high school, so maybe I'll ask Brody, and he'll tell me."

I laugh, and he smiles, shaking his head. "The point is, we're not going to be apart. Besides, we still haven't heard from Stanford. Right? That's because it's meant to be for us. Stanford is where we're destined to go together."

This is what I mean. Noah understands that I don't have financial means, but he doesn't really *understand*. He's not thinking about where I'll live, or how I'll eat. The mountains of debt I'll have to take on, or that it may take me longer than four, five, maybe even six years because I'll have to work.

I can't bring myself to pop his enthusiastically swaying balloon. So I don't. I reach across the center console, run my hand over his cheek, and tell him we'll work it out somehow. The lie tastes sour, even though he swallows it like it's velvety chocolate.

---

"DOES MOM KNOW?" I HISS, CORNERED IN THE BATHROOM I share with Sky. The plastic rings slide across the rod as I shove the teal shower curtain out of my way.

"No," Sky whispers, "but only because I swore up and down I remembered the girl you were spending the night with, and that you weren't going to prom, even though you have a boyfriend." She crosses her arms and stares at me, her mouth a thin, angry line.

"Thank you," I say in an insistent voice. "I mean it. She would've killed me if she knew where I really was."

"Where were you?" Sky asks. Only one of her eyebrows rises on her forehead. I really wish I could do that. My only cool trick is to roll one eye while the other stays still.

"I went to the coast with Noah. His parents have a place."

"Did you—?" I nod before she can finish, and her eyes grow wide.

Sky hates that she's a virgin. In her moments of outrage,

she threatens to go out to a bar and lose it in a bathroom to a random guy. In her next breath, she's hyperventilating about germs.

"What was it like?" She pinches her lower lip and twists it as she waits for my response. Her eyes look wistful. In a world where Sky's anxiety didn't debilitate her, our roles would be reversed and I would've asked this question of her.

"It was..." I purse my lips, trying to come up with a word that can hold the weight of everything I felt.

*Magic*, I think. "Incredible," I say out loud.

"I need more than that." She bugs out her eyes and looks at me in irritation.

"Sorry, sorry." I laugh. "It was worth waiting for. I can see how it would suck to do it with someone I was 'meh' about. With Noah, it was... Wow." The way he pushed the hair from my face, his soft kisses in the space under my ear, his palm running up the length of my thigh. I can't say all that to Sky, because I want to keep some things to myself. I don't want to share it.

"Maybe...one day..." She intertwines her fingers and lifts them, only to drop them immediately.

My hands go to her shoulders, squeezing, as if I could possibly wring out the pain her anxiety causes her. "You can do it, Sky. You can go to college, you can meet someone, you can have a normal life."

"I've been thinking about college. I checked out those scholarships you wrote down." There's a tug on her lips, her face is turning up into a hopeful smile, and I don't even think she knows it. It makes my heart happy. "There's one I think might work. Maybe. I mean, I don't know. It probably won't."

As if she's a balloon, I watch her deflate in front of me.

Her smile slips away, but my hope hasn't left. Sky just took a step, however fleeting, in the right direction.

"Sky, sometimes you have to do things that scare you, just to show yourself you're capable of recovering from the experience." I'm saying the right words to her, trying to put just one tiny hole in the walls her anxiety constructs, but the words hit home for me too.

I wish Noah didn't scare me, but he does. I wish there weren't any reason to fear him, to fear this love, to fear these feelings. I might be a free spirit, but I have eyes. Difficulties lie ahead of us, like roadblocks on the path to bliss.

I'm terrified.

## 13

## NOAH

Ember sees things I don't see.

We will find a way to go to college together. Even if we have to go to community college for two years before we get to a big university. I don't know how it's going work, only that it is.

"Do you want anything to eat?" Ember asks me, grabbing an apple from a bag on her kitchen counter.

"I'm good. I'm saving myself for the wing challenge." Eating a dozen blazing hot wings sounded like a good idea when Brody called yesterday and told me he wanted me to do it with him. Now I'm not so sure having my picture on the wall at some stupid restaurant is that big of a deal.

Ember bites into her apple and chews. "How likely are you to make it through all of them?" she asks, swallowing.

"I'm a sure bet," I say, grabbing her waist and pulling her into me. It's not that I like spicy food, but I love a challenge, and I hate losing enough to push myself through almost anything.

"Are you ready to meet Alyssa?" Ember snuggles her head against me, snapping off another bite of apple.

"Brody talks about her so much, I feel like I don't even need to meet her." Every time the guy is home, he won't shut up about his girlfriend. It's as if he's never met a girl before. Odd, all things considered.

"I think it's sweet," Ember murmurs against me.

"I think you're sweet." I drop my head so my lips brush her hair. "And sexy. And you give the best—"

"Noah!" Ember wrestles from me and starts motioning with her head. Following her gaze, I see her mom standing just inside the door to the apartment.

"Shoulder massages," I finish. I realize how bad that sounded. I was going to say *fake tattoos* but freaked out when Ember said my name.

Maddie stares at me with shrewd eyes. Ember swears her mother doesn't know about our weekend at the coast, but I've been getting a vibe from her since then. Maybe it's my own guilty conscience, but I swear she's looking at me as if she knows every single thing I did with her daughter.

"Hi, Mom," Ember says as Maddie throws her purse onto the counter.

Maddie says hello to both of us, heads to the sink, and turns on the water. She pumps enough soap for three people onto her open palm. Holding a finger to the water, she waits for ten seconds, then picks up a small brush from the back of the sink and scrubs her nails. I thought thirty seconds of warm, soapy water was enough to kill most germs, but Maddie has been going at it for nearly a minute.

I look at Ember for explanation, but she's watching her mom with a pensive look on her face.

Maddie finishes, dries her hands on a clean towel she has removed from a drawer, and takes a deep breath. "Now," she says, "you two looked cozy when I walked in. Are you having sex?"

"No," I say automatically.

"Yes," Ember says.

Maddie keeps her gaze on Ember. She doesn't look mad, or sad, or upset, or *anything*. "Are you being safe?" she asks. Now she's looking at me, and her eyes harden a fraction.

"Yes," I answer. I feel like I owe it to her to speak. "Are you going to tell my parents?" Not that it's the end of the world, but I'd rather not have the conversation with them.

Maddie laughs, taking me by surprise. I don't know what's funny. "Noah, I won't be telling your parents a thing, but don't you think they already know?"

Her words make me think back to the day Ember and I skipped school, and how my dad knew exactly where to find me. "Yeah, probably."

Maddie opens a cupboard, and inside I see a lot of pasta, some canned goods, and packets of dried soup. Tipping her head to one side, she reaches in and pushes things around.

"We're going out tonight." Ember tells her. "A double-date with Noah's brother, Brody, and his girlfriend, Alyssa."

Maddie turns, looking at me with wide eyes. "Your brother's name is Brody?"

"Yeah..."

Ember and I look at each other, and she shrugs. "Mom, are you okay?" She asks.

"Fine." Maddie turns back around. "I'm fine. I just... That would've been my boy name if I'd had one, that's all."

"Really?" Ember asks. "I would've thought you'd choose something like Forest, or Hunter, or..."

"Shades of green?" Maddie asks, a confused smile on her face. Her shock over my brother's name seems to have dissipated. Ember lifts a section of hair with one hand and points to it with the other. "Oh, yes," Maddie laughs. "What can I say? I'm missing a creativity bone. Apparently, I like to state the obvious."

Ember laughs softly, but I'm not sure what the hell to do. Maddie's being so chill about finding out Ember and I are sleeping together, it's disconcerting. Shouldn't she be chasing me out of the place with a kitchen knife, while screeching at me to stay away from her daughter?

Maddie asks Ember a question, something about Sky, and I try to calm my accelerated heart rate. Normally I don't mind hanging out at Ember's place, but right now I can't wait to leave. Suddenly filling my body with flaming hot wings doesn't sound so bad.

———

"ALYSSA, IT'S NICE TO FINALLY SPEND SOME TIME WITH THE girl Brody doesn't shut up about." I lean back in the booth, looking across the table to my brother.

Alyssa sweeps her blue eyes to Brody, her cheeks flushing, and grins at him.

"You don't shut up about me?"

He leans over and pushes his face into her hair, murmuring into her ear. I pretend to vomit, and it gets Brody's attention.

"I've watched you and Ember act like this for almost two months," Brody says. "Deal with it."

I hold up my hands. "Feel free to suck face. I'm not going to stop you."

"I will," Alyssa chimes, playfully pushing away Brody's face when he leans in. "My lips are still burning from the last time you kissed me." She smacks her lips together.

"Mine too," Ember says from her place beside me. We're tucked in a booth in the back of the restaurant. The wing challenge is over, and I won. I ate the wings, even though it felt like real flames were shooting from my mouth. I drank a huge glass of milk after in an attempt to cool it down, and I did it faster than Brody.

I won.

Ember won't let me kiss her now, so I suppose I'm paying the price.

"Did Dad tell you who's coming for a tour next weekend?" Brody sips his beer and licks the froth from his top lip. He looks around for our server, and when he's certain she isn't there, he pushes the glass across the table to me.

I take a small sip. "Who?"

"Anton Dalto."

I freeze. Everything in my world has just come to a screeching halt.

"I know." Brody nods. "I don't think he's coming to try Dad's new varietal."

Maybe he is. Maybe Dalto loves wine. It's probably a coincidence.

"Who is Anton Dalto?" Ember asks.

"The head coach of the soccer team at Stanford," Brody answers. I'm glad he responded to her, because I can't right now. My words are frozen right along with the rest of my limbs. Brody points at me. "He's coming with his family, so you better be there helping dad with the tour." His tone has changed. He's changed into his big brother pants.

"Noah, this is amazing!" Ember tugs my arm, and warmth floods back into my body.

My brain is still grappling with the information. Anton Dalto was one of the best players in the world before his retirement four years ago. His wife wanted to live in the States, and they chose California. I've been watching him play since I was young, cheered him on as he scored four goals in a single World Cup game, and led his team to victory in a stunning shut-out. Last year, when I wanted to work on ball handling with my left foot, I watched old videos of him running down the field, leading his team.

*They've already chosen their team.*

It's important I remember that. Dalto's not coming to the vineyard to recruit me. Brody is wrong.

Finally the fog lifts from my thoughts and I refocus on my brother. He looks worried, and I realize he's waiting on a response from me.

"Yeah, of course I'll be there."

Relief rearranges his features, and he adopts a shaky smile. "I know they've already recruited, but you never know, Noah. You just never know. If anything, this better positions you for a walk-on."

Alyssa snuggles into his side, and he turns to her, taken away by whatever it is she's saying.

I can hardly hear anything. My mind is buzzing like a beehive took up residence in my skull.

*Dalto... At my vineyard... Breathing the same air as me...*

"Are you excited?" Ember breaks through my thoughts. She slips her hand into mine and squeezes.

"Yeah." My voice doesn't give away any of what I'm feeling inside. If I let myself, I'll start running away with half-baked ideas of somehow convincing Dalto to give me a shot.

"Good. You should be." She smiles up at me, the whites of her eyes shiny, her cheeks a rosy hue. They hold no fear of our future. No worry of what a visit from Dalto could mean for me. For us.

"You're better than all other bests," I say. "Even combined, you're better than every best that could ever be."

Does Ember know that? Does she understand how rare she is? How rare what we have is?

Instead of responding, she kisses me. Deeply, sweetly, in that way she has that makes all my surroundings blur.

"Get a room," Brody calls from across the table. Alyssa smacks his arm.

I flip him off, and when Ember tries to pull away I don't let her.

The news of Dalto's visit is shaking my stable ground, and I need Ember to steady me.

## 14

## EMBER

I'm not supposed to answer my phone while I'm on the clock, but Sky has called me three times.

"What's up?" I whisper-hiss. If Gruff catches me, he'll be pissed. He might even write me up. *Teenagers and their cell phones,* he complains. *They can't wait to tell each other every time they pee, or take a bite of food.*

"I just did something big. Really big." Her voice is high-pitched, like she's holding back a squeal. I can see her sitting on her bed, holding a hand over her mouth as if she might surprise even herself by saying the words.

"Uh huh," I say as quietly as I can. "And what was that?" Maybe she has taken up knitting with Mom, or cooking, or collecting porcelain cat figurines. Sky's life is more boring than any of us would like to admit, so this leaves a lot for her to be enthusiastic about.

"I signed up for classes at Northmount Community College next semester." Her words are so rushed they come out on top of the other.

"What?" I say loudly. Gruff looks up from where he's

restocking a display of cheap sunglasses. His narrowed eyes find me in an instant.

"That's great," I whisper, whipping around so he can only see my back. "I'll bring home something sweet to celebrate, okay?"

"Those chocolate Easter eggs with the candy coating?" Sky asks hopefully. "You know I can't say no to those."

"Perfect." Especially since Easter is over and all that candy is marked down seventy percent. "Go tell Mom. I'll see you in an hour."

Gruff taps on my shoulder just as I press the end button. I look back at him and the crooked finger he has pointing back towards the office.

"Okay," I say cheerfully, leading the way.

The write-up is worth answering Sky's call. So is enduring Gruff's lecture about phone usage while I'm on *his* clock.

When I arrive home with three bags of Sky's favorite candy, she's all smiles. My mom had already bought a bottle of sparkling apple cider, and we spend the next hour sipping it from coffee mugs while eating too much chocolate.

---

NOAH WAS CROWNED PROM KING, AND I WAS CHRISTENED public enemy number one—to everyone except Noah's closest friends, anyhow.

I've heard the whispers.

*She's, like, taking Noah away from everyone.*

*I heard they sit at her house in the dark and stare at the wall.*

*What is up with all those piercings? I bet she has her snatch pierced too.*

I laughed out loud about the snatch one. It was pretty funny.

Today I get a break from the rumor mill. It's Saturday, and a normal day for me, although it's anything but a typical day for Noah.

Anton Dalto is arriving at Sutton House this afternoon, and Johanna's going nuts. Ten minutes ago Noah called to tell me he's coming to my place to escape the stressful atmosphere at home.

*Thank god he called first.* I only hope I can get up to my apartment before he arrives. The envelope in my back pocket feels like it's alive.

I'd take the stairs two at a time, but they're treacherous enough already. I'm halfway up when I hear a car door close. I already know it's him. My body can sense his nearness.

He shouts my name and I turn. Leaning onto the black iron rail for support, I wave at him as he jogs from his car. He takes the stairs two at a time, only stopping when he reaches me.

"Show-off," I mutter teasingly.

Noah traces my jaw with a fingertip, but his eyes look frenzied, and his cheeks are flushed. *He's nervous about today.*

"Are you still scared of those stairs?" He asks in a teasing voice.

I stick out my tongue and give the bottom of my shirt a tug, making certain it covers the top half of the envelope. When I'm positive it's safely hidden, I turn and head for the next set of stairs that will take us to my apartment.

"I'm glad you aren't babysitting yet. I really needed to get out of the house. My mom is running around the restaurant and the tasting room like the Queen of England is coming."

"My home is your home," I say when we get to my front door. "And I promise to let you out of the dark at least twice while you're here."

Noah groans. "You've heard that one?"

"Sure have. Did you hear the one about my snatch?"

"That the carpet doesn't match the drapes?"

"What?" I whirl around. Noah's shoulders jump. "Are they suggesting I dye my hair? That's it!" I stomp my foot. Piercings are one thing, but the authenticity of my hair color? "They can talk about my private parts, but they cannot call my hair color into question."

Noah reaches for a strand and twists it around his finger. "Don't worry. I assured them you're monochromatic."

My eyes bulge, and I blink twice.

He leans in until I feel his lips on my ear. "I'm kidding."

Letting out a loud breath, I tip my head back in excruciating relief.

He plants a soft kiss on my temple. "I'd never do that, Ember."

I nod, turning my face to kiss his cheek. "Come on in," I say, reaching for the door handle.

We walk in, and my mom and Sky look up. Sky sits on the floor, her elbows propped on the coffee table. My mom is on the couch, one foot tucked under the opposite thigh, as she leans forward over the table. Playing cards are laid out between them.

"What are you playing?" Noah asks.

"War," Sky answers.

"Can I have the next turn?" he asks, settling in next to my mom on the couch.

"Sure," Sky says at the same time my mom tells him he better not be a *cheetah*.

Noah laughs like he's never heard a joke, but Sky and I

roll our eyes. Despite my mild embarrassment, I'm happy to hear my mom make a joke. The last couple of days, she's been on another planet—staring around, but not really looking anywhere. This morning she snapped at Sky when an open box of pasta dropped out of the cabinet and spilled on the floor.

While Noah plays I go to my room and slip the envelope into my nightstand. I'll open it later. I'm dying to know what it says, but today is about Noah. About Dalto.

My absence goes unnoticed, and when I return I snuggle up next to Noah on the couch. We take turns playing until Noah's pocket rings. He looks up at me, his eyes holding both fear and excitement.

"I better go." He sets down his cards and rises, pulling his phone from his shorts. "I'm on my way, Dad," he says, waiting to hear a response and then hanging up.

I walk him to his car. He's quiet, his hands stuffed into his pockets.

"You okay?" I ask.

"Yeah. Just, I don't know..." We stop at his car, and he turns to look at me. "I'm scared to have the thing I've always wanted. Sounds stupid, right?"

I grab his wrist, turn it over, and run my thumb across it. His fingers flex and unfurl as I run my thumb over the soft skin once, twice, seven times.

"That's not stupid, Noah. It's fear of the unknown. I think working for something your whole life, the way you have with soccer, is kind of like walking up a mountain that ends in a cliff. You have no idea what's going to happen when you step off."

"That's what falling in love with you feels like." He flips his open palm over and grabs my arm, pulling me in close. "I'm frightened for us, Ember. I don't know what's going to happen." The warmth of his sigh travels over the top of my head.

"Everything will be fine," I tell him. Placating Noah is more important than telling him how terrified I am for us. He needs a clear mind right now. "Go," I urge, pulling back. "Call me when it's over."

Standing on tiptoe, I kiss him quickly, then step back.

He drives away, and I go back up the stairs, my fingers tracing my tattoo through my thin shirt.

---

WYATT NEEDS A BATH. HE'S COVERED IN PAINT. WASHABLE paint, thank goodness.

"Come on, buddy." I turn on the faucet in the bathtub and add bubble bath, then peel off Wyatt's clothes and set them in the sink. Drops of moisture hit the wall as he jumps into the tub. The water swirls around him, paint from his body mixing in and creating a watery rainbow.

I watch him play, but I'm wondering about Noah. He hasn't called or sent me a message. I don't know if that's good or bad. I don't even know what good or bad means right now.

Is it good if he goes to Stanford? Or bad?

Is it bad if he stays here and goes to community college? Or good?

All I know is that he can't make choices based on me. That would be—

*Splash*!

"Wyatt!" I leap off the toilet lid and thrust my arms under the water. My hands slide over his chest, but I'm able to grip him under the arms and lift him up. Free of the bubbles and water, he rapidly blinks wide eyes and draws in fast breaths. Pulling him out of the tub, I sit back down and set him on my lap. It was just one second, he's fine, but he's terrified. He clings to me, water drips onto my legs and tufts of soap glide down his face.

"I just wanted to be a dolphin," he cries, his tiny body shaking. I wrap a towel around his back and rock him back and forth.

"Everything is okay, you're fine, I'm here."

We go to his room, where I dry him and dress him. For the next two hours we read and play, and when Wyatt's mom returns, I tell her what happened. She's not mad as I feared she would be, but grateful I was beside him. When I leave, I take a heaping plate of guilt with me.

Yeah, I was beside him, but I was distracted. Thoughts of Noah had taken over my brain, and what would've happened if I hadn't noticed the splash?

For the first time I realize what Noah did by running into the lake when he thought I was drowning. Until this afternoon, I'd thought it was sweet and heroic in an overdone way, but now I see how he must've felt thinking someone was really drowning. He thought someone needed help, and he was willing to pay whatever it cost.

Good people deserve good things.

I hope that coach is coming for something other than wine.

---

MY PHONE MIGHT SOON BECOME A 3D FIXTURE ON MY WALL, like a piece of avant-garde art. *Here is an expression of teenage frustration.* Noah still hasn't texted.

At eight o'clock, I was worried.

At nine o'clock, I'm ticked off.

When my mom opens my door at nine-thirty, her eyes red-rimmed and swollen, her cheeks taut, I stop thinking about my phone and the messages I'm not getting.

"What is it?" Sky asks, sitting up from her pillows and tossing aside an article she'd printed out about cultivating good study habits.

"Mom?" I ask, uncrossing my legs and swinging them over the side of my bed. Sky and I are both waiting for her to say something, but her eyes dart back and forth and she moves her hands around as if she wishes she had something to do with them.

"Mom," Sky's voice is stern, "you're freaking us out. What happened?"

Slowly she walks into our room and sits on the end of my bed. "I've lost four houses in the last few weeks," she finally answers, her voice low. "I know neither of you watch the news, but some things are happening and people are nervous. When people are nervous, the first thing they do is tighten the hold on their wallets. Buh-bye, extras." She shakes her head and squeezes her eyes shut. When she opens them, her gaze stays on the dingy carpet. "I'm an extra."

"No, you're not," Sky and I argue.

I scurry across the small bed and wrap my arms around my mom from behind. Sky comes to sit beside her and piles her arms on top of us.

Mom sniffles. "It will all work out, but in the meantime, things will have to get a little tighter around here."

"I'll call on Monday and cancel my classes," Sky says. "I'll get a second job and go to school when it's a better time. I'm sure those scholarships will still—"

"No," my mom says sharply. "You will not do that, Sky Marie. You will stay enrolled. You will not give up." She untangles herself from our limbs and stands up. Turning around, she points at me. "And you won't either. You're going to college...on scholarships, I guess." Her eyes move away, and I know they're seeing her nightstand with its envelopes of saved money. *College* cash will be moved for certain, going toward *Food* and *Rent*. Not that there was much to begin with.

"I haven't been accepted anywhere," I lie, thinking of the stack of acceptance letters hidden under my mattress. They are all screaming at me, but it's the one that arrived today that sears me with indignation. Stanford. *We're delighted to inform you...*

"You're kidding me?" Sky asks, eyebrows on her forehead. "AP classes, good grades? And nobody wants you?"

I shake my head and shrug, the lie churning in my stomach. "It's tough out there, but I'm happy. I need a little time to think about what I want from life. Who really knows at eighteen what they want to do for the rest of their lives?"

My mother stares at me. Her anguish and disappointment has beaten her down. I can tell. On most days she would challenge me, but on this day, she caves.

"You're going to college one day, Ember. I promise you that." Her face is earnest.

"Yes, Mom. I will."

She leaves with slumped shoulders. Sky and I climb in bed, both too shocked to say much. I wait for Sky to fall asleep, and then I feel it. The sting of salt, the burn at the top of my nose. I'm quiet as can be as I cry. Just because I'm letting go of a dream on purpose doesn't mean I can't mourn it.

## 15

## NOAH

THE FIRST THING I DO WHEN I WAKE UP IS GRAB MY PHONE. BY the time Coach Dalto left last night, it was too late to call Ember. In an apartment that small, it feels like calling her is like calling her mom and sister too. I sent her a message instead, but she didn't respond, probably because she was already asleep.

And she's probably still asleep, because it's six o'clock in the morning. Sleep is but a dream for someone who just found out they're going to put their cleats on Stanford grass in the fall.

I pull on my running clothes and head downstairs, stopping to grab a set of earbuds from a drawer in the kitchen.

It's dark outside and the grass is slick with dew. Turning left, I run on our property until our expansive yard gives way to one edge of the vineyard. The blue of the sky is developing into shades of deep purple, like a bruise, and then slowly changes to light pink and orange, like sherbet.

I love it out here, love the way my lungs take in breath, the way the gentle sloping hills make my body work harder. At the top of a hill I pause, turning in a circle. Grapes forever, it feels like. Behind me, in front of me, and beside me. I reach out and gently pinch a large, dusty purple one that sticks out from the bunch.

Last night my father was ecstatic. He shook hands with Coach Dalto and his wife, Priscilla, thanked them again for coming, and for giving me the opportunity. When they left he said nothing of what this could mean for him. *Four more years of another son who doesn't want to learn about the vineyard.*

It's not forever, it's just for now.

After my run, I shower and eat breakfast. My dad comes in and pours a glass of water. He tosses something into his mouth and swallows the water.

"Too much wine last night?" I ask. Hazard of the job, I suppose.

"Yep. Celebrating your acceptance and got a little ahead of myself." One side of his mouth turns up into a grin, and he shakes his head. "Poor choices are not only for the young." He walks to the pantry and steps in. Boxes move across the shelves, and then he steps out with cereal in hand. "What do you think you'll do about Ember?"

His eyes aren't on me. They're focused on pouring his cereal, as if it's that hard. He grabs the milk from the fridge and adds some to his bowl. Anger flares inside me. When it comes to Ember, it feels like there's always a fire burning in my chest and the flames need only an errant comment to be teased out.

"Did I miss the segue?" My voice is harsh. "Because it sounds like you were talking about bad decisions, and then you asked about Ember." I hate how I have to defend her. I never had to defend Kelsey. My parents accepted her without comment.

Dad rubs a hand over his forehead. "Calm down. I didn't

mean anything by it. I was only asking what your plans are."
He looks at me with somber eyes. "You know she's not going
to Stanford."

I argue without hesitation. "She could. Her grades are
Stanford material."

Dad sets his bowl on the counter and leans against it.
His mouth turns down, not a frown but more a pensive
hopelessness. "Son, I know what a girl like Ember can do to
you. She'll make you think anything is possible even when it
goes against all logic. You'll start thinking maybe you can
work."

What does that even mean? *A girl like Ember?* How is she any
different from anybody else? I shake my head, looking down at
my shoes. The truth is already in my thoughts. She's different,
and I know it. She operates on a different frequency than all the
girls running around our high school. Ember is better. Still, I
want to know just what my dad meant by that. I open my mouth
to challenge him, but stop short when I see his face.

His eyes have gone somewhere, someplace outside this
kitchen, away from this house to another time. What is he
remembering? I feel uncomfortable, because I know
whoever he's thinking of, it's not my mom.

"She'll be something else altogether, a being you didn't
know existed. She'll make you think any dream you ever
had is possible." He turns his gaze back to me, and he's back
from wherever he went inside his memory. "I'm speaking
from experience."

I only nod, keeping my mouth shut. It doesn't matter
what he says. He can't possibly understand. He doesn't know
what's inside my chest when I look at Ember. Tight and full,
ready to explode at any minute.

"You're young," he continues. "I know that's not what

you want to hear, but it's true. You've been given the opportunity you've worked for your whole life. Don't take it lightly." He picks up his cereal bowl and peers into it, his lips turning down slightly. I'm sure it's soggy by now.

He walks from the kitchen, pausing just before he steps into the next room. "Nothing lasts forever, Noah. That's all I'm saying."

He's wrong. He doesn't know Ember. Doesn't know Ember and me *together*. We're not a typical teenage romance. We're deeper, better, more *everything*. There aren't proper words to describe how perfect Ember and I are together. Or how wrong my father is.

We're going to work out.

We have to.

---

"I love it here." The words tumble from Ember's lips.

Sunshine, breeze, birds talking in the trees. I think I needed our spot at the lake as much as she did today. She lays back on the blanket I brought. Her eyes are closed, and she breathes in deeply. Her chest rises, falling back down when she exhales.

"Ember, I love you."

She opens an eye, looks at me, and blinks after a moment. "And I you."

I lay my head back down onto folded forearms, but remain silent.

"You want to talk about it?" Her voice curls into the folds of my arms.

Ember already told me she's not going to come with me to Stanford, but I won't give up so easily.

"I'm brainstorming ways to make you change your mind." My voice is muffled.

"Noah," Ember sighs my name, and it sounds like a tired warning. "We've been through this."

"I'm not giving up." Sitting up, I look at her. "I won't go."

She sits up too, her eyes alarmed. "You better be kidding."

"I'm not. I won't go."

"Noah, you're not thinking clearly. Of course you're going to go. Stanford offered you a spot. *Stanford*. The college of your dreams."

"Soccer won't last forever. You're my forever."

Ember shakes her head. "No way. Not happening."

Her absolution frustrates me. "What's the real problem, Ember?"

"We've already discussed the real problem."

"No. I want to know why you're not coming with me. Why you're not even *trying*."

"I can't, Noah! I can't. My mom needs help. Real help. You don't have the problems I have, and to be realistic, they're not even problems. They're roadblocks. She said the economy has been squeezed, and the first thing people do is cut the excess. Restaurants, gym memberships, *cleaning ladies*."

"Oh." I'm not sure what to say. The threadbare couch, the chipped wood coffee table, plates that don't match. It's clear Ember's mom isn't exactly raking it in. *And all that dried pasta in the cabinet*. Until now, I didn't realize why a cabinet full of pasta and canned goods struck me as odd.

Our fridge is loaded with wild-caught fish and grass-fed meat. Organic vegetables and non-GMO pasture-raised eggs. Our bread might as well have been breathed on by angels.

"What does this mean for you?" I hate that we have to talk about this. I hate that her circumstances are different from mine. I even hate that mine are different from hers. I never thought I'd resent my comfortable lifestyle, but in this moment I do.

"It means I need to get another job. Put all college on the back burner, even community. Not forever. Just for now."

I can tell she doesn't want to. She reaches out beyond the edge of the blanket, scooping, and lets the pebbles drip through her fingers, like sugar through a sieve when Gretchen bakes a pie.

"You don't have to." My words are vehement. "You don't have to give up on your dreams." The things I love about Ember are the very same things making me frustrated now.

How is that possible? How can she drive me to insanity at the same time that I want to wrap my arms around her and pull her tight, press my lips to hers and let her essence engulf me?

"I'm not giving up, Noah." Ember's voice hardens. She's mad too. "I'm pressing the pause button. It's different."

"What if you never press play again? How can you give that up?"

Her expression changes into a soft, despondent look. "Did you know there's a discount grocery store in Brazelton?"

I blink twice. Why in the world is Ember talking about a store in a town thirty minutes away?

"No," I say slowly, my mind racing to figure out how this fits into our conversation.

"When I was ten we had to go there. My mom lost a whole bunch of houses, and we had nothing. *Nothing*. We ate pork and beans from cans. Dented cans."

Ember pulls her legs into herself, resting her chin on the crack between her knees.

"You've never had to wonder what the next month will be like, and I'm happy for that, but I have. And I won't let that happen again. I'm not ten anymore. I can make a difference. You ask how I can give up on my dream, but I ask how I can allow my mother to eat food from a dented can."

Shit. What is there to say? I'm a privileged boy from a wealthy family. Coach Dalto just waltzed onto my parents' vineyard and laid more gold bricks on my path.

How is that fair?

Ember is good. Better than good. She's extraordinary. Why isn't the universe knocking down her door, asking her to come out and spread what she has with the rest of the world?

"I'm sorry." I breathe the words. I wish I had more to offer her in this moment, but I don't.

"There's nothing for you to apologize for. That's just what happened. It's nothing more than that." She shrugs. "But that doesn't mean I'm going to let it happen again."

"Me neither," I declare, an idea forming. It's stupid, and it'll go over worse than a cockroach infestation at Sutton House, but at this point I don't care.

"I'm going to stay here," I say, jabbing the ground with one finger. "I'll get a job, go to Northmount Community College. We'll help your mom, and when you're ready, we'll make the move to a university. Ember, I'm serious. I love you."

"You love soccer."

"I love you more."

"You have a spot on a college soccer team waiting for you."

"I have a vineyard waiting for me too. Not to sound like

an arrogant prick, but it's not as if my alternative to playing soccer in college is shoveling shit at a manure factory. Either way I go, I'll be okay."

"Noah." Ember runs a hand over my cheek, lets it drag across my chest. "You try and stay here, and there won't be a relationship to stay for."

For a second my whole world tilts on its axis. "What?"

"I'm serious. I won't let you pass on an opportunity like this."

"You love me."

"I do. And that's why I'd never allow you to give up Stanford for me."

I look in her eyes and see the strength of a warrior, her resolve hard and cold like steel. I don't want to press the issue. A large part of me wants to challenge her, but seeing her now, I know better.

After getting off the blanket, I reach out a hand and help her up.

I take her to my house. The concert my parents went to won't be over for hours.

Instead of arguing with her, I push her back on my bed. When I want to shout at the injustice of it all, I kiss her instead. And then, because I want to flip fate the stiffest and most heartfelt bird, I don't roll on a condom. Ember sees me without one, and it's like she wants to join me in a grand *fuck you* gesture. Her legs wrap around me, and she guides me inside her.

Fuck you, fate.

# 16

## EMBER

I KNOW IT WAS STUPID.

Tempting fate that way, it was thoughtless and reckless, but it felt good, for more reasons than the obvious. In a small way, it was something we took control of, when everything around us was spinning like debris in a tornado.

It's what I said the moment I stepped from the bathroom that hurt Noah. He's trying to pretend like it didn't, but I see the shadow in his eyes. And now, even though his arm is wrapped around my shoulders where we lie on his bed, I feel like he's a mile away.

Why didn't I keep my mouth shut? I know why. I'm high on his love, and I don't want that to change. I want to keep what we have pure, so I suggested we end on a high note. I didn't really mean it. I don't actually want that. What I want is to create a perfect picture for our future selves. I can't bear to have it any other way.

"Why would you want to break up, Ember? I already promised to take the scholarship. Remember your ultimatum?" His eyes are on the ceiling, and his chest rises and falls in a rhythm, but each inhale and exhale is too long, extended by the effort it's taking him to stay calm.

"Because I'm scared for us." I've finally said it. I've been putting on a brave face but I can't anymore. It's disingenuous, and it hurts. "I want to freeze us in time, while we're at our peak."

He rolls away, dragging his arm out from under my body, only to turn back to me and prop his head in his hand. He offers a grin my mother would call *smart-alecky*. "We're not vegetables, Ember. We don't need to be frozen at the peak of freshness."

I move to pinch him, but he blocks me by grabbing my hand and gripping it tightly. Our interwoven fingers drift down between us onto the bed.

"I'll come home all the time. So often you'll get sick of me."

I watch his face, trying to push away this feeling creeping over me. A foreboding nuisance, like a gnat buzzing around in my head. It's more than fear.

Closing my eyes, I slowly shake my head. "Don't." When I open them, they focus on Noah. "Don't drag us through the mud until we collapse. We'll miss some calls and you'll skip a visit. Then it'll be two missed visits. You'll make new friends, and tell me about them, and to you they'll be real, but to me they'll only be characters. Feelings will get hurt, we won't communicate, and before you know it, we won't talk for weeks." My eyes are stinging now, tightening in that way that tells me tears are imminent. "I can't have that, Noah. I don't want to remember us that way and—"

Noah puts out his hand. "Stop talking." He lowers his head and kisses my temple. "Let's just live here," he whispers against it. "Right now. In these minutes. In these next few months. In the summer of us."

How can I say no?

The boy I love wants only to love me in return.

I'd be a fool to turn that down.

---

WE WERE INSEPARABLE THE WHOLE SUMMER, SQUEEZING EVERY last drop from our precious and rapidly depleting time. August was a deadline looming, a guillotine, blade poised.

Noah gave me a bike for graduation; it was just like the one I saw that morning at the beach. I wanted to ride it more, but Noah insisted he keep driving me to work. Knowing I'd get plenty of time to ride it in the fall kept me from arguing with him.

We spent lazy days together, lying on the shore of the lake, watching puffy white clouds roll across the blue sky. Four more trips to the beach house, and this time we didn't hide it. We were daring and adventurous.

Noah talked Brody into getting him some pot, and I tried it for the first time. Noah was excited over how soft the bud was, something I knew nothing about. I'd needed Noah badly that night. Shapes danced in front of me, turning and swirling until they grew into 3-D forms.

As the days rolled on and August drew nearer, it became harder to ignore its approach. It's whispered beginning had increased in volume, and we both felt the impending yell.

---

*TWO DAYS.*

He leaves in two days.

We're at the lake again. We've been other places this

summer, but we always come back to the lake. This is where the magic began.

The clouds are dark, but we decided not to let that deter us. We're lying on a blanket on the sandy bank, and neither of us speak. Perhaps we're so full of thoughts, emotion, and fear, that if we let even a drop of it out, the floodgates will open. Besides, the quiet is nice. Is there anything better than being close enough to someone to sit with them in silence?

Eventually, Noah reaches for me. I turn into his touch. His eyes reflect the way I feel. We are both drowning on the inside. I meet his lips in the middle, and we take, hungrily. We have sex all the time, but it doesn't feel like this. Where we are usually unhurried, today has an insistence. There's a finality to it. When the raindrops fall, we don't stop. It's a gentle rain, the kind that touches your skin in a casual, almost comforting way. Intoxicated by the scent of wet air, I tilt my chin to the sky and savor the feel of my hands skimming Noah's damp back. When it's over, we dress and lie back down, me with my head on his chest, his hand running over my hair.

"I love you so much, Ember." His voice is thick and sad.

"I love you too," I say, my words tumbling onto his chest.

It's the saddest, most perfect day ever.

---

It's here.

Noah and I drive the two hours to Stanford in his car, his parents following. When we arrive, Noah looks out his windshield and smiles. I mimic him. I smile so damn hard, there's no way he'll see my insides breaking into a million pieces.

His dorm is red brick and three-stories high. People are everywhere. We climb from the car and join his parents.

"Let's go this way," Johanna says, taking charge.

I follow. All day long, I follow. Campus tour. Meeting this person, then that one. Smile, smile, smile, but it feels more like marching to the gallows. My internal timer counts each second.

Not until it's time to leave do Noah and I get a moment alone. His parents say goodbye and tell me to meet them at their car.

He pulls me into a tight hug the instant his dorm room door closes behind them.

"Are you excited to start next week?" he asks.

I most certainly am not looking forward to my new job working mornings at a cafe. Or going to my old job at night. Gruff is getting on my last nerve.

"Sure," I say, thinking of the dwindling cash in my mom's envelopes. "Are you excited for your first practice?"

No response. His chin comes to rest on the top of my head. "Fuck this small talk."

My body trembles with my empty laughter. "It's painful, isn't it?"

"The conversation or the good-bye?"

"Both."

His breath bolts from him in one swift exhale. "Excruciating."

"How are we supposed to say goodbye?" I'm aware of his parent's waiting for me in their car. The timer is ticking off its final moments.

"I think it's like anything else. You just do it. You force it to happen, even when you want to fight it."

He runs his fingers through my hair and I squeeze harder, willing myself not to cry.

"I'll see you soon, okay? I'll be home before you know it." He cups my face and I rise on tiptoe to meet him. Our kiss is short and sweet. Kissing longer will only hurt more.

I leave on a promise to talk that night when I get back to Northmount. The door shuts behind me and I put one foot in front of the other, never looking back, too afraid I'll abandon my responsibilities, run straight back to his arms, and never leave.

I climb into his parents' car. At first they make small talk, and I swear I try to engage. I must suck at it, because they stop bringing me into the conversation. I want to pull out my phone and text Noah, but I know he has things to do, and I don't want to take away from his first evening there. I stare out the window and try to keep the tears at bay. When they drop me off in front of my apartment, Johanna makes a comment about still seeing me even though Noah is gone.

It's a sweet gesture, but an empty one.

Before I reach the landing I'm sobbing.

---

EVEN THOUGH WE HAD MAGIC AND THE KIND OF LOVE I'M certain someone could write a book about, it all happened like I said it would.

That first month I was glued to my phone, waiting for his call. He came home every weekend. I stayed the night at his house, not asking either of our parents if it was okay. We did it because we could, because we wanted to punish someone, or something, for the way we missed each other. We joked I'd develop problems walking because of how much we had sex. The misery we felt during the week was soothed by the time he arrived home on Friday afternoon, only to begin again when he left on Sunday.

The second month he missed a visit, and my mom had the flu. Sky and I cleaned houses for her while she lied on the sofa with aches she swore were cancer, and I dropped into bed at night, physically exhausted.

Noah grew busier. He made new friends. Soccer practice was more intense. He had to travel around California for games. There was always something to do, a person to see, a plan to make. *Have fun*, I'd say when we were hanging up, but I didn't really mean it. I felt sad and left out. I was frustrated at the universe, at circumstance, for making this so damn hard. We loved each other. Why couldn't that be all we needed to survive?

He'd call when he could, but I was working *all the time*, and seeing those missed call notifications tore at my heart. We began to fight. We missed each other, but it manifested as criticism, one of us finding fault with the other nearly every time we talked. We were reaching for something to save us, not communicating properly, and sinking fast.

I hung up the phone on a cold, bleak day in January. Actions brought us together, but all it took to sever us were words. *This isn't working*. We'd both said it. We were broken, desolate. We were bringing each other more pain than pleasure. We agreed it was over. Love wasn't enough.

I lost him, when all I wanted was to have him.

# 17

# EMBER

*ONE YEAR LATER*

MY FEET.

My poor, aching feet.

I reach down, rub a hand over my heel and up my instep, kneading as I go.

"No more doubles," I tell Dorothy, the middle-aged woman whose shift I covered last night.

"You're the one who wanted my shift," Dorothy points out from across the booth. Reaching down, she pulls her cash tips from the front of her apron and lays the small pile on the table. She separates the bills by denomination and stacks them.

The breakfast rush has just ended, signaling the end of my shift. The cafe is mostly empty now. Jack, who has been coming here every morning for years, sits at the counter sipping black coffee.

"I know." I slide my foot back into my shoe. "Christmas," I add.

"I feel you, honey." Dorothy rearranges the salt and pepper shakers, so they're in their proper place.

Her kids are teenagers. Her husband is a mechanic. *Always has grease under his nails,* she says, *but God help me, I love him.* One day Dorothy told me how their family got started early, and not because they chose it that way. After she told me their story, I'd never been so happy fate didn't take us up on the devil's dance we did that day at Noah's parents' house. We were reckless and foolish. We got lucky. In that one way, we got lucky.

"You going to be okay?" Dorothy's concerned gaze pins me against the brown vinyl seat.

"Of course."

"You seem sad."

"I'm tired. That's all." I smile. I am so fine. Better than fine. I'm dandy. Freakin' dandy. The whole place is covered in Christmas decorations, and people are in a seasonally-induced good mood.

Everything is great.

GREAT.

It's been almost a year since I last heard from Noah. He disappeared from my life, like a magician in a puff of smoke. I had fantasies he would come home for the summer, we would see each other and instantly we'd know we'd done everything wrong. We'd form a plan, do better. This time I'd come to visit him at Stanford. Sky had a car, and I'd borrow it. We'd make it work, because we'd learned not to rely on love alone.

But, no.

Noah didn't come back. Or, if he did, he didn't find me.

I'm still here with relics of him. The yellow bike I ride every day. The lake I avoid at all costs. My lips feel seared by his kiss. Some days I wish I didn't still love him. Other days it's all I have.

That and my jobs, of course. I'm still saving money, stashing away as much as I can so that when I take courses at the community college next semester I can work less, and focus on school more. By all accounts, I'm okay.

Things got even worse for my mom after Noah and I broke up, but she's better now. I constantly doubted my decision to stay, but when she lost two more houses, I knew I'd made the right choice. Sky worked evenings doing her medical billing, even though we told her to spend that time studying, and we made it through. Mom printed flyers, posted them around town, and eventually rebuilt her clientele.

I might be okay, but this time of year is hard. I keep picturing Noah at his parents' house next to a Christmas tree, or vacationing on a tropical island for the holiday. Each time he has a girl next to him. She's beautiful, and her head is tipped back in laughter while Noah grips her around the waist with one arm. The image knifes my heart every time, yet I can't seem to make it go away.

Even now, talking to Dorothy, I see them together. *Stab, stab, stab.*

"I better go," I say in a high-pitched voice, jumping up.

Dorothy looks at me as if I'm transparent. She has the knowing gaze of a mother who doesn't believe a word coming out of my mouth.

I leave, my hands stuffed in my jacket pocket, but when I reach my bike, I don't feel like getting on it. So I don't. The windy day makes the cool air feel colder, and it's a good match for my heart.

I wander along the main streets in town, past the storefronts and offices. Turns out, walking without a purpose sucks. Without something to focus on, my mind wanders. Straight to Noah. The very place I don't want it to go.

Without looking, I duck into a store. The warm air envelops my face. I pull off my jacket, drape it over my forearm, and peer around, curious at what I've gotten myself into.

Round racks of clothing, shoes falling over one another haphazardly on shelves, and an odd smell. Not terrible but slightly musty. A multitude of smells mixing together to make a blasé scent, like too many colors added together make brown.

"Welcome to Zee's." The voice reaches me before the person. It has a soft, Southern lilt. He comes from an open door at the back of the small place, his purple velvet blazer shiny under the overhead lights. From his forehead to his neck, his brown hair is spiked in intricate rows.

"Hello," I say, unable to take my eyes off his hair.

"I'm getting ready to shave it all off," he says, continuing behind the counter. There's a stool there, but he doesn't sit.

"Okay," I respond, not sure what I'm supposed to say.

Turning his head, he glances out the window and then back at me. "Did you come from Friendly Little Place?"

I look down at my uniform and laugh. "What gave it away?"

The guy steps back out from behind the counter. "Can I help you find anything?"

"Oh...umm." I look around. "Probably not. I was just... I don't really know." I laugh, embarrassed. "I wound up here."

The guy walks closer, and I gaze at his blazer. It looks soft. He extends a hand.

"Dayton Mann," he says, grinning. One of his front teeth turns in slightly, and it makes me feel like I can trust him.

"Ember Dane." I return the smile, my first in weeks that

wasn't immediately followed by *What can I get you*, and my face stretches with the effort.

"What do you think about me putting the 'closed' sign up and taking you for a drink?"

"Are bars open in the middle of the day?" Never mind that I'm not twenty-one.

He sends me a derisive look, but it's playful. "Honey, bars would stay open during an apocalypse." Dayton laughs at his own joke and wanders to the front door. He flips the open sign and reaches over the counter, coming away with a set of keys.

"Let's go," he says.

I don't quite know what just happened, but I'm not going to question it. We walk out and I wait for him to lock up. He leads the way and I fall into step beside him. He tells me about his teacup Chihuahua until we reach the door of a little bar on the corner.

---

My new friend slips into the booth across from me. Very different from the booth at Friendly Little Place. This one has a high wooden back, creating the notion of privacy.

He sets down the amber colored beers we ordered from the bartender before claiming our spot. I wasn't carded, thank god. Maybe it was the uniform.

"Are you going to get in trouble for closing the shop like that? It's the middle of the day." I reach for the beer and take a small sip.

Dayton shakes his head. "I own Zee's."

I raise my eyebrows. He looks too young to own a store.

"Where are you from?" I ask.

"Did my accent give it away?" He laughs, twisting a light-blue corded bracelet around on his wrist. "I followed love here, all the way from Alabama." He raises his eyes to the ceiling. "Lord help me, I was dumb for that man. And blind, because I couldn't see how confused he was. My momma would've said he didn't know whether to check his ass or scratch his watch."

"I take it things didn't work out?"

"He decided he didn't want what I have, if you catch my drift."

"Ah." I nod. "Drift caught."

"And you? Why do you look like your grandma just died?" His eyes grow wide. "Oh, shit. Please tell me she did not just die?"

"She did not." I laugh softly. "Why did you close the shop in the middle of the day? Don't you want to make money?"

He shrugs. "Nobody else was in there and I was bored. Why did you wander into a store when you didn't know what it sold?"

I bite my lip and look away. I don't want to talk about Noah. "My mind was occupied. I wasn't paying attention."

"What did he do?"

"What makes you think someone did something to me?"

"Because looking at you is like looking at a mirror image of myself at this time last year. You look *sad.*"

"I feel sad," I whisper, the emotion coming to the surface because it was named, like Dayton called roll and it stood up to announce its presence.

"Tell me all about it," Dayton coaxes, making a *come on* gesture with his hands. "It'd be nice to hear someone else's shit right now. This time of year makes me think of Diego." He scrunches his face and shakes his head quickly. "I don't want to think of him, or his new wife. So come on. Talk to me."

I start talking. Dayton nods often, interrupting me twice to ask questions.

"It was probably just puppy love." I tuck my hands between my thighs and lift my shoulders, then drop them slowly. If I attribute our feelings to being young, maybe it'll make me feel better.

"That's possible," Dayton says, drawing out the second word. "No matter the age, real love is intense. You drown in it, and if it goes away, it hurts. But not any less just because you're young."

"How old are you?" I remove my hands from the warmth of my legs, wrap them around the beer glass, and take a long drink.

Dayton smirks. "Twenty-six. And based on your story, I'm aware I supplied alcohol to a minor."

I glance at the bar, fearful the bartender heard Dayton, but he's watching the TV in the corner and paying no attention to us.

"I should go," I say, looking back at Dayton. "I have to work at my other job this afternoon."

"You have two jobs?"

I nod.

"Are you in school?"

"I'm starting classes at the community college in January." Pride fills me. I'm late to the party, but at least I got there.

"When is your next day off?"

"Wednesday."

"I think you need yoga. Take a class with me? There's a good studio a few streets over."

"I've never done yoga before," I murmur, standing and grabbing my jacket.

Dayton stands also. "First of all, you don't *do* yoga. You *practice* yoga. And second, I can feel the stress rolling off you in waves." He leans in to me and sniffs. "I can even smell it, and it's not pleasant."

Laughter tumbles from my lips. Real, no holds barred, unadulterated laughter.

He grins, proud of his joke, and hands me his phone. "Put your number in," he tells me.

I do as he says and hand the phone back to him. "I'll give it a try."

"You won't regret yoga," he promises. "Nobody does."

"Can I bring my sister? Isn't yoga supposed to calm you down and stuff?"

Dayton eyes me. "Is your sister hyper?"

"She has severe anxiety. Struggles to be in public sometimes. If she can learn some ways to manage it, she might have a happier life."

"That's the beauty of yoga." He spreads his arms wide. "It's for everybody."

We step from the bar and say goodbye, then go in opposite directions.

"I'm calling you tomorrow," he yells behind me.

I turn around, raising a hand above my head and waving it his way, then keep walking.

My heart feels just a little lighter, my step a tad bouncier. For a short while, my new friend made me forget about my aching heart.

And about my aching feet.

# 18

# NOAH

*TWO AND A HALF YEARS LATER*

I WAS RAISED IN NORTHMOUNT, BUT FOR THE PAST FOUR years, I've stayed the hell away. Mostly, anyway. I came for Christmas morning, to appease my mother. My parents understood why I spent my summers traveling, and visiting friends at their family homes. I couldn't come back and face Ember. She'd tried to tell me from the very beginning, and I was stupid and stubborn, believing we were stronger than we were. Sincere, but naïve, an eighteen-year-old who didn't yet know the external dangers a relationship can fall prey to.

This is my first time being back for more than a day since I started college, and nothing feels quite right. Not even my old room, with its charcoal gray bedspread, and framed and signed Lionel Messi jersey. As soon as I walked in yesterday I looked at the desk, seeking out that picture of Ember. It wasn't there. Probably my mom's doing. I didn't know whether to thank her or ask for it back. This room is a snapshot of a period of time in my life, and now it looks like Ember was never a part of that.

It feels just as weird to wake up here as it did to walk in yesterday. I never thought I'd miss Tripp's music that he plays at all hours of the day. Waking up to the quiet of this big house feels loud. By the time I make it downstairs, the sun hangs high in the sky. I squint and rub my eyes, as if I can somehow rub out the pain from the hangover.

*Tripp and all his goodbye shots.*

He's headed to South America, to see the Peruvian girl he met on Spring Break. I told him Cancun would only lead to trouble, but Tripp gave me a one finger salute, then told me not to forget my denture ointment while he was gone.

Thanks to multiple rounds of shots with weird names, I now want to put a mask over my face to protect it from the laser beam focus of the sunshine streaming into my parents' house.

All the windows are thrown open, and that means my mother is in a good mood. That shouldn't surprise me. Tomorrow is kind of a big deal.

Through the large dining room window, I see my brother. He's standing on the back porch, his back to me. Alyssa stands beside him, gazing up at him like he's made of puppies. Or diamonds. Or whatever she would like enough to make her look blindingly devoted.

I'm about to pull open the door to say hello when Brody's arm winds around Alyssa's waist. He pulls her against him and leans down. Quickly I back up, moving away from the door and their tender moment.

They're getting married tomorrow. Maybe that's why they're being so loving and vomit-inducing. Maybe I'm being the love-Grinch because I'm back in town and as much as I want to track down Ember, I also don't want to see her. I don't know if she's dating someone else, and I don't think I can handle the answer to that question.

I shouldn't want her, but I don't want anyone else to have her either. The thought of her giving someone else those feisty, cute looks... My fists ball at my sides. She's no longer mine, and she hasn't been for a long time, but that doesn't stop me from despising the idea of her being anybody else's.

Leaving my brother and Alyssa to their sweet nothings, I stomp to the kitchen and head straight for the coffee maker. After I've shoved a k-cup into the machine and hit *go*, I search the contents of the fridge, hoping somehow there will be breakfast leftovers even though it's so late I should be eating lunch.

"Do soccer stars normally shove their noses into fridges as if they've never seen food before?"

My smile springs up instantly. I back out, letting the door fall shut as I go to Gretchen.

Her arms are open, waiting for me to step inside. Her eyes are full of pride, and happiness shines from her wide grin. Like a child, I bury myself into her embrace. I'm older now, and much bigger, but the warmth of her hug still permeates my chest. It's the physical equivalent of being told everything will be all right.

"I wouldn't call myself a star," I argue, stepping back. I was ecstatic when I was invited to play at the MLS Combine. The four-day showcase led to an invite to try out for the Atlanta MLS team. Try-outs were a few weeks ago, and I thought I did well, but I haven't heard back from them yet.

*Nothing.*

*Nada.*

Not even a phone call. Every day I tell myself to chill out, but it's getting hard as each day passes.

She gives me a knowing look and makes a *tsk* sound.

"Play humble with someone who doesn't know you like I do."

All I can do is laugh. She's right. I'm kind of a stud on the field. I played well in college. I worked harder than ever, trained harder than ever, gave up everything from alcohol to girls. Despite what I've accomplished, I try hard to be humble. Nobody like's an arrogant prick. A part of me wonders if I keep my ego in check because Ember would hate an inflated head. *All these years later, and her grip on me is still firm.*

"Any chance there's some breakfast left over?" I ask, changing the subject. It's easiest.

"There would be if you'd gotten your ass out of bed at the time of day when people eat breakfast."

I turn toward my big brother's voice. Beneath a big beard is a smile, his teeth being the only thing to let me know he's grinning.

We hug, clapping each other on the back. "I thought you were getting rid of the face pubes?" I deliver a couple of *thwacks* to his cheeks with open palms. Last weekend, at dinner after my graduation ceremony, he told me he was going to cut off his beard for his big day.

He bats my hand away, grumbling. "Not you too."

Alyssa stands beside him, rocking back on her heels. She hugs me and whispers *thank you* into my ear. I'm confused, and when we pull back she points at Brody's face and pretends to gag herself.

"I'll shave him tonight when he's asleep," I promise.

"I'll supply the razor." Alyssa pokes Brody in the side until he laughs.

He walks to the pantry and grabs a bag of tortilla chips. "Breakfast," he says, pushing them to my chest. "Mom wants us to run an errand for her."

I'm not buying it. "She said I need to go with you?"

"Yep."

Liar.

I open the bag and toss a chip in my mouth. "Let's go."

Brody pecks Alyssa on the cheek. I wave to her and Gretchen on my way out.

"What's the errand?" I ask as soon as we're driving. I crack my window and let the warm May air filter in.

"Mom's kind of embarrassed about it, so don't say anything." Brody uses a button on the steering wheel to turn down the volume of the music. Reaching over, he sticks his hand in the chip bag and takes out an overflowing handful. A few spill onto the floor and into the cup holders in the center console, but the majority of his haul makes it into a pile on his lap.

After shoving three into his mouth, he crunches and says, "Mom needed me to grab her prescriptions. She's going through menopause."

Brody makes a face as he says the final word. It's probably the same face twisting my features right now. Remembering your parents are human is uncomfortable.

"What prescription?" I don't know why I asked that question, but I can't think of what else to say.

Brody shrugs, using the back of his thumb to wipe his upper lip. "I don't know. I'm not a doctor."

I roll my eyes. Brody is a day trader. He has a degree in accounting, but said he's more successful sitting in his underwear in front of the computer. Alyssa swears he wears shorts, but the shirt is fifty/fifty.

"Okay, then. To the pharmacy we go." I toss the bag of chips into the backseat and try to calm my racing heart.

*Who says my mother even uses the same pharmacy?* Even if

she does, surely Ember doesn't still work there. *What if she does?*

What if she got stuck under the fluorescent lights, unpacking box after box of random children's toys and hair products? Guilt consumes me because now I'm convinced she still has her high school job and never got to experience life, and the worst part is that I didn't know.

I didn't know because I never checked.

"What's your deal, Noah? You look like your dog was just run over." Brody crunches the last of his chips.

"Nothing," I mutter, staring at the crumbs stuck in his beard.

It's all too much. The chewing, each crunch like Brody is tearing through bones. The chip fragments caught in his tangled facial hair. The manifested reality that I'm about to see Ember wearing a yellow vest better suited for a canary, like the past four years never happened.

I roll down the window a few more inches and let the air whip my face.

That fucking beard is living on borrowed time.

MY FREAK-OUT WAS FOR NOTHING. EMBER DOESN'T WORK here. I discreetly asked an employee while my brother stood in the pharmacy pick-up line at the back of the store. I'm so relieved I want to shout and run through the aisles. Of course, now that I know at least one thing she's *not* doing, I'm wondering what she *is* doing.

I text my brother and tell him I'll be waiting outside in the car. Curiosity took me in the store, and now there's nothing keeping me there. Eyes on the ground, I'm reaching for the door handle of my brother's car when an explosion of laughter breaks into my thoughts.

Picking my head up, I follow the sound. Across the street and a few doors down, a group of women have their heads thrown back. They're dressed in tight leggings and tank tops, something that resembles a quiver strapped to each of them. If it weren't for the red hair cascading down from a thrown back head, I'd continue getting into the car.

I can't help it. I'm not the one telling my legs to move. Right now, they have a mind of their own. After a break in the cars, I hurry across the street. By now the group has moved on, and the redhead walks with her arm wound around the waist of a man. I didn't see him in the group, but he must have been there too.

The same curiosity that took me into the pharmacy pulls me to the store they were all standing in front of. *Mind + Body*. Beneath the words is a lotus flower. I pull open the door and get blasted by heat. It smells earthy and salty, but also like eucalyptus.

"Hi," chirps a girl behind the counter. "We don't have another class until four."

"Class?" I ask, unsure of what this place is. I'm not even certain that was Ember. Redheads are uncommon, but she's not the only one in the world.

*Even if she is the only one who's made me crazy.*

My phones buzzes in my pocket, but I ignore it. Brody can wait for a minute.

"Yes." The girl draws out the word. Her eager smile has turned wary. "This is a yoga studio."

"Right, right," I smile and raise my eyes to the ceiling, as though even I can't believe how unobservant I am. "Sorry. May I see a schedule?"

She points up at the wall behind her head. Following her pointed finger, I see a giant chalkboard. A grid has been drawn onto it with the week's classes written out. "This"—she stands on tiptoe to point at a box—"is the next class. Giovanni is teaching, and he's amazing."

I nod and say, "Uh-huh." I can't manage anything more than that. I'm too transfixed by the name in the box above Giovanni's. It's the same name written in a box for Tuesday at six-thirty, and Sunday at noon.

"Whitley, thank goodness you haven't left yet." A breathless voice comes from behind me. "I left my wallet in the studio."

My breath slams up my throat. My heart bounds around my chest like an unbroken stallion. That voice has haunted me, shown up in my dreams, infiltrated my thoughts. I turn around, unsure what to expect but willing to take whatever Ember dishes out.

Her hands fly to her lips when she sees me. Through her fingers I hear her gasp. The girl at the counter, Whitley, is saying something, but to me it sounds like she's speaking in slow-motion.

"What are you...?" Ember hands move from her mouth to her hair. She runs her hands through it. "Why are you...?" Her head shakes as if she's clearing it. "Hi," she says, then laughs.

"Uh...Uhh." It's all I can manage because I'm seriously that dumb. The language center of my brain is mush.

And then she does the most unexpected thing. But it's Ember, so maybe it's expected.

Full speed, she runs to me. Like 1,424 days haven't passed. Like our relationship didn't end in almost exactly the way she said it would.

Her legs wrap around my waist, and I thread my arms around her, holding her up. Her fingers caress the back of my neck, and she presses her nose into the space beneath my ear.

Now I'm home.

## 19

### EMBER

How can hurt disappear in an instant? My relief at seeing Noah, the end of his absence, tossed my old, wounded feelings out the window and right onto the concrete sidewalk.

I'm still in his arms. My heartbeats haven't yet slowed to a normal pace. He looks like my Noah, but different too. Baby fat has melted from his face. His shoulders, *the ones I'm currently clinging to,* are wider. Beneath his thin cotton shirt I can feel the hardness of his body.

Tempting as it was, I've made it a point not to look him up. He's the reason for my *two glasses of wine maximum,* rule. Anything more than that, and down the rabbit hole I'll go.

A throat clears. Noah and I both turn to the sound.

Dayton stands in the open door, eyes wide.

Unhooking my legs from Noah's waist, I slide down his body. My eyes meet his and my cheeks catch fire. He grins when he sees the pink. Damn my traitorous fair skin.

The door softly falls into the frame as Dayton walks closer. He's squinting, eyes critically appraising Noah. I know Dayton knows who this is, but he's trying to make

Noah sweat. There's no one else whose arms I would jump into. I may have downplayed our relationship the first time I met Dayton, but since then I've bared my soul to him. There's nothing Dayton doesn't know.

"Who are you?" Dayton can make his voice very deep when he wants to.

Noah's hand extends. "An old friend." If Dayton's voice was soprano, Noah's voice is baritone. He says the word *friend* like it's a challenge. *I challenge you to matter more to her than me.* Noah thinks Dayton is my boyfriend, and he's being cocky.

And I really, really like it. But I'm not going to allow this pissing contest to continue.

"Dayton," I say, crossing to stand beside him, "is my best friend. He's also very gay."

He huffs. "Just gay, Ember. There is no *very* gay. You're either gay or you aren't."

I laugh. "Dayton, this is Noah Sutton."

"I knew that already." Dayton takes the hand Noah has re-extended. "Why are you back?" Dayton's voice is back to normal, but he's still defending me and being possessive.

"My brother is marrying Alyssa tomorrow," Noah answers, facing me.

"Aw," I say. "College sweethearts."

Noah stuffs his hands in the pockets of his jeans, glancing at Dayton. I do too.

"Well," Dayton says, getting the hint. "I have to run something by Whitley. Excuse me." He sidesteps Noah and hurries behind the tall, white counter.

I forgot about Whitley. She watched the entire exchange, the one that happened before Dayton arrived. The one where I forgot myself, and catapulted into Noah's arms, and then stayed there. For a really long time.

"So..." Noah starts.

"What do you want?" I blurt out.

He shrugs, stuffing his hands in his pockets. "I don't know."

"Why are you here?"

"I don't know."

I'm out of questions. The ones I'm willing to ask, anyway.

"Can I see you tonight?" Noah's eyes burn with hope.

I don't respond, because I don't know either.

"After the rehearsal dinner, I'm taking my brother out for a drink. Will you meet me? He'll only stay for one. Then we can talk."

There's nothing to discuss but the past. The way we ripped our relationship apart instead of letting go at a high-point, and preserving the memory. I'd wanted to look back on us and see the innocent, first love, remember the rush and first-times that could never belong to anyone else. I'd let Noah talk me into a long-distance relationship, and with that we took away our chance at remember-when's that don't hurt. Instead of being my high-school sweetheart, Noah is the man who broke my heart.

As if the all-encompassing hurt doesn't still sting, I hear myself agree.

It's a masochistic move, but I can't help it. The pain is worth it.

"Can I have your phone?" he asks, hand out. "I'm assuming you got a new number in the last four years?"

I place it in his palm without a word. I kept my number the same for two years, and then Dayton talked me into changing it. He said it would be a fresh start, and eliminate the possibility that Noah could be on the other end of my ringing phone. Changing the number took my very last hope, but I begrudgingly admitted that was a good thing.

Noah keys in his number, and a second later his pocket vibrates.

"There." His grin reaches his ears. "We've officially exchanged numbers. Now I can call and tell you where we're going tonight." His pocket starts vibrating again, and it doesn't stop.

"My brother's waiting for me." He backs up a few steps. "Tonight, Ember." His deep voice strokes my name, taking me back to our final day at the lake, the day Mother Nature's tears fell over us for what we were about to do to ourselves.

"Tonight," I echo softly, watching him go.

The door closes and Dayton walks up behind me. "Ohhhh, sweet girl." He rests his head on my shoulder. "He's better than you let on."

"He wasn't always that big." I want to bring Noah's clout down a smidge. Make him a little less overwhelming.

"Was he always that handsome?" Dayton reaches around me with my wallet in his hand.

I take it and stuff it in my purse. "Yes."

We leave Mind+Body, Whitley in tow. She hasn't said a word to me since Noah walked in.

"Sorry about that." I reach for her hand and squeeze.

"It's okay." She bumps my shoulder with her own. "We all have one."

"One what?" We come to a stop at the corner. Whitley's car is parked in the last space on the street, and Dayton and I are around the corner.

She and Dayton exchange a look as he grabs his mat strap and hoists it higher onto his back. The kind that says *Can she seriously not be aware of this?*

"One that got away." Whitley explains, waving goodbye

and walking across the street to her car. Dayton and I keep going around the corner.

While we walk, I tell him about tonight. He looks at me with pity. "I'll be by tomorrow at eleven, to pick up the pieces," he says, then pecks me on the cheek and gets in his car.

I climb into my car and lean my head against the seat. Closing my eyes, I picture Noah's lips saying my name, and the look on his face when he turned around and saw me standing there. I start the car and try to shake off the image of the tousled light brown hair, and the baby blue eyes. Seeing him just now was a gut punch right to the feels.

Tonight's not looking like such a good idea after all.

# 20

# NOAH

"Did you see her?"

Brody takes the turn onto the road that will eventually lead us back to our parents' house. These are the first words he's spoken since I left Ember. Until now all he's done is given me wary looks. His silence worked for me. I was reliving the moment I saw Ember again. Until three seconds ago, anyway.

"Yes." My voice is calm. My insides are anything but. "She's going to meet us tonight, after the rehearsal dinner. I know you don't want to drink much and—"

"You think that's a good idea?" The doubt in Brody's tone tells me just what he thinks.

"Why wouldn't it be?" A defensive edge hardens my tone.

Brody sighs, shifting in his seat.

"Just say it." My excitement is waning. Brody's attitude has ruined my buzz.

He pulls up to the iron gate, and waits for it to retract. "History belongs in the past."

The car rolls forward and I'm considering slugging him.

This isn't what I want to hear. "That dumbfuck beard doesn't make you an authority on the universe."

Brody strokes the scraggly bits that hang off his chin. "It might."

I shake my head. "You look like a poor excuse for a wizard. Get rid of it before dinner."

"Let's go." He parks and nods out the window behind me. "Dad's here."

I follow his gaze to my dad's car. "Don't tell anyone about Ember."

Brody opens the car door and pauses to look back at me.

"I don't want anyone's opinion about it." *Including yours.* "I've made up my mind."

"I won't say anything." The words float behind him as he exits the car.

I get out, too, and walk beside him to the front door. He claps on my back twice, letting me know everything's okay.

"My boys are here," Dad thunders when we step inside.

He hugs me first, roughing up my shoulders a bit when he pulls back. His hair has thinned a bit on top, but he's aging well. It gives me hope for my future.

"Where'd you guys go?" He's looking at the bag swinging from Brody's hand.

"Mom's medicine."

Dad makes a face. "I wish she'd at least tried some alternatives first." He shakes his head.

"Like what?" I ask.

"Exercise. Meditation—"

"Fish oil?" Brody snickers.

Dad points a finger at him. "Joke all you want. That stuff is good for you."

I laugh. "Did you get your crunchy gene from your mom? Or your dad? And why did it skip me and Brody?"

"Very funny." Dad takes the medication from Brody and turns around. "I won't tell you where I got the crunchiness, but I can tell you which one of you has it too," he says, over his shoulder.

"Who?" we yell after him, but he's out of earshot or ignoring us.

Brody looks at me. "Obviously it's you. Ember teaches yoga, she's pierced and tatted, and you still love her."

"Shut up. She only has the nose ring now. All her earrings were gone. And for the record, I never should've told you about her tattoo."

Brody shrugs and walks away, off to find Alyssa. She's supposed to be with my mom and her mom, running through last-minute items.

Fine by me. I need space. For a second, I consider heading for the lake, maybe even to the exact spot, but I'm not sure that's a great idea. I have to maintain some kind of control. I showed none today, darting across the street and into the studio like that. What was I thinking asking Ember out tonight? I don't have a goal, or a plan. I don't know what I'm doing.

At the moment I saw her, all I knew was that I wanted to see her again.

I'll go into tonight with an open mind. Old friends catching up. High-school sweethearts reminiscing.

---

TWICE IN MY LIFE I'VE BEEN STOOD UP. EACH TIME COURTESY of a certain red-haired, feisty female. The first time, I hung my head, and then fate had me stopping at the drugstore for medicine.

This is the second time, and I'll be damned if I'm going to

stand by and lick my wounds. The first place I thought to go was that old apartment she lived in with her mother, but I'm guessing she no longer lives there. At least, I hope she doesn't. I'll try it if I have to, but first I'm going to do some research.

It's not hard to find out where someone lives. The Internet doesn't have secrets. When my query for Ember comes up empty, I type in her sister's name.

*Bingo.*

After Brody heads home, I leave the bar and follow the directions spouting from my phone. The house it takes me to isn't palatial, but it's nice. Well-kept. The porch is hedged by eucalyptus, manicured into near-perfect rectangles. Four steps lead to the front door, and I take them two at a time.

I haven't stopped to think through what I'm doing. I have no idea if Ember lives here. Maybe she lives with Dayton. It doesn't matter. Sky will know where she is.

My knocks on the wooden door land one on top of the other. Not a casual knock. I'm not feeling exactly nonchalant right now.

Nobody comes to the door. From the corner of my eye, I see movement in the curtains. Lifting my eyes to the porch ceiling, I send up a quick prayer that Sky remembers what I look like, and that she answers the door.

The sound of the lock brings my eyes back down. *I owe you one, God.*

A red-haired girl opens the door. A red-haired girl smiles at me. A red-haired girl fills my vision.

"Should I even ask how you knew to find me here?" Ember steps back, opening the door all the way.

"I could tell you, but I'd have to kiss you." I take one step inside, halting when I see Ember's frown.

"Behave," she warns with a pointed finger.

"Am I allowed all the way in?" I nudge the toe of one foot forward, inching my way into the answer I hope she'll give me.

She sighs, her eyes roaming my face. In her gaze I see reluctance infused with longing, fear mixed with need. The magic of Ember washes over me again, drowning me. Doesn't she know I can't get away from her? No matter the physical distance, she is never far from me. Suddenly her hand is in mine, and I don't know how it got there. It's soft and warm, and when I rub my thumb against the heel of her palm, she sighs. A different sigh this time. Delicate.

Her head leans against the open door. "We haven't spoken since we broke up." Her voice is soft but her gaze is hard.

I gulp. I knew I was going to have to answer for that. "That's how breakups usually work."

"But didn't you...I don't know...come home at all in the last four years?" Little lines form around her lips, a sure sign she's getting angry.

"No. Not really."

"You stayed away?"

"I came for Christmas."

Her anger deflates. "You didn't come back because of me?"

"Seeing you would've torn me apart, Ember."

"But you're here now."

"Because I have to be. Then when I thought I saw you, something took over. It was like I couldn't help myself. I had to know where you'd come from."

With one finger I touch her temple, my finger free-falling down her face and ending at her jaw. Hooking my finger below her chin, I tilt her head up and gaze into the eyes of the woman who made me *feel* music instead of *hear* it.

"For the past few years I've been imagining you, seeing you in different places, my heart beats speeding up each time. In my mind I knew there was no way I was seeing you, but today, it was possible. It wasn't just a daydream anymore." My thumb traces a design on the plumpest section of her lower lip.

"Noah," Ember whispers, her eyes worried, "You shouldn't be here."

I shake my head. "Don't say that."

She lifts her shoulders, holds them, and lets them drop. "It's true." The simplicity of her words pierce me, a sword swiftly vanquishing my hope.

"Do you want me to leave?" I focus on the painting hung on the wall behind her. I can't stand to watch her lips form words that will push me out of her life. Again.

She doesn't say anything. Not with her mouth, at least. Instead, she is a flurry of action.

The door slams, locking in place. With two flat palms she pushes against my chest. I stumble backward across the small room until something soft but large stops me. Ember presses into me, her hands on my neck, her breath against my cheek, her lips finally finding their way to mine.

My mind is going haywire. I feel like I'm eighteen again. All I can see is Ember, all I can feel is Ember, all I want is Ember. Suddenly, we're new. We haven't experienced the pain of hurting one another. We never missed phone dates, never cancelled trips home to visit, never hoarded hurt feelings until they grew into the monster that ruined us. We are whole again.

She steps back. "Sit. Couch."

I drop onto a cushion like my ass is on fire.

Ember sinks down onto my lap, her knees pressing into the outsides of my thighs. I grab onto her hair and tug, dipping her head back and kissing her throat. She moans as my lips travel down, her hasty hands fumbling with my belt buckle. She pauses, lifting her arms in the air so I can pull her shirt over her head.

"Take off your pants," she tells me.

I don't know when she became this authoritative, but I'm not going to question it. I do as she says, while she slips off her pink pajama shorts. Standing in front of me is the woman I dream about, naked, but she doesn't give me the chance to drink her in. Before I can ask her to slow down, she's on top of me.

In seconds, we are one. In minutes, she tips back her head and loses herself. When she comes down from her high, eyes hooded and face dreamy, I stand with her in my arms and walk from the living room to the hallway. She points at the door on the left, and I carry her in.

I have not forgotten the curves of Ember's hips. The contours of her arched back. The soft skin at the base of her neck. The red hair brushing against her creamy skin.

I could try for a hundred years to forget this woman, and it would be futile.

The saying is true.

You never forget your first love.

## 21

---

## EMBER

"Mmmmmm." Noah's moan reverberates through my back. He tightens his arms around my waist and pulls me closer, though I'm not sure it's possible.

"I'd love to wake up like this every day," he says, his voice making the little hairs on the back of my neck stand upright.

He shouldn't say things like that. This was a break from reality, a dip into the past.

It was fun though. Unexpected. When he stared at me in the open front door last night, daring me to tell him to go, I felt the old enchantment, invoking me to enjoy him for the short time I could have him. Time hadn't lessened the magnetic pull. The only thing time had done was turn us into a man and a woman.

Rolling over, I drink in his bedhead and squinty-eyes. Without thinking, I lift one hand and trace his profile with my fingertips, starting at his temple and going down to his hips. Across his ribs is something the dark of the night kept from me.

Gaping down at the inked skin, my mouth falls open.

"You got a tattoo." The three-inch-high Sutton name stares back at me.

He glances down at himself. "I did."

"Were you afraid you'd forget your last name?" I bite my lip to keep from laughing.

Noah grabs my hand and twists, showing the inside of my forearm. "Did you mistake yourself for a bird?

I snatch my hand away, laughing. I happen to love my newest tattoo. "It's a dove. A symbol of purity. And love." My hand returns to his hip.

"You haven't been too pure recently." He peers down at my hand, where it sits on his hipbone.

The sheet covers him from the waist down, and it would be so easy to let my hand disappear under it. Instead my fingers *bump bump bump* their way up his rippled torso.

"I take it you're still playing soccer?" His abs are enviable. His thighs are muscled. From his scapula to the bottom swell of his backside, he is all cut muscle and sinew.

Noah moves his head to the side and studies me.

"What?" I ask.

"You haven't searched for me on the internet once, have you? Not in all the time we've been apart." The hurt is evident when his eyes drift down to the sheet between us.

"No," I say, though I don't think he needs my answer. I don't want to tell him why I haven't kept tabs on him. "You haven't looked for me, either."

"You don't have any social media profiles," he argues. Which is true.

He rolls onto his side, tucking his hand under his head to prop himself up. I sit up, and when I do, the sheet falls away from me. Noah stares unabashedly at my breasts.

"Enjoying the view?" I smirk.

"Immensely." He reaches for me, his hand cupping my

left breast. "You've always been comfortable in your own skin. I loved that about you."

Loved...past tense.

It's good he said that. It's a needed reminder of what we're doing here. This isn't a rekindling. It's a fun twelve hours between two people who desperately needed a release.

He traces the swell of my breast with the pad of his thumb. "I tried out for Atlanta's team a few weeks ago."

Happiness is my first emotion. Sadness is my second. I can't help it.

"How did it go?"

"Good," he says, letting go of my breast and grabbing my hand. His stomach grumbles and he laughs, a stream of warm breath fanning my skin.

"Do you want breakfast? I usually eat fruit or oatmeal. I'm vegan now."

"I'm definitely not telling Brody that." Noah laughs at the look I'm giving him. "Don't ask," he says, waving one hand. He sits up suddenly, grabbing me by the shoulders and pushing me down on the bed. Moving over me, he rubs the tip of his nose along my jaw.

"I'm hungry for something else right now."

"Me too." I bite my lip and raise my eyebrows. He grins down at me, and it's like the sun wants to shine from my chest. I love who I am when I'm with him. Wild and free, the Ember from his high school memories. Suddenly, I'm not worried about the fall-out from our trek down memory lane.

I'm all in, for as long as it will last. We used to believe we created magic when we were together. If this isn't magic between us right now, then I don't know what is.

I DIDN'T ACCOUNT FOR SKY. DIDN'T EVEN THINK ABOUT THE possibility of my sister being in the kitchen when we walked out.

"Holy shit," she whispers, frozen in place on a square tile halfway between the fridge and the small butcher-block island.

"Umm..." I search for words but come up empty. "Oops." I make a silly, bared-teeth face.

"Hey, Sky. How are you?" Noah strides past, brushing against me as he goes. My toes curl as if just his touch cues up their muscle memory.

"Uh, fine." She shakes Noah's hand and peers past him, wide gaze settling on me. "Four years ago called. It wants Northmount's resident soccer asshole back." She points to Noah as she speaks.

Noah doesn't get mad. Or hurt. Or embarrassed. He laughs, a big chortle, bowl-full-of-jelly laugh. "I see the Dane spirit hasn't taken a hit since I left."

Sky glares at him and hurries to me, grabbing my arm and yanking me down the hall. "What the fuck, Ember?"

"I..." My hands tangle in my hair. "I don't know. He's here to watch Brody get married, and I just...just...gave in. It felt good, okay?"

Sky gives me a look.

"Not just the sex. Everything. He's...Noah. He came back." I softly breathe the words.

I can't take the pity in Sky's face, so I look away.

"Ember?" Noah calls from the kitchen. He knows better than to come down the hall and find me. Sky might tear his head off. "Do you want a bowl of fruit?" I hear the faint suction sound of the fridge being pulled open.

"I'm making bacon and eggs," he yells, when I don't answer right away.

Smiling, I leave the hall. Sky follows.

Noah's back is to me, his gaze on the contents of my fridge. Placing my hand on the small of his back, I rise on tiptoe to set my chin on his shoulder. "You couldn't make that if you wanted to. Those food items cannot be found here."

"I had to get you back out here somehow. I have to leave soon." Noah pulls his phone from his jeans' pocket and looks at it. "I need to be at the church soon."

"Are you leaving, then?" Sky asks.

Leaning back to see around the open fridge door, I shoot her a glare.

She's sitting stiffly at the table we keep in the corner of the kitchen, her legs crossed at the ankle and her hands folded on the tabletop.

"I'll make you breakfast," I offer, fisting my hands in his T-shirt and pulling, so he backs up. Stepping into the space he vacated, I pull cartons of fruit from the bottom drawer.

Noah's doubtful eyes never stray from me the entire time I'm putting together breakfast.

"What's that?" he asks hesitantly as I pour a little coconut oil on the fruit mixture.

"Grease." I smirk.

"Haha."

I hand him the bottle and grab the cinnamon from a cupboard.

"Coconut oil?" His face is a cross between fear and having smelled something foul.

"Don't knock it. It's full of health benefits." I grab a spoon, toss it together, throw a handful of slivered almonds on top, and give it to Noah.

He doesn't say another word about it. In fact, he inhales the whole concoction, and when I hand him mine after I'm done, he finishes that too.

Sky hasn't said much in the last ten minutes, but she breaks the streak when she asks, "Is graduation over?"

Noah nods. "Last weekend."

"Does that mean you're back for good?"

I look away. We haven't discussed this. The question has been lurking in the recesses of my mind since the second I saw him, but I can't bring myself to ask. The answer, no matter what it is, carries a heavy weight.

"I'm supposed to head back to Stanford tomorrow. My roommate left yesterday for South America, and our apartment is empty. I tried out for Atlanta's MLS team, but I haven't heard back from them yet."

I close my eyes and shut out the room. I might as well be eighteen again, waiting to hear if he will keep chasing the carrot being dangled in front of him. In this analogy, the carrot is a dream, and the person dangling the dream is Noah himself, the part of him that needs the glory of the sport to feel successful.

Under the table, Noah squeezes my knee. I meet his eyes and his gaze intensifies, unspoken words swirling around in a frenzy. What is it he's trying to say?

*I'm sorry.*

*I already miss you.*

*This may have been a mistake.*

*Let's do things right this time.*

Noah drops my gaze, stands, and clears all three of our bowls. The back of my chair catches my slumping body as I realize those are all things *I* want to say, and maybe things I want *him* to say.

"I have to go. Hair appointment." Sky runs her hand

through the blond locks that hang almost to her belly button. She closes the distance between our faces, until her nose is six inches from mine. "Are you going to be okay?" she whispers.

I roll my eyes, an *of course I'm going to be okay* gesture. Except, she knows me well enough not to buy what I'm selling.

Before we can go any further into this conversation, before she can lecture me like big sisters do, I gently push her by the shoulders and tell her to go before she's late.

"Get more than a trim," I say, making scissoring motions with my fingers. "Do something crazy. Change up your style."

She frowns at me, but I can tell she's considering my words. "We'll see." She backs away from the table, glancing at the sink where Noah stands, rinsing the bowls. "Will I see you at class this afternoon?"

I look over at Noah. "I'm not sure," I say quietly. "But you should go no matter what." Yoga has provided Sky with a grounding feeling, and taught her how to breathe when she starts sensing that familiar tightness in her chest. At first she would only go with me, then, slowly, she began taking classes on her own.

For a moment she watches me, then mouths, *Good luck*. In a normal voice, she says "Bye, love you."

"Love you too," Noah says, smirking.

Sky shoots daggers at him before taking her purse from the counter and leaving the room.

I hoist myself onto the counter beside the sink where Noah is working. He dries his hands and stands between my legs. Gripping my waist, his thumbs graze the top of my stomach.

"Why does she hate me?"

Wrapping my arms around his neck, I cock my head to the side and smile. "It's a sister thing. She's being protective."

"She thinks this is bad? You and me, again?"

I nod. "She saw how upset I was the first time, that's all."

"You don't have the market cornered on heartbreak when it comes to us."

My eyebrows rise. "No?"

Noah grunts, a sound of disbelief. "How could you even think that? Of course not."

He rests his forehead against mine. His eyes flutter closed, and I allow mine to do so also.

"Nobody has ever matched you, Ember. Nobody. I tried to forget you, but at some point I realized it was useless, because every person I met had one big fucking flaw. *They weren't you.* Eventually I stopped trying to move on and focused only on soccer." His words wash over me, warm on my face and fiery in my heart. "Your first love isn't supposed to be your last, right? I tell myself that every time I think of you, but my heart won't be talked into getting over you." He stops talking , dragging in a ragged breath with his intense gaze on mine.

My breath. My heart. Where did they go? I think they're having a party, rejoicing at what Noah has just said.

It would be so easy to let his words carry me away, and *oh my god* I want to. I pull back and search his face, trying to understand why he's saying all this to me. When I come up empty, I ask "Why now, Noah?"

"Why not?"

"You've only come home for a wedding. You're not staying."

"I could," he says with earnest. "I could go back, pack up all the things from my apartment, and leave. Tripp's already gone. I don't have anything to go back to." Light brightens his eyes as he speaks.

How many times have I replayed a reunion? How many times have I fallen asleep wondering what it would be like to see Noah again? My stomach tips, excitement flickering deep within me. Could we have a second chance?

"I like the sound of it all, Noah. But your try-outs... We've been through this once before. Someone can call you back at any minute."

He flicks his hand as if batting away a minuscule but annoying gnat. "It's been too long. I don't expect a call."

The glimmer in his eyes decreases by a small fraction. It's his dream and it might be over, so he's mourning it the way he did four years ago, when he thought he wasn't going to play in college. I wonder if it's even worse now, because he's an adult. If it had happened before college, he could've focused on doing something else instead of continuing to make his whole life about the sport.

Noah's pocket buzzes. He pulls out his phone, only to silence it.

He captures the side of my head in a cupped hand. "Come to the wedding. Be my date." His voice is urgent. "I have to go, but I don't want to be without you. Will you come?"

"Won't it mess up Alyssa's seating chart?" I don't know much about weddings, but Sky watches a reality TV show about a wedding planner, and I've picked up a few terms from it.

"I don't know if she has one of those, and I don't fucking care." To prove his point, Noah retrieves his phone and presses two buttons. He watches me while he waits for someone to pick up.

"Brody, tell Alyssa I have a date today after all."

Brody's deep voice streams out of Noah's phone, and it's loud. Noah presses the end button and grins. "Problem solved."

"You're crazy."

"I am."

"I like crazy."

"I know."

He presses a kiss to my mouth, and I respond, wrapping my legs tighter around his torso. After a minute of noisy kisses and wandering hands, Noah pulls away. He sucks in a deep breath. "I better go. Brody will kill me, resurrect my body, and kill me again if I'm late for his wedding." He steps away and helps me off the counter.

I walk him out, and he tells me where to be and what time.

"You better not stand me up for a third time," he warns, his face stern.

I laugh and cross my heart. "I won't. I'll be the one in..." My closet flies through my head. I have no idea what to wear. I live in yoga clothes. "I'll be the one in anything but white."

Noah leans in for a quick kiss. "Thanks for narrowing it down."

"See you soon," I call after him.

He throws me a wave and a smile before climbing into his car and driving away.

───

As soon as he's gone, I call Dayton. "No need to come pick up scattered pieces of Ember off the ground," I say when he answers. "At least not until tomorrow."

"Why?" His tone is suspicious.

"I'm going to his brother's wedding with him this afternoon."

"Ember—"

"Don't."

"Stop acting like you knew what I was going to say."

Cradling the phone between my ear and my shoulder, I pick up cartons of berries and stick them back into the fridge. "You were going to tell me how a one-time thing is only a one-time thing, but a two-time thing is never a two-time thing. Am I right?"

"Well—"

"And you were going to say that a two-time thing makes a way bigger mess than a one-time thing."

"Yes, but—"

"You were also going to say—"

"Stop interrupting me!"

I pour a fresh cup of coffee, sit at the table, and blow across the top of it. "Sorry."

"I was just going to tell you that I'm coming over to help you get ready. You are terrible at doing your own hair." He waits for my response, but I don't need to see his face to know how pleased he is with his insult.

I sip my coffee. "Don't be a drag, Dayton. Just be a queen."

"Stop quoting *Her Majesty*."

"I take it you're not referring to Queen Elizabeth."

"Not unless she wears dresses made from meat."

I bark a laugh. I love how Dayton can banter, but I don't have time for it right now. If I don't put an end to it, he'll never stop.

"Are you coming over?"

"Does my momma put sugar in her tea?"

My eyes roll upward even as a smile overtakes my face.

"I've never met your mother, but I'm guessing she likes her tea sweet."

"Of course she does. She's a proper Southerner."

"I'm getting off the phone now."

"Yankee." He practically spits the word.

"Is that an insult?"

"What do you think?"

"Bye, Dayton."

The line goes dead. Dayton likes to hang up first. He says it makes him feel powerful.

Twenty minutes later he walks into my house holding a garment bag and a bottle of pink champagne. I never drink during the day, but I'm relieved to see the bottle. I need some liquid courage.

I sit facing the bathroom wall, straddling the closed toilet, while Dayton blow-dries my hair. He's focused on his task and not talking while I replay last night's events in my head. What is it about Noah that makes me unable to control myself? His scent, his face, his voice, they all cause a knee-jerk reaction in me.

I bite my lip as Dayton yanks my head back with the tug of the round brush. All of this isn't a good idea. I know that. Nothing good can come from seeing Noah again. But what's the purpose of *good*? Where does *good* get people? And what if *good* and *right* aren't synonymous?

Exposing my heart to Noah is the opposite of good.

But it's not wrong.

And that's why I'm letting Dayton yank on my head with the torture device he's wielding. It's also why I've agreed to wear the emerald green dress he brought from his shop. The bodice is so tight I'll be short of breath the entire evening, but while I'm gasping for air, I'm going to look amazing.

## 22

## NOAH

"Alyssa wants to kill you."

"Hello to you too," I say to Brody, walking into his makeshift dressing room at the church.

Reaching out, I rub his newly hair-free cheek with an open palm. "Smooth as Grandma's ass."

Brody's lips turn down even further. "Fuck you. And don't disrespect the dead."

"I thought it was more of a compliment," I mutter, turning away. "I'll find Alyssa and apologize." Is it really that hard to find a chair and squeeze someone in at a table? This wedding stuff sounds like a bunch of high expectations and nonsense.

Brody's rapid head shake stops me before I can walk out the door to find the blushing bride.

"What?"

"Don't do it." He grabs his beer from the little table. "She's crazy today," he pauses, lips poised for a drink. "Lie low and behave. She's happy she'll get to see Ember again, and she already had the planner rework some stuff to accommodate, but she's on a warpath."

I grab a bottle of beer from the mini-fridge Brody brought and sit. "I never saw Alyssa as the bridezilla type."

"Me neither. Just nerves, probably. She put a lot of work into today."

He's still talking, I think about how much planning this all took, but my mind has already moved on to long red hair and that damn dandelion tattoo.

She liked my tattoo, even though she teased me about it. She'd tease me mercilessly if she knew about the tattoo I almost got one night two years ago. Copious amounts of vodka and a broken heart don't mix well, and I almost had the permanent *Shmily* to prove it.

Thanks to Tripp, I am *Shmily* free. Not completely, though. My heart bears the word.

"And that's when the alien switched Mom's head with a gerbil. It was too much weight for the gerbil to carry, so he was crushed and then—"

"Brody, what the fuck are you talking about?" His words sink in and I feel guilty. How long was he spinning that yarn?

He gives me a dirty side-eye. "I hope you listen better to Ember."

I don't answer. I just finish the beer. It's like my brain has stepped out of my body, and my heart is doing all the deciding right now. Every move I've made since I saw her on the street yesterday was brainless, but damn if it doesn't all feel really, really good.

"What's up with you two anyway? Are you going to come back and start up again?"

The couch catches me with a nice *thud* as throw myself back. "Didn't you already give me your opinion on that?"

"Yes. But I talked to Alyssa about it last night. She pointed out that maybe it's the universe's way of giving you a second chance. There was pretty much no hope for you guys before, but now..." He shrugs. "You're back. And single. She's still here. And single."

"I haven't officially moved back. I could still get a call." Always on the hook. Always waiting for something that may never happen.

"How likely is that?"

I sigh and eye my empty beer, wishing I had another full one in my reach. "Not very. They should've called by now."

Brody hooks an arm around my shoulder, and for a second, I think he's going to rub his knuckles on my hair. Instead he pulls me in roughly. "I want whatever you want. Got it, little brother?"

I nod. "I want whatever Alyssa wants for you."

He chuckles and lets me go. "Smart man."

When the wedding planner pops her head in and tells us it's go-time, I follow Brody into the sanctuary and take my place with the other groomsmen at the front. Dad comes up and hugs Brody first, then me. My stomach drops as I search the crowd for red hair. I scan the aisles, every pew, and *nothing*.

I pull my phone from my pocket to send her a message, and at that second one pops up on my screen.

**Lose something?**

Grinning, I look up to see Ember waving from the back of the church. She's standing in front of the open doors. The breeze slips in from the outside, causing the lower half of her dress to swirl around her. She laughs, rolling her eyes, and pushes it down. She chooses a seat on the grooms side and sits gracefully. Shoulders pulled back, gaze on me, her lips are full and begging to be kissed.

I type out a quick response. **Your lips look lonely without mine on them.**

She pulls her phone from her purse, her eyes on the screen for only a moment. She grins, looks up at me, then back to her phone.

The response bubbles pop up on my screen, and her message comes through.

**Interesting. My lips were doing okay until you showed up yesterday.**

**Just okay?**

**Okay is not a bad place to be.**

**Okay is not good.**

**Good isn't always right.**

**Did you major in philosophy?**

Shit.

My fingers freeze, hovering above my screen. I rub my eyes with my thumb and pointer finger. Why can't life have a rewind button? *Just rub it in that she didn't go to college, idiot. Way to go.*

Apprehension sticks in my throat like some kind of foul-tasting gelatinous substance. When I remove my hand, my eyes find Ember. She's poised, her expression unchanged, but in her gaze I see disappointment.

In me?

In herself?

The room is full of people, happy voices coming from all sides, but it's as if there's a film between us and everyone else in the room. Ember and I could be alone right now, having a conversation with our eyes.

*I wanted you to come to college with me.*

*You know I couldn't leave my mother and Sky.*

*You didn't have to give up your future for them.*

*I didn't. My future hasn't gone anywhere. Anyway, sacrifice doesn't have to hurt.*

*How so?*

*When you sacrifice to make someone happy, and their happiness makes you happy, then it doesn't hurt.*

It's easy to imagine Ember's bright, full eyes communicating with me. I wish I could touch her right now. My fingers ache to press into her skin, to leave my imprint.

"It's okay." Ember mouths, her face full of unspoken emotions.

And suddenly, it is okay.

Everything that has happened between us is okay. Like a wave sweeping in, crashing at the shore, and pulling grains of sand back with it, welcoming them back into the fold.

Yesterday, last night, right now—these are moments that comprise the story of us.

Noah and Ember.

The ceremony starts, and it's impossible to take my eyes off Ember. She watches the bridesmaids, the maid of honor, the flower girl, the bride, and I watch her.

She's captivating.

---

"How long do you think we have to stay here?" I nuzzle my nose against the side of Ember's head, soaking in the scent of her. We're seated at a table but I'm facing her, my legs wide, while she leans back into my chest. Her shoulder bumps against my chest with her chuckle.

"Long enough to watch their first dance, cut the cake, speeches... You know, all the stuff you're supposed to be here for."

I'm high on Ember, on the vanilla-and-orange scent of her shampoo, on being with the woman who never gave my heart back after she stole it when we were eighteen. "Our wedding won't be such a fuss," I announce quietly.

She sits up, turning weary eyes on me. "Noah." Her tone of voice has turned my name into a warning.

I don't care. Not right now. "What?" I ask, defiant. What's so wrong with my words? Nearly four years apart didn't dull the glimmer of our magic. That means something. I want to be reckless right now, make plans, and keep them.

For the first time since I tried out for the professional team, I'm hoping my phone never rings. If they don't come calling, I won't have to choose between Ember and the one thing I've been working for my whole life. We could have a normal relationship. I'll get the kind of job that will have me home everyday and we could build a life.

Ember tucks a strand of hair behind one ear. The small gold stud earring she wears shines in the strings of lights hanging over our table. "I don't think you should be talking that way."

"I know. I want to though. Do you understand? I want to." My eyes squeeze shut, the frustration grabbing ahold of me. I want to make Ember a million promises.

"You're not in a position to make big statements like that. It's not fair. To me, or you."

She's right. Of course she is.

"Ember!"

Alyssa's voice rings behind me.

Ember stands, smiling broadly, and steps into Alyssa's open arms. "Congratulations."

My brother is by Alyssa's side, and when Ember pulls back, she turns to him and repeats herself.

Brody opens his arms and doesn't give Ember a choice. He pulls her into a hug and says something into her ear. She glances at me and laughs. I frown immediately. There's no telling what that fucker said.

Alyssa pulls Ember into conversation, while Brody zeros in on me.

"You doing okay?"

"I'm better when my brother isn't talking shit about me to my..." The sentence falls short.

Brody raises his eyebrows but keeps his mouth shut. Ember hasn't heard my floundering sentence, or if she has, she's pretending it doesn't bother her.

"Relax, man." Brody steps closer, leaning in so were face to face. "I told her she's the only thing besides soccer that makes you crazy."

*Oh.*

Well, that's true.

Stepping back, he slips a hand around Alyssa's waist. She stops mid-sentence and gazes up at him.

"We should probably keep greeting people." Brody looks around. "It's awkward, but necessary."

Ember and I send them off and sit back down.

"Now can we go?" I ask, setting my hand on her knee and grabbing a handful of the silky green fabric.

Ember shakes her head. "We have the rest of the night, and I'm not going anywhere. Just enjoy the wedding."

I sit back, sip from my water, and try to rein in my eagerness. Everything feels more urgent, more important, like every minute I spend with Ember carries more weight than the one before. I can't help the feeling that there's a timer on us. More than just me having to go back to Stanford because I have an apartment there. That can be easily dealt with. Break the lease, put Tripp's stuff in storage, and move back. Dust off my hands and be done with college.

I sit through all the reception rituals. Ember and I find my parents and talk with them. My mother almost falls from her chair when she sees us approaching. Maybe I should've told her I was bringing Ember, but I went straight from Ember's to find Brody at the church, leaving no time for conversation with my mom. My dad is as jolly as ever, but he's probably had a few glasses of wine. He hugs Ember and tells her she looks just like she did when she was eighteen.

Finally, people begin to filter out. My parents say good-night, and my dad pulls me aside.

"Is that where you spent last night?" He stuffs his hands in the pockets of his rented tux and ducks his chin, talking quietly.

I glance at Ember. She's in conversation with Alyssa, and they're laughing and touching each other's forearms.

"Yeah. I stayed at Ember's."

"Hmm." He rubs his chin. "You sure that's a good idea?"

An angry breath jumps out of me. "I'm not having this conversation with anyone else. I'm an adult. So is Ember."

His hands go up in the air between us, palms out. "Don't get mad. I'm a concerned parent." He sighs like he's letting go of something. "Go have fun. Spend some time with your high school sweetheart. Don't let your old man stop you."

I soften a little. "Thanks, Dad."

He pats my shoulder before he turns away from me. "Johanna," he calls to my mother, "Take this tired man home."

When my parents are gone, I tug Ember's hand.

She gives me a look, and I notice her pink cheeks. "Yes, now we can go," she says.

"Why are you flushed," I ask, stopping at our table. Ember grabs her purse and waits, watching as I hook my suit jacket from the back of my seat with one finger and sling it over my shoulder.

"This dress is incredibly tight." She looks uncomfortable

even as she says it, running her hands over the flatness of her stomach.

Together we head for the parking lot. "Take it off."

She throws me a derisive look. "Um, okay, yeah. Sure."

"I dare you to drive home without that dress on."

Her eyes widen, but her tongue darts out to lick her top lip, exhilaration rippling across her face. "A dare? How old are you?"

I wiggle my eyebrows and say nothing.

She stares at me, her lips twisting as she considers it. "It would be nice to breathe again."

I take a deep breath and exhale loudly. "Feels good. Bet you'd like to feel that good."

"Okay, okay." She flicks out a hand and smacks my chest. "You're overselling it."

"So you'll do it?"

"If I did it I would keep my underwear on. Wouldn't want to show off my hiney."

Laughter tumbles from my chest. "Am I still ass-y?"

"Oh, yes." Her expression is solemn. "Ass-y still defines you." She looks pleased as she stops and digs through her purse. Producing her keys, she points them into the night and presses the button. A few rows away a car beeps and lights flash.

Relief flits across her face. "I forgot where I parked." She starts for her car.

"Do you do that often?" I ask, falling in step beside her.

Her gaze briefly meets mine before returning to the sidewalk. "Only when I'm meeting the ghost from love life past and it makes me feel weird things."

We get to her car and I pull open her door. "Get in and disrobe. Then you won't be nervous anymore. Like picturing people naked when you're nervous, but the opposite."

She steps into the open space between her door and her car. "I'm not nervous." Defiance makes her chin jut out.

"I am." The admittance flies out, dodging my filter and shooting into the thick, uncertain space between our bodies.

She lowers herself into the seat without responding. She's thinking. I haven't moved. I feel stuck, hovering in some weird haze, and I'm not sure how to move forward. I need Ember to take the reins now. She needs to tell me how this will go. She stares up at me, studying my eyes. She's always been able to pierce my defenses, pin me with her gaze, and strip away the layers until I'm left bare.

"Follow me home, Noah."

So I do.

This time, she lets me into her house without hesitation. My hand in hers, she pulls me through the place, into her room, and shuts the door.

Like last night, she takes charge. Her hands are on me first, pulling at my tie and lifting it over my head. Fingers nimbly open buttons, skim my torso, reach down and unzip me. She works her dress over her head, and then I take over.

I'm slow with her, savoring the curve of her backside, the way her belly dips low and her hip bones jut out when she's on her back. This is the way last night would've gone if carnal need hadn't engulfed us.

She falls asleep quickly when it's over. I'm exhausted too, but the wheels in my mind are turning, excited by the prospect of Ember being mine again.

It's easy to see that happening, as long as my phone doesn't ring. If I get a call from the recruiter, I don't know what I'll do. Soccer is like a drug. Playing is like a drug. Like any other addiction, the hit of dopamine is strong and powerful. The reality is, I'm only as good as my last shot. And so, I chase the dream, the possibility that every shot can be better than the last, every hit of dopamine can feel just as good as the one before it.

Maybe being in love is the same way. The addiction, the dopamine, the desire for more.

Ember, snuggled into my arms, makes an incoherent sound but doesn't wake.

My eyes close and I drift. Sleep is coming on quickly, but ahead of it are thoughts of high school. Of sneaking off to my parents' beach house, the way she showed me how to dance without music, and how long she waited to tell me what *shmily* meant.

There hasn't been a minute, not since the day I pulled her from that lake, that I didn't love her. Back then, and today.

I love this girl.

## 23

### EMBER

Day two waking up like this.

Noah snores softly, his chest rising and falling in a rhythm. I trail a hand over the expanse. His muscles are well-defined but not bulky. If there is one thing I know for sure, it's that his body was made for soccer.

His eyes flutter open, and a low sound reverberates through his chest.

"Sorry I woke you," I whisper.

"No you're not." His voice is scratchy.

"You're right," I say, grinning. I'm not sorry at all.

He rolls over so he's facing me. "I don't know about you, but I'm hungry. I worked up an appetite last night."

My stomach growls as if it's in on the conversation. Swinging my legs around to the edge of the bed, I stand and pull a shirt over my head. "Basic needs first. Then I was thinking we could go to the lake. Maybe laugh about how you thought you were being a hero." Noah tosses a pillow at me, and I dodge it. "Get dressed," I call out, heading for the bathroom.

Just as I close the door, I hear his phone vibrating on my dresser.

A few minutes later I open the door, hoping to hear who he's on the phone with, but I can only hear the baritone of his voice, not the words. Sighing, I stick my toothbrush in my mouth. I'm spitting out toothpaste when he comes to find me.

He props one arm on the jamb above his head and watches me rinse. He's dressed in last night's clothes, his white shirt untucked, and the top two buttons are undone. On his face is resolute sadness, like his heart has been carved out and he's hollow. I know that look. It's the one that prompted me to tell him to go four years ago. For Noah, sacrifice equals anguish.

"Congratulations." I try to smile.

"Ember—"

"You're leaving." My gaze rests on his in the mirror.

"Come with me?" Noah's eyes are bright, the corners of his lips turned up with the hint of a hopeful smile. His tone is urgent, making the question sound more like a plea.

"Noah…" I tip my head to the side and slowly shake it.

"Please. Think about it. What do you feel?"

I turn to face him, lifting myself up so I'm sitting on the counter. I know what he's getting at. It's still there. The pulse of electricity, the seismic activity of an off-the-scale earthquake, and the extraordinary power of attraction that bound us together when we were fresh-faced and new.

"Magic," I say with a lift of my shoulders. That one, simple word is the tip of the iceberg for us, and yet it's powerful enough to encompass everything hidden beneath the surface.

"Yes," Noah breathes, stepping in to the bathroom so we're only a foot apart. "Exactly. We could do this every day."

He places his hand over my heart. "We could have magic every day. Not like in high school when we had to be home, at work, or at practice. Not like now when we only have a little more time together."

My heart twists at the mention of our dwindling time.

"We could have magic all the time, Ember. Let's do it." He's talking fast, excited by his idea. He comes even closer, so that now he's standing in the space created by my open legs.

"Where would I stay, Noah? You'll be on the road. A new city every other week, maybe more often than that." As much as I want to let myself get wrapped up in this fairytale idea, I know better.

My words have hit their mark. Like a deflating balloon, Noah's excitement shrinks before my eyes.

"I'll keep a permanent place in Atlanta. The coach said there's a building a lot of the players live in." His voice is smaller now. Crestfallen. "I don't want this to be over." He tucks my hair back behind my ear, his fingers trailing down my neck.

"I know." My voice trembles with the tears I'm holding back. "But I don't want to give us half a shot. I move across the country to be with you, and then you travel all the time? We can't fail again. I won't be able to stand having us not work out a second time." Does he understand how much I need to preserve him, even now? I love him far too much to stain us a second time. "It sounds romantic and audacious, and it would make a great story, but the reality is different. I was right the last time, Noah. We fell apart, and we were just kids. I don't want to know what it's like to fall apart as adults."

We both hear the phone buzzing in his pocket.

"You better go." I hate the words as I say them.

"We can still go to the lake. The day doesn't have to be over. I don't have to go back until tomorrow."

How easy it would be to continue this game, pretend like each kiss, each touch, each look, isn't one of the last. "No," I say. My voice is low in volume, but strong.

Noah pulls his hand back from my neck, and the air that replaces his touch singes me. He steps away from the counter, his hips pulling away from their spot between my knees.

Our eyes locked, he offers me a hand getting down. Ignoring it, I hop down on my own. He walks to my room and emerges a moment later with his wallet and jacket.

Neither of us speaks. Words are too much right now. Like the first time we parted ways, we might make well-intentioned promises that can never be kept. This time, we're leaving it good. On our terms.

I follow Noah to the foyer, my eyes on his light brown hair, his strong neck, the way it flows seamlessly into broad shoulders, curving in to a chiseled torso. I'm committing his body to memory, filled with the knowledge this will probably be the last time I see it.

He pulls open the front door, pausing at the threshold. When he turns to me, his eyes hold sadness. My own are tightening, the burn of tears threatening. This is where Noah should kiss me once, gently, a soft good-bye kiss.

That's not what he does.

Wrapping one hand around my back, he tugs me into him. His other hand wraps around the back of my neck, and his lips find mine. I hold onto him for dear life as our kiss deepens, him trying to fight the circumstance, and me desperate for just one more minute with him.

He finally drags his lips from mine, but he doesn't move

further than an inch away. His ragged breath blends with mine, and together we create a palpable thickness.

With eyes that scream for rebellion against our choice, he turns and leaves. Unmoving, I watch him go. When his car disappears past the line of trees, I whisper my thoughts out into the evergreens.

*I'm sorry.*

*I already miss you.*

*This may have been a mistake.*

*Stay and we'll do things right this time.*

———

NOAH HAS BEEN GONE TEN SECONDS AND I'M ALREADY LOSING it. Sky isn't here, so I text Dayton.

**Pieces of me are scattered everywhere.**

A moment later, he responds.

**I'm on my way.**

I don't have to wait long. Dayton makes it in record time.

"Baby girl," he says, descending upon me the second I pull back the front door. Putting my hands up, I fend him off, but he gives me a reproachful look. "I know you need a hug."

"I'm okay." I try to sound strong when all I feel is weak.

Dayton ignores my protest and pulls me to his chest. We're almost the same height, so he turns his face to me and smells my neck.

"You smell like sex." He takes one more, longer sniff, and I feel the air move across my skin. "And regret."

I tip my head to the side and grin sadly into his hair. "Yes to one, and no to the other."

"No sex?" He lifts his head from its inspection, wary eyes pinning me. My cheeks warm as I think about the many

times Noah and I were together. Sheets off the bed, toe-curl-
ing, soul-satisfying, mind-bending... Dayton runs a bent
finger over my cheek. "So yes to the sex then. And no to the
regret." He winks at me. "That's my girl."

I try to smile at his praise, but I can't. The sadness of the
morning is taking over, and my control slips further and
further from my grasp.

"Tell me everything." Dayton rolls his eyes, well aware of
my refusal to share intimate details. "Well, your version of
everything, anyway."

I don't say anything. I simply can't speak. The sorrow in
my heart wells up and out, snaking through my system and
overtaking me. The tears I was successful holding back with
Noah come bounding forward now.

Dayton stares at me in horror. He may be gay, but he has
the same deer-in-the-headlights look of any guy who has a
weeping female in front of him. I grab a tissue from the box
on the coffee table and blow my nose. I'm blotting my
cheeks when Dayton pseudo-apologizes.

"I've never seen you cry before. I didn't know you had
tears in your body. I guess it makes sense, since I've seen you
sweat like a pig more times than my momma has pulled a
Sunday roast from the oven."

Despite my splintered chest, I smile.

Dayton sinks onto the couch, grabbing my hands on his
way down. He pulls me from where I sit on the coffee table
and into his arms.

Snuggled next to him, my head rests on his chest while
his hand strokes my hair. "I thought I could do it. I was so
high from the rush of seeing Noah. It's like I kept going up,
up, up." My free hand reaches out, lifting higher and higher,
mimicking a roller coaster on its ascent. "Each minute was
better than the last while he was here, and then he left,

and... crash." My hand fists, dropping onto Dayton's thigh. "Go ahead and say it."

"What?"

"That thing you're dying to say to me."

"I'm not dying to tell you I was right."

I smack his knee. "I see how you slipped that in there."

Beneath my head his chest shakes.

"It was worth it though. All of this." I palm my chest. "The last two nights were worth it."

"Then that's all that matters."

Dayton holds me until my neck begins to hurt.

"I'm going to grab a shower," I say, standing. I'm teaching in two hours, and I need to get ready. I could still get a sub, the way I planned to do when I thought I'd be spending the day with Noah, but it will be good for me to work.

Dayton pinches his nose and makes a face. "Please do." He waves an open palm in front of him. "You smell like things that would make you blush if I said them."

Halfway across the living room I pause and look over my shoulder. "Two nights ago I had sex right where you're sitting."

Dayton is quiet for a beat. "Who's bare ass was on the cushion? Yours or soccer stud's?"

"Soccer stud."

"I'll just get cozy then," Dayton jokes, wiggling his hips and burrowing deeper into the couch.

I grab a throw pillow from the chair and make good use of its name. The pillow hits Dayton squarely in the head.

He laughs and rises from the couch, following me down the hall. "Want me to wash your sheets?"

I stop, one hand on the bathroom door handle, and consider his offer.

"Yes," I say, before hurrying into the bathroom and closing the door behind me.

Sagging against the wall, I slide slowly and the floor catches me. As much as I want to keep Noah's scent on my sheets, I want to get rid of it in equal measure. Clean break this time, right? That's what I tell myself through the silent sobs. I chant it without a sound, as the curtain of tears falls from my eyes.

I knew what I was getting myself into. Yet, I went through with it. There is no love without sorrow. Rising from the floor, I reach into the shower and turn on the water. I undress, and the tears that are in free fall hit my bare skin.

It's not much of a leap to say these are both happy and sad tears.

Happy because I had Noah again.

Sad because it was likely the final time.

"Dayton," I yell through the shower curtain.

A few seconds later, I hear the door open. "Yeah?"

Pulling back the shower curtain, I stick my head out and take in Dayton's uneasy expression. My sheets are balled in his hands, one of them spilling onto the floor. "Starting today, don't ask me to get dinner out more than twice a month. No more daily latte's, and I need to see if I can find a better rate on car insurance."

"Are you saying that—"

"It's time, Dayton."

A satisfied grin parks itself on his lips. His face has the look of a proud mother. He backs out of the open door, and I put my head back under the spray. The water runs over me, taking with it Noah's scent, his touch, the invisible trails of his intoxicating kisses.

In my mind I see a stack of textbooks, smell the woody scent of fresh pencils, hear the *tap tap tap* of computer keys.

I've been waiting so long I don't even know what I'm waiting for anymore. My mother is happy and settled, no longer in need of financial help. Sky has her anxiety under control. My yoga teacher certification was finished a long time ago. I have enough credits from community college courses that it should only take me two years, maybe even eighteen months, to graduate with my bachelor's degree.

Noah is out there, accomplishing his goals and going after more.

I'm long overdue.

# 24

# EMBER

To-Do List

- Graduate college
- Buy a yoga studio
- Meet someone new
- Start a YouTube yoga channel

## 25

# EMBER

MY BODY SAGS ONTO THE UNCOMFORTABLE, PLASTIC SEAT. I wish it were a bed. A big, soft bed, with even bigger pillows, and cool sheets.

"Do you want anything to eat?" Matt glances at the watch I gave him for his birthday last month. "We have almost an hour before boarding starts." Bending down, he rummages through his carry-on.

"I'm fine," I say, yawning. My body clock is so messed up, all I really want to do right now is pass out. I swear, I switched over to Greenwich Mean Time our first night in London. It's nine o'clock in New York, where we now sit as we wait for our next plane.

"I'll grab something for you anyway." Matt stands, looking down at me. He smiles a little, but I see through the façade. Deep down, he's questioning our relationship.

Just like I am.

How could I not? We've been dating eight months, and

everything was going great. When Matt said he wanted to take me to London to celebrate my graduation, I said yes immediately. And then... Well, Dayton warned me this would happen. *Traveling with someone is like a glimpse into the bare bones of your relationship.* He wished me luck, but the look on his face made it clear he doubted it would go well.

As soon as I get home, I'm going to pinch him for letting me go in the first place. He obviously knew it was a bad idea for Matt and I to travel together. Sighing, I shift in the uncomfortable seat, bringing my knees into my chest so my feet dangle on the seat edge.

I feel bad. It was too soon for us. If we can just get back to California, slip into our normal life, everything will be okay. He'll pick me up for dinner after my Wednesday class, and I'll stay over on Friday night. We'll visit his grandmother at the nursing home, and it'll all be normal again.

Except, it won't, because now I know things. Things like—

*Holy fuck.*

My stomach is gone, slipped right out through my feet. The throngs of people walking past me, suitcases rolling along behind them, turn to vapor. Through the mist I see *him.* He's six feet away, leaning on crutches, gaze fixed on me. His right leg sticks out in front of him, immobilized in a brace.

My head is thick and hazy, and now he's coming over. Slowly. My breath slams up my throat at the same time I attempt to swallow the pooled saliva in my mouth, and I cough.

He stops inches from me, and I feel his heat. It might be twenty-seven degrees outside, but my body is an inferno. Only he can do this to me. Only Noah can take my world and shake it, emptying from it my secrets and fears, my insecurities and pleasures. It piles up around me like little mounds of coins.

"I'm a gimp, you know. You could've at least come to me."

Noah leans into his crutches, his voice faintly playful. He doesn't smile, but his eyes look full, like he has words and emotions in triplicate, and they might all come tumbling out in an instant.

"I...couldn't." It's not enough, but I know he'll understand. My shoulders lift a fraction and drop.

"I get it. I saw you first. I had more time to recover."

My whole body wants to reach out, touch him, run my fingers over his lips. Two years since we last saw each other. Two years since I've felt him, smelled him, tasted him.

*Noah*, my heart screams.

"Are you okay?" I point to his leg.

"Yeah." He looks down. "Torn ACL. During a game."

When his gaze returns to mine, I see it. His vulnerability, the trademark confidence missing. It wrecks me.

"You didn't see it?" His voice is soft, tinged with hope.

I know what he's really asking. *Do you watch me?* And with the answer to that question comes a confirmation neither of us need. *You still care.*

"No," I lie, looking out into the crowd of nameless faces. I saw his injury, but it's best not to go down that road. Any question of residual feelings and it leaves us wide open to possibilities we should no longer have.

"Um, hi." Matt's voice bursts through my thoughts. "Here, Ember." A bag of something lands on the seat beside me. Matt holds out a hand to Noah, and Noah shakes it. It takes Matt less than a second of looking straight at Noah to place him. "Shit! You're Noah Sutton!"

Noah smiles tightly, pulling his hand away.

"Man, we were watching the game where you got hit." Matt's talking quickly, his excitement bowling over any desire to appear cool in front of his favorite soccer player. "That was low. That guy deserved more than a red card."

Noah's hair brushes his forehead with his nod. Murmuring his thanks to Matt, his eyes remain laser-focused on me. I shift, uncomfortable, and look away. *Yes, I lied to you.*

Matt comes to his senses and says my name. I meet his confused gaze. "Do you guys know each other?" He glances from me to Noah.

My legs finally feel strong enough to stand on, so I rise. Two pairs of eyes study me, waiting for my answer. "We went to high school together. Noah, this is Matt." I gesture between them.

I'm trying not to let guilt flavor my words too much, but it's there anyway. Matt and I watched the game where Noah was injured. Sort of, anyway. I don't watch sports. Instead, I was curled up in the sheets of our hotel bed, reading a book. Every so often Matt leapt from the couch and yelled complaints at the game on the TV, and I looked up. He yelled when Noah was injured, even told me Noah was carted off the field, and I didn't say a word. Not because I didn't care. I spent the next day furtively looking up every article I could find about Noah's injury, and still I didn't tell Matt anything.

I could've told him I knew Noah. Matt wouldn't have cared. He's not the jealous type. The problem is *me*. I don't speak about Noah. I don't even allow myself to think about Noah. The knowledge that my one great love won't be my forever love is too much for me, so I just don't go there.

And yet, here he is, standing in front of me, *again*.

Noah sucks in a quick breath, but I don't meet his eyes.

What did he expect me to say? *Matt, this is Noah Sutton, my high school boyfriend?* I can't reduce us to a juvenile relationship, personified by hand-holding at a Friday night football game and making out in someone's parents' car after a date. We were so much more than that.

I look to Matt, not Noah, because I can't bear to see the hurt in his eyes. Matt's not looking at me, though. He's still star-struck by Noah.

"I need to find something for you to sign. The guys at my firm won't believe me if I don't have proof." Matt grabs his bag off the seat and unzips the front section.

My gaze shifts as Noah mouths something at me over Matt's back. *Boyfriend?* He gestures with a thumb. I nod. Why do I feel guilty? I've done nothing wrong. But still, I feel it, the flicker of shame, like I wasn't supposed to move on.

Indignation flares. Noah moved on. I saw the stupid magazine cover. He dated a model, someone who was my genetic opposite. I glare at him. He's not going to make me feel like I've done something wrong. I open my mouth to tell him so, but Matt stands up. *Thank goodness.* Extreme emotion conveys passion.

"I can't find a pen. Ember, do you mind taking a picture?" Matt looks at Noah. "Is that okay with you?"

Noah nods, and I want to laugh. Throw my head back and let loose an unladylike howl of a laugh.

In what universe is this happening?

Matt positions himself beside Noah, lifts his arm like maybe he's going to throw it over Noah's shoulder, decides not to, and drops it. The whole thing is awkward.

"Smile." I hold up the phone. Matt's grin reaches his ears, but Noah's is barely passable.

A woman's bored voice comes over the intercom system,

and we all three listen. I stop paying attention when she doesn't say Los Angeles, but Noah tells us they're calling his flight. Matt steps back to my side, taking his phone from me and sliding an arm around my waist.

For a nanosecond Noah looks as if he wants to rip Matt's arm off, but he changes course quickly. "It was nice to see you, Ember. It's been... a while." Now he grins, a real, knowing smile, and I want to melt into the floor. Whatever he's recalling from the last time we saw each other, it's most definitely not for anyone else's eyes.

"Bye, Noah." It's a struggle to make my voice nonchalant. Like it's no big deal that I've seen him, and even less of a deal that he's leaving.

He skillfully navigates a turn with the crutches, and I wonder if he's used them before. The thought makes me sad. He's the most significant person in my history, and I know so little about him now.

A rhythmic and slow progression carries him through the crowd. He requires a lot of space, and most people give it to him when they realize he's injured. Others stare in recognition. Twice on the way to his gate he's stopped to sign an autograph. Inside my chest, a peal of acerbic laughter erupts. *He's autographed my heart. My soul. My memories. Do they count?*

Matt and I watch until the crowd swallows Noah and we can no longer see him. Shaking his head, Matt turns to me. "I can't believe you know Noah Sutton. That is so cool."

*Oh yeah? Do you want to know what is not cool? How fanboy you sound right now.*

I bite my tongue and push down the scathing remark. I'm angry, and not at Matt. If Noah would treat me as if I'm nothing more than an old friend, this would all be so much easier. But, no. He has to look at me with eyes that *see* me. Eyes that *know*.

"He was my first," I blurt out. I can't stand it. Keeping it hidden makes it feel illicit, and maybe that's the problem. If I tell Matt, maybe it will take away Noah's hold on me. A smidgen of it, anyway.

Matt looks surprised. "First kiss? Or, like, *first* first?"

"*First* first."

He pushes out his lips and nods, hands in his pockets, as he thinks for a moment. "Violet Crabtree was my first."

"Okay?" It comes out like a question. Why is he telling me this?

"Now we know that about each other. Check it off the list." Removing a hand from his pocket, he places it on my arm and squeezes. "I'm going to run to the bathroom before they call our flight." He starts to leave but turns back around. "I grabbed something for you to eat. It's on the seat beside you. It's not healthy, but beggars can't be choosers." He shrugs and walks off.

That went...well. Like, really well. *You got lucky with Matt.*

Resolve runs through me. Matt is a good person and deserves more from me. Noah is a part of my past, but I don't have to romanticize it so much. That's all I'm doing. Looking back wearing rose colored glasses. I'm sure if I think really hard, I'll remember things about Noah that weren't great. I can't think of any off the top of my head, but I'm certain they're there, buried somewhere deep in the recesses of my mind.

From now on, I'm going to focus on Matt.

Yep. That's what I'll do. I feel good about that decision already.

My stomach grumbles and I cover it with a hand. Good

thing my really sweet, mature, kind *boyfriend* Matt got something for me to eat. I reach into the seat beside me and wrap my fingers around the crinkling bag.

*I can do this.*

Opening the bag, I crunch through three potato chips and try to stop feeling like I've been punched in the stomach.

# 26

# NOAH

*FUCK*.

I stare at the ceiling and growl.

It's hard to remember not to move. The pain is an instant reminder. I look down at my traitorous leg, buried under my gray comforter. *Thanks a lot, asshole.*

It was a routine play. Left foot, right foot. Left, right, left, right. Step over. Pass to Terence. Terence back to me. Then came the defender, who on any other day shouldn't have been a big deal, but this guy was out for blood. He apologized in a post-match interview, saying he meant no harm, and wished me a speedy recovery. I responded with goodwill in my post-match interview, telling the reporter that injuries occur in sports, and blame is unnecessary.

*Lies.* That fucker wanted me on the injured list.

As if the torn ACL weren't bad enough, I had to run into Ember. With her *boyfriend*. Apparently, my low point wasn't low enough.

Throwing an arm over my eyes, I try to block out Ember's image. Of course it's useless. Ember exists on a reel tape in my mind. Why should this morning be any different? *Because she has a boyfriend and now you can finally get over her.* Despite her relationship, one thing has been bothering me since I hobbled away from her stare.

She lied about watching my game.

Why?

It's a question I can't answer myself, so I don't even try. Instead, I sit up and inch out of bed, reaching for the brace on my nightstand. After it's fastened, I grab the crutches propped against the wall and lean them on the bed next to me. Slowly swinging my good leg to the floor, I use my hands to lift the injured leg to the edge of the bed. I rise, balancing on one leg, and prop the crutches under each arm.

All that work just to get out of bed.

Everything is slower. It takes me four times longer to fucking do anything. Breakfast? Not if I want toast. The toaster is tucked in the back of a bottom cabinet. Eggs? Good luck reaching a pan. It's also in a bottom cabinet. I ended up with an apple, stale tortilla chips, and then I found a protein drink.

Have I mentioned my career might be over?

And the love of my life has moved on?

Fuck my life.

---

MY LOW POINT JUST GOT LOWER. I MEAN, I KNEW THE LIKELY prognosis from my internet research, but hearing the team doctor say it is somehow worse.

"Sorry, Noah. I know it's not what you want to hear." Dr. Clafin claps me on the back. He's nearly all gray hair now, but when I started with the team he was only just beginning to gray. It took two years for his hair to lose pigment. The same amount of time it took my professional career to be in jeopardy.

"I'll give the report to Marcus," Dr. Clafin says, one side of his mouth upturned in a resolute smile.

I nod, picturing the displeasure I know will cross my head coach's face.

Backing away from my couch, Dr. Clafin gathers his things and packs up the little bag he brought with him. When he's finished, he looks at me. "I'm sorry, Noah." His eyes hold a mixture of compassion and disbelief, as if even he can't believe I'm injured this badly. He means well, but his pity only aggravates me.

An irrational urge rises up, but I manage to suppress it. The doctor can't change his report, no matter how much I wish he could. There wouldn't be a point. My obvious brokenness would give me away in seconds. I can't play tough like I have in the past. A steroid shot won't fix me this time.

"What now?" I ask, leaning back against the buttery soft, overstuffed couch cushions. Automatically, I drape an arm across the back and try to lift my right leg with the intention of crossing my ankle over my left knee. As soon as I try, I remember I can't. The swift shot of pain is not nearly as agonizing as the blow to my fragile ego. I feel fucking worthless.

"Well, you're going to need surgery for certain, but we have to allow time for the swelling to go down. Probably about three weeks? In the meantime, I'll call a friend of mine in Arizona and see when he can get you in. You need the best if you want to play soccer again."

"And until then?"

"Pre-hab it. The first thing you'll lose is your quad

muscle, and it'll go fast. Don't let that happen. I'll email you a guide with exercises you can do."

I dip my head back and bring it up slowly, two times. It feels like there's a weighted blanket covering me. It's all so big, so heavy, so *excessive*. The world is a blender and my life is the smoothie.

"Try to keep in good spirits, Noah. Call your parents. Call your brother, and FaceTime with his new baby. Try to get out of here once a day." Dr. Clafin raises his eyebrows. He's waiting for me to agree.

"Sure, sure." I say it to placate him. I'm not interested in hobbling around downtown Atlanta. Enough people were inadvertently tripped by my crutches in the New York and Atlanta airports already, I'm not trying to send anyone else sprawling onto sidewalks. Or be the recipient of any more irate looks. Some of them turned to compassion when they realized the person who accidentally tripped them was injured. Some of them... Well, not so much.

Dr. Clafin sends me one final wave on his way to the door. "I'll be in touch about your surgery."

I say good-bye as the heavy door swings shut behind him.

For the next week, I do the opposite of everything Dr. Clafin suggested. I order in every meal. I sleep all day, stay up all night watching stupid movies. Sometime around two a.m., I use the video app on my TV to find the recording of my injury. It's only one minute and thirty-seven seconds long, and I watch it more than sixty times. My injury comes at fifty-two seconds in. Then I'm on the ground, holding my knee, my face scrunched. Every person who has seen this probably thinks I was trying not to cry about the pain.

Physical pain doesn't bother me. It's fleeting, a blip in time.

The stadium lights were bright, even through my scrunched eyes, and I could hear the footfalls of my teammates cleats as they ran to me. Even in that moment, I knew it was bad. Maybe it was the searing pain, maybe it was the popping sound that I still can't stop hearing. The physical pain was nothing compared to my fear.

The tears I was holding back came from panic.

What if I lose it all?

Have I already?

---

"NOAH?"

Her voice comes from behind me. I'm sitting on the couch, because where the hell else would I be? She rounds the couch and comes to stand beside the coffee table. Holding two bags of groceries in each hand, she looks at me like she's trying not to tell me I'm pathetic.

Miranda is my right hand. She handles everything for me, including all personal travel and my apartment when I'm away with the team. She's a nice person, and an even better assistant. Two guys on the team have asked me to pass her their numbers, but I lied and said she has a boyfriend. I don't need the headache of dating drama, but I see the attraction. She's in her early twenties, intelligent, and her white-blonde hair gives her an angelic effect.

Miranda was on vacation when I got hurt. When she heard what happened and that I was back in Atlanta, she offered to come back early. I told her to enjoy the rest of her time, and when she returned she jumped right into her role. She's the reason someone came to clean up behind my lame, feeble ass yesterday. I hobbled into my room and shut the door while a cleaning person hauled away all my take-out boxes. I was too embarrassed to look them in the eyes. I feel like a jack-ass for acting like an invalid.

"Thanks for buying groceries," I say, trying like hell to sound like my normal self and not some depressed asshole.

She shrugs. "After all those take-out boxes I saw in the trash yesterday, I thought you might want a fresh and healthy meal."

"I can't do much cooking right now." I probably could, it would just take a thousand times longer and piss me off.

"Lucky for you, I can." She walks away. In a few seconds I hear the fridge open and the sounds of food being put away.

"I broke my collarbone in junior high," Miranda says, "and my mom made me chicken marsala. So that's what I'm making you. I know you love mushrooms."

I can't turn all the way around, so I settle for turning my neck as much as I can and nod. "Thanks," I tell her, and listen to the sounds of her moving around in the kitchen.

My phone rings beside me and I reach for it. I learned to keep the damn thing pretty much glued to me, so I didn't have to swing my broken ass around the apartment to find it every time it rang.

I sigh when I see who it is. I knew his call was coming, but answering makes all this even more of a reality. "Hello?"

"Scottsdale," Dr. Clafin says, his voice scratchy as he coughs. "On the twenty-third. Miranda is arranging everything."

I wish I could turn around and give Miranda a dirty look. She knew about the surgery when she walked in.

It's quiet, then there's a muted sound of nose-blowing, and more throat clearing. "You'll be in good hands. My friend in Boston didn't hesitate when I asked him. Dr. Cordova is in high-demand, but he's making room for you.

Doesn't hurt that he's a huge soccer fan." Dr. Clafin chuckles, but it turns into a cough. "Damn cold," he growls, when he's able to speak again.

I smile at his words, and realize it's my first smile in more than a week. *Since I saw Ember in New York.*

"I'll wait for Miranda's itinerary," I say loudly. "She's the boss."

She walks from the kitchen and stands in front of me, smirking and shaking her head.

Dr. Clafin laugh-coughs again. "She's already getting things in order," he says. "She is gold, you know? Never let her go."

We chat for a few more minutes, and I wish him a speedy recovery before saying good-bye.

"I was going to tell you after you ate," Miranda says from the kitchen when I hang up. "You're grumpy right now, and I knew Clafin was going to call you."

I nod. Miranda is right. I need to stop being an asshole. It makes me feel better to know my surgery has been scheduled. The listlessness was eating at me. I needed a plan. A goal. Something to look forward to.

Maybe I'll go out tomorrow morning. Get breakfast at my favorite restaurant. The team will be back in town soon, we could go to happy hour.

This emotional high I'm on feels so good, so refreshing, that I pick up my phone and bring up Ember's name in the contacts. I'm not sure if it's still her number, but I can try. Friends can call each other, right? Friends care about the general well-being of one another. If Ember were injured, I'd want to know the outcome.

Before I can think about it any longer, I press send.

The phone rings. Once, twice, three times.

"Hello?"

I freeze. I have no words. My thumb presses down hard on the end button, as though it's really a button and not a red circle on a glass screen.

Why am I surprised?

Why am I this angry?

He's her boyfriend. He has the right to answer her phone. Still, it fucking tears me up inside. Is this how people are supposed to feel when they learn their ex has moved on? Is this normal?

"Dinner will be ready in ten minutes, Noah. I'll refrigerate the other half and you can have it tomorrow."

I scoot to the edge of the couch and hoist myself up, grabbing my crutches from beside me on my way up.

"You just made your mom's recipe, Miranda. Aren't you going to stay and enjoy it?" I look out the black-paned window beyond the dining room table. The lights of downtown Atlanta are taking over the pink and purple sky, and I know there are people out there, gearing up for a Friday night. "I'm sure you have somewhere to be, and spending twenty more minutes with an invalid doesn't sound like much fun, but—"

"I'll stay, Noah." She gives me a reproachful look and shakes her head.

"What?"

"Nothing." She stirs the contents of the pan.

"Just say it."

"Maybe you should try and reframe the situation." Keeping her eyes on the food, she says, "I know things look bleak, but you still have a lot going for you."

"Are you saying I'm being a baby?"

She glances at me. "Kind of," she admits.

She's probably right. Maybe I should look at what I still have, instead of what I think I might lose.

I go to the table and sit down, feeling like an ass because I can't help her set the table or finish the food. She brings her laptop to the table, and we go through flights and hotels while we eat.

Focusing on the surgery should help take my mind from Ember. But it doesn't. I'm nodding and giving input on dates and times and car rentals, but I'm only halfway in the conversation.

When Miranda leaves, I lay down in bed and try not to think about what a red-haired female is doing across the country, or who she's doing it with.

---

"Do we know where the doctor's office is, Miranda?" I fold myself into the rented SUV, ass first, then use my hands to lift my leg into the car. We landed in Phoenix last night, and my pre-op appointment is this morning.

"Yep." Miranda places my crutches in the trunk, then climbs into the driver's seat and brings up the address on her phone.

We crawl along with morning traffic. I grab my phone from my cup holder and find some music. "Why are we staying so far from his office?" My voice is irritable and petulant. I'm in a bad mood. The team is playing a match today, and I won't be there. It's my first miss in two years.

Miranda casts a cool glance my direction. "Because it's close to the hospital where the surgery will be performed."

"Sorry," I mutter.

"It's okay, Noah. I know this all must suck."

We arrive at a big medical center. Miranda hops out and goes to look through the directory, then gets back in the car and finds a spot on the other side of the place.

"Good thing I looked," she says, getting out and retrieving my crutches from the back. "I don't think a stroll is what you want this morning."

"Thanks." I work to keep my voice light. She's right. I don't want a *stroll*. I want a sprint. I want high-knees. I want my lungs to burn with exertion.

Miranda waits for me to get out of the way, then closes the door.

We make our way to suite twelve, to a door that reads *Dr. Isaac Cordova* in block letters, with the words *Valley Orthopedic* and a phone number below it. The eyes of the person at the front desk sparkle in recognition.

After my x-rays are finished the technician asks me for an autograph for her son. She thanks me profusely and drops me off in the exam room. Miranda smirks when the door closes, because she knows I get a little embarrassed. I've never become used to signing autographs.

Dr. Cordova comes in right away. I'm surprised by how young he is. Maybe I'm used to Dr. Clafin, so I was expecting someone older. He extends a hand to me and smiles wide.

We chat for a minute, until he confesses he watched the match where I sustained my injury, and knew right away how bad it was.

"I told my wife it was your ACL. You were going one way, the guy was going another. Opposing forces like that? No chance." He grimaces. "He deserved that red card."

"Yeah, I've had better days." I shrug.

I'd really like to tell Dr. Cordova exactly how I feel about the situation, but I have to be careful what I say. The team spokesperson already lectured me on how to present myself when asked about what happened. *Everyone has a phone,* he'd warned, *and you don't want to be caught on record saying something bad.*

"Well, let's get to it." Isaac completes the exam, talks to me about my x-rays, and we iron out the details for the surgery. Miranda takes notes, which is good because there's little chance I'll remember everything.

We're about to leave when I throw one more question at the doctor. "Do you have kids?"

He beams. "Yep. My daughter is seven, and we have a boy due in three months."

"Congratulations. That's great." I pause, feeling stupid, but forge ahead. "I've spent my whole life on soccer. I never thought about much aside from that, and suddenly the possibility of having a real life exists. House, wife, kids, the whole nine yards. Is it as incredible as it looks?"

My brother is the only other person I know who has a normal life, but he doesn't have a demanding job the way Dr. Cordova does. I guess that's why I'm asking him. Between my teammates and brother, my sample size sucks.

I make it a point not to look at Miranda. Admitting all of this makes me feel weak.

Dr. Cordova nods. "It's even better than it looks, I promise. Things happen the way they're supposed to. I know it sounds trite, but it's true. Although you shouldn't count yourself out. I'm going to do my best to get you back on that field. Maybe I'll invoke some black magic, and give you some kind of super scoring power." He laughs. "Sorry, my daughter is into superheroes right now."

He walks us out and tells me he'll see me tomorrow.

It's a silent drive back to the hotel. My mind is flooded with thoughts.

This ACL tear doesn't mean the kiss of death for my career, but it could be the beginning of it. Every missed play, errant goal, any mistake made will be accompanied by someone wondering if I've lost my edge.

What if I'd chosen differently, two years ago? Let the call from the Atlanta recruiter go to voicemail and never returned it?

Like Dr. Cordova, I could have a family. A wife, maybe even a kid, and a career that won't end just because I'm human and breakable.

I could've chosen Ember.

And that's when the truth smacks me right in my face.

I turned down lifelong magic to chase an ephemeral dream.

# 27

# NOAH

"Is there anything else I can get you, Noah?"

Miranda hovers near the door of my hotel room. She looks tired. Her hair is tied messily on the top of her head and she's wearing sweats. She always wears black slacks and button-up shirts, but on this trip, she's let loose a little. Last night we went out to a restaurant, and she had two glasses of wine. I had nothing to drink, since I'm still on painkillers. She giggled a few times and told me she's thinking about going back to school for her Masters degree. This morning she apologized. I don't think she wanted me to know about going back to school.

I hate the idea of losing Miranda. She's intuitive, trustworthy, and intelligent. I told her I would make it work, that she could go to school and still work for me. Assuming there's even a reason to work for me anymore.

Miranda waits for my response. "I'm good. Thanks for everything. Getting my parents out here and all that." I hadn't expected them to come, but they arrived the morning of my surgery. It was good to have them, but three days with my parents hovering over me was enough. My mom was oddly nurturing. Maybe the arrival of her first grandson smoothed out her edges.

"Wild horses couldn't have kept your mother away." Miranda chuckles. I wonder if my mom gave her a hard time. It's safe to assume she did. "I'm going to pack everything up in the morning. Flight's at two."

"Sounds good." I nod. I've had enough recovery time in this hotel room. It's nice, but I want my own bed. My own stuff.

Miranda opens the door and backs up until she's standing in the dimly lit hallway. "Let me know if you need anything tonight."

I wave at her from my bed. A mountain of pillows prop me up, and additional pillows keeps my leg elevated. I might have all the extra pillows in the hotel. White bandages hide my knee and the incision.

The TV is on low, playing some sitcom re-run I'm seeing but not really watching, when my phone rings. It's just out of my reach on the nightstand. Annoyance flares. Why didn't I ask Miranda to hand it to me before she left? Normally I'd let the phone call go, but something tells me I should answer it.

Stretching, scooting, and being mindful of my leg, I get my fingertips on the end of the phone, walking them forward until its firmly in my palm. It's on the fifth ring and I know soon it will go to voicemail.

Flipping it over, I look at the name flashing on the screen. My stomach flops.

"Hello?" I answer quickly. For weeks I've been fighting the urge to call Ember again, but here she is calling me.

"Noah?"

My excitement fades. It's a man's voice.

"Yes?" Then I think about why someone would be

calling me from Ember's phone, and fear cascades through me.

"Is Ember okay?" My voice is rough and demanding. Panicked.

"She's fine. This is Dayton, Ember's friend. We met—"

"I remember," I interrupt. I know it's rude, but I'm not interested in cordial greetings. "Why are you calling me?"

If Ember's fine, why isn't she the one using her phone?

"Ember's mom is in the ICU. She was thrown from a motorcycle earlier today. The doctor isn't certain how bad it is just yet, but Ember is losing her mind. And—" he sighs, pauses, then continues "—if she falls, you should be there to catch her."

The news sinks in.

"I'll be there as soon as possible. Tomorrow morning." I look down at my leg.

"Good," Dayton's voice is pleased. I get the feeling I just passed a test.

"Ember told me not to call you, but I know her better than that."

"Are you going to tell her I'm coming?"

Dayton snorts. "Have you ever been punched by her? It hurts. Even when she thinks it's a friendly smack."

A short laugh escapes me. "I'll take that as a no then."

Dayton tells me the hospital where Maddie was taken, and I tell him to expect me in the morning. We hang up and I call Miranda.

"Change of plans," I say sharply when she answers. "I need to get back home to Northmount ASAP."

I wait on the line while she pulls out her laptop and looks up flights. "I can get us on the nine a.m. It's the first one out in the morning. There's one that leaves at eleven tonight, but that's in, like, three hours. So we'll plan on—"

"Tonight," I say. I want to hold Ember tonight. I want her to know she has me. Years have passed, but I haven't gone anywhere.

"Okay," Miranda says, her voice reluctant, but she doesn't ask any questions. She tells me she'll need fifteen minutes to book our tickets, get dressed and throw her things in her bag.

I hang up and do as much as I can on my own. The crutches slow me down, and more than once I get upset and take out my frustration on a table leg. Miranda arrives and helps me finish up.

Soon we're on the freeway, heading for the airport. Miranda finally asks the reason for this change of plans. I tell her a truncated version of Ember, without mentioning the magic part. Miranda places a hand over her heart and sighs wistfully. "It's so romantic."

"She has a boyfriend." I have no idea why Dayton called me. He probably shouldn't have.

Miranda gives me a look as we coast into the drop-off area of the rental car lane. "That makes it even more romantic."

I'm going because Ember is hurting. I want to be there to catch her, and I have an awful, gut-wrenching feeling that Ember is about to fall really, really hard.

---

"Are you sure you don't want me to go in with you?" Miranda asks me again. It's almost one in the morning, and we're nearly at the hospital.

"No." I feel bad for my tone, but I've already told her that a handful of times. She's not usually this pushy.

"I'll head to the hotel and get us settled in then."

I hear it in her voice. The hurt. Sighing, I rub my eyes with the heels of my hands. Miranda has been a mother hen since I arrived home after my injury, and it's getting old. Still, I don't want to hurt her feelings.

"I'm nervous about seeing Ember. I didn't mean to snap at you."

"Don't worry about anything. Ember will be happy to see you."

I shake my head. "You don't know Ember." I picture the Ember I saw in the airport, how standoffish she'd been, how stiff. How she'd lied to me.

"You're saying she has feelings for you?"

"No."

"That's what I heard."

"That is not what I said."

"I'm aware. I'm just telling you what I heard."

We're quiet until Miranda pulls up to the hospital entrance. "Visiting hours are over, you know."

"But what if she's in there?"

"What if she's not?"

"Then I want to be the first face she sees when she arrives tomorrow morning, or, this morning, technically." I peer through the sliding glass doors at the entrance. Someone sits behind the reception desk, staring at a computer screen.

"Alright," Miranda says, defeat in her voice. She comes around to my door, crutches in hand, and waits patiently for me to climb out and get the crutches situated under each arm.

"Let me know when you want me to come get you."

She walks around the car and opens her door. Turning, I begin my now-familiar pace. I'll be happy when I don't have to heave, haul, and swing my body anymore.

"Good luck, Noah," Miranda calls.

It takes a lot of work, but I slow and pause, throwing up a hand to send her off. She drives away, and I resume my slow walk all the way to the reception desk.

The woman is surly. Her frown seems permanent. She informs me in an acerbic tone that visiting hours have been over for a long time. When I tell her my plan to wait, the frown lines around her mouth grow deeper, like chasms on the earth's surface. I don't even ask for an update on Maddie. Snakes might sprout from her head if she has to unnecessarily remind me I'm not next of kin.

Hobbling to the far corner, I prop my crutches on the wall and pull another chair over in front of me. Once my legs are up on the second chair, I remove my sweatshirt and roll it up. It'll make a decent pillow.

Before I fall asleep, I take out my phone and go to a special folder in my photos. In it are all the pictures I've ever taken of Ember. Most of them are snapshots of real pictures, but there is one from two years ago that I took while she was sleeping. Her rose-colored lips were parted only slightly, and her whole face was relaxed. I wanted to remember her that way. She'd had so many expressions that night, beginning the moment I surprised her in the yoga studio, but this was the first time she looked serene.

Stuffing the phone in my pocket, I lean my head on the make-shift pillow and close my eyes. I'm exhausted, but it takes forever to fall asleep. I don't know how Ember will act when I see her.

But Dayton called me.

*Me.*

Even though Ember has a boyfriend.

Dayton knows Ember will need me.

*Me.*

FOUR HOURS. I SLEPT FOUR HOURS ON THAT CHAIR. THE cushion became a pancake somewhere around hour number two, but the person who replaced the surly lady has made up for her nastiness.

"Noah, here's another cup of coffee."

I thank her when she sets it down.

The shift change occurred at five a.m., and with nobody else in the waiting area, and me being awake, I explained why I've been here all night. She promised to whistle when a redhead walks in. I'll probably see Ember first though. There's a reason I chose this seat. It's next to a wall of windows, and those windows look out onto the parking lot and entrance.

Deanna, the nice receptionist, goes back to her desk, as a yawn escapes me. Reaching for the coffee, I resume my vigil. My stomach is in knots.

As I watch, a man parks a sedan and climbs out. He looks up at the building, shuts his door, and starts for the entrance. I blink twice to make sure I'm seeing things clearly. Walking in, he heads straight for the elevators. I struggle to my feet, my coffee forgotten, and try to catch up.

There's no use, and the elevator doors shut long before I can get there. But there's only one place my dad could be going, and it makes no sense. I ride the next elevator to the ICU. The nurses station is empty and I have no idea what to do. Across the hall is another waiting room, this one just for this floor. I go in there, choose a seat in view of the door and the nurses station, and wait for my dad to pass by.

Ten minutes.

Twenty minutes.

My leg is killing me. It's time for my medicine, and I

need food to go with it. There's a vending machine in the corner, so I hobble over and choose a bag of pretzels and water.

When I get back in my seat, I pop a few pretzels in my mouth and take my pill. Leaning my head back, I close my eyes for a second.

"Please call her doctor. We want to know how she's doing."

I lift my head, blinking. *Shit*. Damn pain pills. How long have I been asleep?

"Noah?"

Ember stands in the doorway, her feet planted, her body shifting forward like someone pressed the pause button on her stride.

I try to get up, but I'm a mess. My hands are shaking as I reach for my crutches, but one of them falls. I growl in frustration, then hear a sound. A sweet, throaty, amused sound.

Ember is in front of me, reaching down for my fallen crutch. "Here." She extends the stupid fucking crutch between us. I take it and shove it under my arm, along with the other one, and stand.

Ember stares at me and pinches her bottom lip with two fingers. Behind her is Sky, arms folded in front of herself and eyebrows lifted high onto her forehead.

"Dayton called me," I explain.

"I see." Ember nods slowly. She looks tired. The skin beneath her eyes is puffy and faintly purple.

"How is your mom?"

"She has a severe concussion, possible bleeding on the brain. They need the swelling to reduce before they can assess her accurately." Tears spring to her eyes, but they don't spill over. "I haven't been updated since last night. No news is good news, right?" She tries for a smile, but it fails.

"Yes, definitely." I try to sound upbeat. Sky walks away and sits down.

"Why are you here, Noah?" Ember squints up at me.

Her ability to pierce me with her eyes is still the same as it was the day we met.

"To catch you if you fall."

"I won't be falling, Noah, because my mom is going to be fine." Her fists ball at her sides and her lower lip quakes. "I don't know what romantic notion Dayton put into your head, but I don't need you to catch me." Her eyes flash, filled with thunder and lightning. "Besides, you've met Matt. What is he going to think about you showing up here?"

"Probably nothing." I lower my voice. "You reduced us to friends from high school."

Ember crosses her arms. "I told him after you left."

"Everything?"

She glares at me. "Enough."

"What does that mean?"

She takes a step back and rolls her eyes. I hate that she's keeping distance between us, and I don't want it there anymore. I want to press her body against mine, hold her, and whisper to her that I'll be here for her, no matter what happens. I can't do any of that, because I need fucking help fucking standing. Like a goddamned toddler.

"Ladies?"

We all turn to the door. A nurse in purple scrubs looks from Sky to Ember. "Your mother's doctor will be here soon."

"Okay," Ember whispers, and the nurse walks away. At once, the fire in her has been snuffed out. Her shoulders droop with the weight of it all. She stands rooted in her spot and presses two fists to her eyes.

"Ember?"

We all turn to the confused voice. Red colors the surface of Ember's cheeks. Sky looks like she doesn't give a shit about anything that's happening right now. I don't know what I look like, but I'm guessing if my expression reflects what I'm feeling, I want to punch Ember's prick of a boyfriend for not staying the night with her when she needed him the most. If she was mine I never would've let her go last night, and I would have come here with her this morning.

Matt and Dayton stand beside one another. Matt stares at me. Dayton stares at me.

I don't do a damn thing. My chin *might* be raised a fraction. I *might* be thinking about the nearest exit I can point Matt to.

He strides in, Dayton behind him, and pulls Ember into his arms. I look away. They exchange a few hushed words and he leads her over to a chair a few seats away from me.

Dayton sits down beside me. "What happened to flying in this morning?"

"Wasn't soon enough."

His head tilts as he watches me. "What did arriving in the middle of the night do for you?"

"It put me here first."

Dayton crosses an ankle over the opposite knee and leans back. "I'm glad you're here," he says under his breath. "Matt proposed."

# 28

# EMBER

MATT'S GRIP ON MY HAND IS STARTING TO HURT. Instinctively, I pull it away, but he only pulls me back. Why the hell is he holding me so tightly? My eyes find his, but the question stays stuck in my head.

The lights in the waiting room are bright, the sharp smell of astringent fills my nose. I wish I could close my eyes and make this all go away.

My mom. In the ICU. How can this be?

*A morning ride on a friend's motorcycle*, she'd told me two nights ago when I called her. Not a normal mom thing to do, but when was my mom ever normal? So I told her to have fun, and wear her helmet.

When I woke up yesterday morning, before I knew what had happened to my mom, I felt sorry for myself. Thoughts of Noah filled me. Was he okay? Did he have surgery? Would he crash my wedding, confess his love, and refuse to allow me to marry anybody but him?

And then the guilt came. The wretched, consuming guilt. Could I get any more pathetic?

Matt proposed.

He went the whole nine-yards. On one knee, his eyes shining, the ring box teetering on an outstretched palm.

My first thought was *Why didn't he propose while we were in England?* That would've been more romantic. My living room wasn't exactly exciting. Maybe that's why I didn't see it coming. Then came the second thought, but I guess it was more of a feeling. Crushing sadness. Not what I was supposed to experience during a proposal. *So this is how we will finally end.*

It had to end someday. Noah was never to be my forever.

It was time. *Move on with your life. First loves are not last loves.*

I swallowed the pain, pushed down the denial, and said yes.

A few hours later, it all stopped mattering. My mom was thrown from the back of the motorcycle. The friend she was riding with broke both legs. The helmet I told her to wear? She didn't. I was in my backyard finishing up a yoga video when Matt came outside to hand me the phone. Stress over the proposal consumed my thoughts until I put the phone to my ear, and my sister's teary voice spoke.

Then everything else fell away.

———

IT's AWKWARD. NOT THE WAITING ROOM IN THE ICU, BUT THE assortment of people in it. The knots in my stomach are tied into their own knots. Dayton sits beside Noah. My sister is on my left, Matt on my right.

Noah looks awful. His eyes are bloodshot and sunken.

"Did you sleep here last night?" I ask him, no opening sentence or casual conversation to start.

Sky's shoulders jump at the sound of my voice. It's the first sentence anyone has spoken in a while.

Noah looks up from his phone. He's been typing on it since the nurse asked us to wait in here for the doctor. His lips twitch. He looks unsure.

"Well?" I press.

He nods.

I look back down at my hands. My bare hands. One very bare finger in particular, and I hope Matt doesn't take that to mean anything. Leaning my head back on the chair, I close my eyes, and think of bridesmaids dresses. Sky looks amazing in light blue, and purple, and magenta, and red. All colors, actually. It's that blond hair of hers, it goes with everything. I'll let her choose her own color. I don't want a big ceremony. I'll wear flowers in my hair. Not a flower crown, maybe just one pinned behind my ear. Understated.

This is how I distract myself for the next thirty minutes, while Dayton plays a game on his phone. Twice, Matt steps out to take a call. Noah has his eyes closed and his head tipped back, but I know he's not sleeping. The rise and fall of his chest is uneven. Sky sits like me. Lost in thought.

Finally, the doctor walks into the room. He's a smaller man, almost my height, and the bald spot at the crown of his head is close to converging with his receding hairline. He strides past the first two rows of chairs, and Sky and I get to our feet.

"How is she?" Sky asks first, her voice anxious.

"I'm most concerned with her brain swelling. She's on medication to reduce it, and we're using additional methods to assist. We'll be monitoring her closely, and I hope to see improvement. If her brain continues to swell, she'll need a decompressive craniectomy." He speaks the words in an unaffected tone, but to me they sound big and scary, and it's still unbelievable that it's my mom he's talking about.

"Yes, yes. Okay. What is that? A...decompressive cranie... cranie..." Sky drops her head into her hands instead of finishing.

"A decompressive craniectomy means a section of her skull is removed to allow her brain to swell without being squeezed. That is a last resort though."

Sky begins her rhythmic breathing while I rub circles on her back, and try to get ahold of my own emotions.

"Your mom was in a bad accident. She may have a long and difficult road ahead of her. Physical therapy, speech therapy, maybe even behavioral and emotional struggles. Traumatic Brain Injury is very serious."

Sky breathes deeply, and I count with her in my head. Inhale *one, two, three, four, five*. Exhale *one, two, three, four, five*.

"She doesn't have insurance," I whisper. Why, in this moment, is that what comes to mind?

The doctor eyes me. "I've been told all her expenses will be fully paid by someone who prefers to remain anonymous."

Sky lifts her head, clearing her throat as the tears begin to slide down her face.

"What?" she asks, looking to me for knowledge I don't have. I shake my head.

"Now what?" I ask the doctor.

"We wait, and we watch. Closely." He nods to all of us and walks out.

The air in the room is tense, thick, and full of questions nobody wants to ask. My mind runs over everything I know, over and over without end, until I have the urge to scream.

My mom is in the hospital.

My mom is in a coma.

My mom might need a surgery that will remove a piece of her skull.

I ball my hands into fists to hide the shaking. Dayton and Matt stand, their arms outstretched, waiting for me to fall into them. Noah's crutches make protesting noises against the linoleum floor in his frantic attempt to grab them.

I don't give him the chance to get up. I don't fall. I climb onto his lap, fold myself into his big, warm front, and dissolve.

# 29

# NOAH

I'm wrecked. Ravaged. Someone has reached inside me and yanked, turning me inside out.

I cannot subdue Ember's guttural sobs. My whispers into her hair are met with more tears. The stroke of my hand on her back does nothing to soothe her. I've never seen anyone experience pain so deeply. So openly. Ember has never shied away from emotion. With her, everything is felt in its entirety. Her highs are mountaintops, and her lows are underwater caverns. Even when it hurts, she allows the emotion to sweep her, to have her thoroughly, to run its course.

I've always known this, but to see it in action, to feel it alongside her, reminds me how much I love it.

So I hold her. When Matt stomps from the room, I hold her. When Dayton releases Sky, and she blows her nose, I tighten my hold on Ember.

Softly, Sky calls Ember's name, and only then do I ease up on my grip. Ember nods, acknowledging her sister with almost imperceptible movements. She climbs from my lap, her eyes locked on me. Red-rimmed and swollen, swimming with more pain and fear than I've ever felt in my whole life.

Fiery anger burns across my chest with the injustice of it all.

Ember drags the back of her hand under her nose and wipes it on her jeans. Sky winds her fingers through Ember's, tightening until both their hands grow pink. She whispers something in Ember's ear, and they walk out of the room together.

I stare at the space they left behind, and Dayton plants himself in the chair opposite me. He looks despondent, and I probably do too.

"Noah, we need to talk about something."

I swing my gaze back to him. "What?"

Leaning forward, his elbows come to rest on his knees. "Ember will be pissed, but I can take it. One day she may even thank me. I don't like Matt." Dayton pauses, holding up one finger. "Correction, I don't like Matt *for Ember*. He's not a bad guy. The real problem is that he's not you."

I'm stunned.

Dayton leans forward, his elbows resting on his knees. His eyes are earnest.

"Ember is settling. She might not even know it, but it's true. Matt is not the guy for her." He flashes me a bitter look. "Hell, maybe you aren't either."

I send him a *fuck you* with my eyes. There is nobody better for Ember than I am.

Dayton holds up his palms. "But maybe you are. I don't know." He sends me a second bitter look. "You left her twice."

My lips become a hard line. I know what I did. I know what I chose. And if I could go back, I would choose differently. I'm here now, and I want to keep showing up for Ember.

"Why did you ask me to come here?" I ask Dayton.

"You came here on your own, Noah. Remember? I didn't ask you. You showed up the second you thought Ember needed you. And she did. She chose you, Noah."

In a moment when emotion ruled, Ember chose me. She settled into my arms. Not her boyfriend's, not her best friend's. *Mine.* Doesn't that say more than anything else could? Accepted proposals be damned.

*Wait.*

"Is she engaged?"

Dayton lets out a loud, obnoxious stream of air and throws up his hands. "Details."

I glare at him. "Kind of an important one."

"But is it really?" Dayton scrunches his face, answering his own question with a shake of his head.

"I'd say so." Matt's voice filters in behind me, and Dayton stares over my shoulder to the entrance.

I twist, watching as Matt stalks into the room and stands between our seats. He leans over, clapping Dayton twice on the shoulder. It's hard enough that Dayton winces.

"Thanks a lot, buddy."

He straightens and pivots on one heel so he's facing me. He bends and puts his face way too close to mine. A snarl pulls his lips from his mouth. I don't think he'd be this aggressive if my leg wasn't hamstrung. The fumbling guy who took a picture with me in the airport is long gone.

"You're not going to win," he says slowly, as if that's what I'm here for. Competition.

Dayton's phone dings loudly. He looks down at it and back up to us. "It's Ember."

Matt's body swings around as Dayton scans the screen.

He glances between Matt and me. "She wants you both to go." Matt walks out, muttering, and I look at Dayton. He shrugs. "She said this is stressful enough, and she wants to wait alone with me and Sky."

I nod. I don't want to add to Ember's stress level. I tell Dayton where I'm staying as he walks with me to the elevator. Matt is long gone. "Tell Ember," I pause, not sure what to say. "Tell Ember I'm here for her."

"I will."

We say goodbye and I step onto the elevator.

It takes fifteen minutes for Miranda to arrive once I text her and ask her to come get me. While I'm waiting, I watch Matt march his haughty ass right over to his car and drive away.

When Miranda pulls up I get in, tossing my crutches in the back. I avoid her concerned gaze, but there's really no point. I'm stuck in this rented SUV with her for the next fifteen minutes. The stifling air is thick with her questions, glutted with my thoughts, and saturated by my confusion. It's a bitch trying to breathe in here.

"How did everything go?" Miranda asks tentatively.

How should I answer that? I almost want to laugh at the insanity of it all, the complete unfairness.

"Do you ever think that maybe there's no reason for all this?" My hand flies out to gesture at the world around us. Restaurants, a bus stop, people in cars going different directions as they navigate different lives. What is it all for? What is the point of any of it?

"What do you mean?" She's still using her tentative voice. I can't blame her. She's never heard me talk like this. I don't know if I've ever even thought like this.

"We work hard, we make plans for our lives. We love, we hate. We win, and we lose. We do things in the present to make up for the past. We do things in the present to control the future. But why? What is the point of any of it? What are we living for?" My hands drop to my thighs, where I can feel their clammy heat. I stare out the window and wait for my breath to slow.

"I don't know," Miranda answers quietly. Her thumbs tap on the steering wheel as she slows to a stop at a red light. Her gaze swings to me. "If you ever find out, will you tell me?"

I nod.

"Was she happy to see you?"

"She was relieved, I think."

"And the boyfriend?"

My blood boils the second I think about Matt. How could he have left? He should have stayed in the big waiting room next to the entrance, even after Ember asked us to leave. If I were her boyfriend, there's no fucking way I would've listened. Even just the chance to be there for her again would've been enough reason to stay.

"Miranda," I say abruptly. "I need to see my dad."

I spend the rest of the drive giving Miranda directions to my parents' house, and her question about Matt goes unanswered. A few minutes before we get there, I call Sutton House and get Miranda into a tasting.

She drops me off at my front door, and heads down to the guest center at the entrance to the vineyard.

I find my dad in his office, which is thankfully on the first floor. He's bent over his iPad, squinting. His glasses are on the table beside the tablet, but he refuses to wear them. I think he keeps them there so he can throw them on if my mom walks in.

"Hey, Dad." I swing myself in.

My dad's eyes bulge when he sees me. He stands and

hurries to me. We can't really have a proper hug, so he settles for patting my back. "Noah! What are you doing in town?"

My mouth opens to respond but shuts again when I see realization dawn. I close the office door with my foot and hobble to one of the two chairs in front of his desk. Dad sinks down beside me.

"Ember's mom was in a motorcycle accident, but you know that already." I'm going for nonchalant, but it's hard.

"I—"

"How long have you been cheating on Mom?"

Dad holds up his hands, trying to pacify me. "Whoa, Noah. That's not what's going on."

"Then why were you at the hospital this morning? I was in the waiting room, Dad. I saw you."

My dad sighs, swaying his head slowly from side to side. "Maddie is an old friend."

*Bullshit.*

"Why didn't you ever tell me you knew Ember's mom?"

"I didn't know for certain that Ember was her daughter, but I suspected. That red hair had to come from some-where." His lips twist into a half smile. "The past can be murky. Sometimes it's best not to re-visit it."

"Until today, you mean?"

"She's an important piece of my past. I couldn't *not* go see her." His eyes shine as he speaks.

"Does Mom know you went to see her?"

"It was she who insisted I go."

*What?*

"Why didn't Mom go with you?"

He shifts in his seat, crossing one leg over the other, and then dropping it back to the floor. "Maddie wouldn't want your mother there."

I nod, my head spinning. "Are you paying her medical bills?"

Dad leans back in his chair. His belt cuts into his midsection, and his white undershirt peeks out from the top of his denim button-up. It's what he wears when he walks through the vineyards on his own. I've always thought of him as young, but for the first time I'm seeing his age. It makes me uneasy, knowing he is susceptible to time.

"Noah, you're still young. You may not understand this until you get older, but sometimes people can't see things for what they were until they've traveled far enough from it. We tend to romanticize our experiences, and that changes how we look back on them. Kind of like a tinted lens."

"Is that a yes?"

He nods slowly. "Why are you here?"

"Ember's mom."

He leans forward. His eyes penetrate, like he's diving into my thoughts. "Why are you *really* here?"

Pulling my gaze away, I look out through the large window behind the desk. Blue skies stretch on and on, and the breeze presses through the trees, causing the leaves to tremble.

"You don't need to respond, son. I know the answer. She has haunted you every minute of every day since you were eighteen. What if you...just...let her go? I know you don't want to, but you've both been hanging on for so long. You've been gone, but you never really left. She stayed here, but part of her was wherever you went."

In my head his words make sense, but in my heart they're gibberish. He's speaking as though Ember is a choice. She's not.

She's inevitable.

Inescapable.

My forever.

And I'll be damned if I ever let her marry someone else.

"I don't know what happened between you, Maddie, and mom, and I don't want to know. But Ember and I aren't you and Maddie. I'm not going anywhere without her."

"What about when Marcus calls you and asks you why you aren't in Atlanta rehabbing your knee?"

"I'll rehab here."

"And then? When you're ready to play again? What will you do? Drag Ember with you? She has a business here. That yoga studio is hers now, Noah. She bought it."

I fall back, quiet. I didn't know she took over the studio. I'm an ass. Why do I assume Ember hasn't moved forward? Why do I expect everything to be as it was two years ago?

She's a business owner. She has a boyfriend now, a *fiancé*, but still, she turned to me. In her time of need she came to me. Fell into me. Crashed into me.

Because magic doesn't die.

Maybe magic doesn't have to be loud and consuming. Not all the time. Maybe magic dims and simmers, but remains crackling quietly beneath the surface. I felt it when she chose me today.

Eyes locked on my dad, I pull my phone from my pocket and press a couple buttons.

"Miranda," I say when she answers. "I need to get rehab set up here. I'm going to be here a little longer."

"Okay." She sounds uncertain. Either that or she's tipsy.

"And I'll deal with Marcus soon."

That's not a call I'm looking forward to. I'm in the middle of my contract. He's going to want me back as soon as possible, if only for media efforts. A happy, united front. Too bad. Soccer took my free time, soccer took my energy, soccer consumed my thoughts and determined the direction of my life.

No more.

I gave up everything for my passion, and what it gave me in return is so little compared to what I could've had. I'll always be grateful I had the chance to make my dream come true. Not everyone does. But things are different now. For the first time in a long time, I don't feel pulled in opposite directions. I'm pointed one way, staring ahead at one path, and it's the only one I want to be on.

I let Ember go two times. There will not be a third.

# 30

# EMBER

I SHOULDN'T BE DOING THIS. I KNOW THAT. YET, HERE I AM.

I'm here because I can't think of anywhere else I'd rather be. After a day spent at the hospital, I need comfort. My hand is up, poised to knock on the thick white wooden door, but I stop when I hear voices coming through from the other side.

*Two voices?*

*A woman?*

Oh no. I've completely misread why he's here.

I turn to go, but the door opens. I'm frozen in the arc of light that spills into the hallway.

"Hi," I sputter.

An immaculate blonde with a severe bob and an even more severe look on her face stares at me. She holds onto the edge of the door with one hand and purses her lips. A stack of papers is gripped by her free hand.

"Ember?" Noah calls out. Peeking past the blonde in her black sheath dress, I make out Noah's legs. A stack of pillows holds up his injured leg, and the other lays flat on the bed.

My eyes switch to the blonde.

"Miranda, can you please let Ember in?" Noah sounds irritated.

Miranda stares at me for another second before stepping out and darting around me. Quickly, I reach out and palm the door so it doesn't close.

"Ember? Come in," Noah calls.

I step inside and let the door swing shut. Rooted in place, I stare at Noah. He's propped up by half a dozen white pillows. They fan out like a peacock's plumes.

"Hi," I say.

"She's my PA."

I put up my hands and shake my head. "None of my business."

Noah grins. I don't want to like his smile, but I do. I especially don't want to like the laughter in his eyes, yet I do.

"You look mad." His lips twist with contained amusement.

"I'm not mad." I fix him with a dirty look.

"Perturbed?"

"Nope," I deny swiftly with a jerk of my head.

"You never were a good liar."

"I'll take that as a compliment."

Noah's toffee-colored hair falls into his eyes, and he pushes it back. "It was meant as one."

I clear my throat. "No news on my mom."

Noah sighs slowly in response to my non-update.

My hands hang in front of me, my fingers knotting. I'm not certain why I'm here. The thinking, the crying, the what-if's, they were all driving me out of my mind. Where else am I supposed to go?

*Matt's house.*

"I should've gone to Matt's house," I blurt out. "I don't know why I'm here. It's wrong. I shouldn't have come." My hands run through my hair, grabbing at the ends and pulling it over one shoulder. I scrunch my eyes and groan. "Why am I here, Noah?"

Noah's laughing eyes are gone. His features rearrange as he grows serious.

"Magic." One simple word, spoken without pageantry, yet it holds so much between each of its letters.

My head shakes. "Don't. Don't say that. We were kids, Noah. Hormonal teenagers. Everything is bigger when you're eighteen. All the emotions are"—I stretch my arms as wide as they will go—"gigantic. They take you over."

Noah's mouth sets in a grim line. "You're arguing too much."

I point a finger at him. "You still believe in magic."

"And you don't?" His voice is loud now.

My feet propel me, until I'm standing at his bedside. "Magic doesn't exist. Neither does reason. The whole world is made up of little things that happen every minute of every day, and all it takes is one person to change his mind, and the picture shifts again." I lift a hand to my face, discovering tears on my cheeks.

Noah reaches for me, but he can't quite close the distance. He's hampered by his propped-up leg. It doesn't matter anyhow, I wouldn't accept his pity. Being angry is keeping me together.

Noah leaves his hand there, extended between us. "Please."

I crawl on the huge, soft bed until I'm beside him. He wraps an arm around my shoulders, and I curl in. He feels good, and he smells even better.

"Noah?" I say softly, looking up.

He looks down.

We stare at each other, and I feel it. The very thing I just denied existence. Like a sparkler on Fourth of July, it sizzles and pops.

Noah's gaze darkens, his chest hollows out with a deep breath, and his face lowers.

My tongue darts out of my mouth, wetting my lips in anticipation. My toes flex, pushing me closer to his face. His lips hover half an inch above me, and I smell the sweet malt scent of a beer he must have had earlier.

"Noah," I say again, this time like a request. I want his mouth on mine. I want to go back to when we were kids. Back to when my mom was healthy, and everything was fresh and new.

"We can't," Noah moans, his tone frustrated. He pulls back but doesn't break eye contact. "If you did this, it would tear you up inside."

He's right. I'd never be able to live with myself. Matt loves me. "I should probably go." I start to rise, but Noah tightens his hold.

"Stay," he murmurs.

Defeated, I lay my head on his chest. His heart hammers out a beat against my face.

"I was accepted to Stanford." The truth floats out and hangs in the air. "I didn't tell you because I knew I couldn't go, and I didn't want to make everything harder on you. I wanted you to stay on your path. I was afraid you'd deviate for me." His heart is beating faster now. "I'm sorry. Back then it seemed like the right choice."

"What's right isn't always what's good."

I turn my head, placing my chin on his chest, and look up at him. "Are you angry?"

He looks down, studying me. "No," he finally answers. "And I'm not surprised. You have a thing for self-sacrifice."

He's right. I do. I like that about myself. I lay my head back down.

"I hear you're engaged." His steady voice washes over me.

I gulp, nodding my head. My fingers automatically reach for a ring I'm still not wearing. I remind myself that it's too big for my finger, but part of me wonders if that's a convenient excuse. Shame snakes its way through me.

Neither of us say anything, though my mind is racing. I should be with Matt right now. He's kind and caring. He supported me when I wanted to buy the studio. He helped me create a business plan, introduced me to a client of his who works in advertising. Yoga's not his thing, but he accepts that it's mine. He thinks my aversion to throwing away food is weird, and I've learned not to proudly announce I made dinner from items the average person would've tossed. My nose ring is non-negotiable, and I think he finally gets that.

*Noah...* My heart pounds out his name. This is the crux of the problem. Matt is a lot of good things, but he can never change the one thing he is not. *Noah.*

Noah might be back for right now, but what does that even mean? He'll rehab, he'll go back to Atlanta. He'll choose soccer again, and I won't stop him. I could never stop him from chasing his dream, even if I want to. He needs to see it through, as far as it can go. I can't be responsible for an unfulfilled aspiration.

The knowledge of this is enough to un-do me. It shatters my insides, and I cry again. Noah holds me closer, brushes his lips across my hair and says all the right things. *Your mom will be okay. She'll make it through all this. She'll have a good life, and be able to walk, talk, and be happy.*

He doesn't know I'm mourning *us.*

"WHERE HAVE YOU BEEN?"

Matt's shiny leather shoes sound like thunder on my wooden floor. He's coming from the kitchen, and he's angry.

"I—"

"You were with him, weren't you?" Fury makes his lips quiver. I've never seen him so upset. Then again, I've never spent the night with another guy.

"Yes, but—"

"You have got to be fucking kidding me," he yells, throwing his hands in the air.

Sky comes from her room, glancing between us with frightened eyes.

"Matt, calm down." My palms meet in front of me, and I make a pleading motion. "Nothing happened. I promise. I fell asleep at his hotel room. I know it sounds bad."

"It sounds pretty fucking bad, Ember."

"I know, and I'm sorry, but nothing happened. I promise."

Matt blows out a long, heavy breath. "Why were you there?"

I look down at my hands. This is the question I still don't know the answer to. I was hurting, and I went to him. I don't know how else to explain it, but I do know that reason won't do anything to make Matt feel any better.

"He's an old friend—"

"This again?" Matt tips his head back and laughs, though the sound is anything but happy. "*He's an old friend,*" he says in a girlish voice, making air quotes with his fingers.

"He is." My words slip through clenched teeth. It would be nice if Matt would sit down and hear me out.

"I'm a pretty smart guy, Ember. Watch me do the math."

He lifts a finger to his chin and tips up his head, pretending to think. "Ember's high school virginity plus one soccer star rushing to her after his surgery, divided by the annoying-as-fuck pleading looks you give one another, equals Matt and Ember are no longer engaged."

Sky slipped from the hall while Matt was talking and now stands beside me. She opens her mouth but I'm faster. "Matt, if you would calm down and listen, I can explain."

"Are you going to explain where your ring went?"

I look down at my bare finger. "It's too big for me, Matt. I need to have it sized."

Saying the words out loud makes me consider why it's so big. I have other rings in my jewelry box, he could've taken one and had the engagement ring sized correctly. But that would've taken time, and it's becoming clear to me something had lit a fire under Matt.

"Maybe you need to think about what you really want, Ember. You don't seem too clear on the matter."

"Matt—"

"I'm going to the office. You have until close of business today to tell me what you want." He storms past me. "Your breakfast is on the table," he mutters.

My shoulders jump when the screen door slams shut.

I blow past the kitchen and head straight out into the backyard. I've planted flowers everywhere, and a big tree sits in the corner. A vegetable garden is opposite the tree, and in the middle is a little couch. It's not an outdoor piece of furniture, so I have to keep it covered. The antique wooden back is painted blush pink, and its ornately carved legs curl into the soft green grass. I added polka-dot cream colored cushions. It's impractical but I love it.

Pulling off the tan cover, I brush off some stray dried leaves and lie down. Sky follows me out, folding herself into a seat right on the soft green grass. I wish my mom was here too, but right now she's fighting a battle nobody knows the size or duration of yet. Her problem is infinity times more important than mine.

Looking up into the blue sky, I open my mouth and talk into the warm, moist morning air, telling Sky everything.

I talk until I'm spent. Then we go inside, and get ready to head back to the hospital.

# 31

# NOAH

I NEVER THOUGHT I'D REACH A DAY WHEN THIS WOULD MAKE me happy. What I just did should have me shaken to my core. I should be looking back over a lifetime of practices, games, sweat, and dedication.

All my life spent working on this one thing, and all it took to end it were a few words.

*"Playing professionally was my dream, and you helped me achieve it. I will always be grateful you chose me, but it's time for me to move on."*

*After a moment of stunned silence, Marcus spoke first. "We'd love for you to rethink your decision, Noah. You'll still be a valuable member of the team once you're healed. I hope you're not making this choice based on your injury."*

*I shook my head, even though nobody could see me. "I'm not, Coach. There's something at home I need to focus on."*

*There were well wishes all around, and that was that.*

I quit the team. Soccer. I quit soccer.

"What now?" Miranda asks. She's sitting at the round table in the corner of the room. Her laptop is out, her fingers poised above the keys.

"It's over." There are loose ends still—papers to be signed, lockers to clean out, lawyers who need to draft documents, pending media releases—but, effectively, I'm retired.

Miranda sucks a breath deep into her lungs. I can tell this is unsettling to her, yet for me, it's not. It's exciting.

Shackles have been cut. Shackles I placed upon myself.

"I still need you, Miranda." How can I explain this appropriately? She's a lifesaver. I'll need help getting my Atlanta place packed up and sold. Assuming I'm staying here.

I don't know. I don't know anything. Ember left my bed quickly this morning, flustered and chagrined.

*"We did nothing but sleep,"* I reminded her as she shot from my bed once she realized where she was.

*"At this point, I'm not sure if that's worse,"* she fired back, stumbling to slide her feet into her shoes. She ran out the door without another word.

I have no idea where Ember and I stand, but I don't have to lie down and accept that. Yes, she has a fiancé.

But there is no way in hell I'm going down without a fight. I made that mistake already.

"Miranda." I sway to my feet and tuck a crutch under my arm. "I need to go somewhere."

She sends me the telltale look of a woman who does not approve. Her eyebrows pull together, and her gaze dips to her computer, but her lips remain tight.

"What?" I ask.

"She's engaged." Miranda keeps her gaze on her keyboard.

"You let me worry about that." I change into a fresh shirt and start for the hotel room door.

Miranda drives me, and I feel like a fool. What I

wouldn't give to drive myself right now. So fucking ridiculous.

"Do you want me to wait?" she asks when we pull up.

I peer into the green front yard with all the cute potted flowers lining the walkway. A thought occurs to me. "She might not be here. She might be at the hospital." In my haste, I didn't think to check with Ember. "I'll text you in five minutes," I tell Miranda as I get out. She hands me my crutches with a frown.

"I just don't want to see you hurt," she says quietly. "It's really nothing against her. You're going way out on a limb, and I…" she trails off, shrugging and twisting her lips.

"I appreciate your concern, and you get a raise because I'm certain I didn't include driving me around and tending to my injury as part of your job description."

I start up the driveway without waiting for Miranda's response.

She gets back into the idling car, and I knock on the door. When nobody answers, I go around the side of the house and find a gate. Lifting my hand over the top, I flip up the latch, using my shoulder to prop the door open and finagle my way inside. My crutches are silent on the soft grass. I'm so quiet, Ember never hears me. Neither does Matt.

I stop right where I am and watch them. They're on the far side of the yard, seated on a couch. Heads bent toward each other, they talk in low voices. A light breeze picks up a strand of Ember's hair and sends it flying. Matt catches it, tucking it behind her ear. Ember's face turns up in a smile, and she presses a cupped hand to Matt's cheek. He leans into her touch. Her lips move, more words, and the tenderness of the moment spears my heart to the wood fence behind me. My chest fills with fire, but it's an empty flame. If this is what Ember wants, I have to give it to her. She has stepped aside for me. I should be strong enough to do the same for her. What is good, and what is right, aren't synonymous. Ember was correct when she said that.

The silence of my retreat matches the silence of my arrival.

Pulling open the passenger door, I get in and drag my crutches behind me. Miranda ducks when I lift them and toss them into the back seat. They don't fit, so they stick awkwardly between us.

I feel her stare but I don't look at her. I can't. I'm certain there's a gaping hole in my chest where my heart used to be.

"Your mom wants you to go to their house for dinner. Do you want me to take you there now or back to the hotel?"

"Let's go there now, and you're staying for dinner. You don't need to eat alone." My voice is gruff. I don't mean it to be, but *fuck, fuck, fuck.* I'm a fool. Ember has moved on. She made a life for herself. Of course she couldn't wait forever for me.

Honestly, I deserve it. I deserve to feel ripped open. Bare and exposed. She let me go twice, even when she knew she loved me. Even when she knew *I* loved *her.*

Miranda doesn't say anything more the whole drive to my parents' house. When we get there, I head straight to my dad's office and grab the decanter of bourbon off a shelf. Two thumbs of the brown liquid spill into a tumbler, and I take it like a shot.

A throat clearing at the door draws my attention. My mother leans against the frame, her arms folded. "You okay?" She tips her head to the side and gazes at me with concerned eyes.

"No," I say roughly, pouring more bourbon into my glass. Just one thumb this time.

"Is it about Ember?"

I trace the edge of the glass with my fingertip and nod.

"You know she has a boyfriend?"

Confusion pulls my eyebrows together. "How do *you* know she has a boyfriend?"

My mothers emits a tiny, sardonic laugh. "You're not going to believe this, but I go to her yoga studio."

I bark out a laugh.

"I know," she says, tucking her hair behind her ear. "Ironic, right? But it's helped me a lot. She's a great teacher."

I laugh again and shake my head. Of all the things I could've been told, my mother becoming one of Ember's yoga students would have never entered the realm of possibility.

"She's engaged," I say.

My mother tilts her head again, and pity comes into her eyes. I look away.

"The guy seems nice, Noah. He comes into the studio sometimes."

"She's settling," I respond, louder than I intended.

My mother pushes off from her place against the door frame and strides to me. She takes the tumbler from my hand and sets it on my father's desk. With her hands on my upper arms, she levels me with a penetrating, parental stare. "Is it settling if it's anybody but you?"

"Maybe," I admit with a disappointed murmur. She gives me a small smile and backs up a few feet, setting her hand on the back of a chair.

Suddenly my conversation with my dad pops into my head. "You sent Dad to see Ember's mother."

Surprise makes her eyes grow big and her lower lip drop away from her upper. "Yes."

"Why?"

She walks around to the front of the chair and sinks. Folding her legs up, she wraps an arm around her knees and peers up at me. "I never particularly cared for Maddie Dane, but your father sure did. I was jealous, of course, but it was high school. Everyone is jealous of someone. They weren't good together. She was impulsive and headstrong. She made him crazy."

Her eyes look far away as she talks, one hand waving in the air.

"Your grandparents died the summer after high school graduation, and your dad needed to grow up. Fast. The vineyard had been my summertime job for three years in a row. That summer, one item on my to-do list was teaching your dad everything I knew about the back office. Maddie didn't like it. She wanted him to spend the summer with her, doing whatever it was Maddie liked to do at the moment. She was a bit all over the place."

Mom wrinkles her nose. Even in memory, she doesn't appreciate that trait.

"He told her he couldn't, their fights became bigger and more frequent. The rest is history."

Sometime while my mom was talking, I grabbed the tumbler and drained the contents. Setting the empty glass down, I carefully lean a hip against the side of the desk and look at her. She's watching me, waiting for me to react. I see the parallels between my dad and Maddie, and Ember and me, but we aren't the same people. Ember is not like her mother.

"I sent your father there because it was the right thing to do. When I heard about Maddie, I knew he'd want the chance to see her. Not because he still loves her, but because I love him. When you love someone, you try to do what's right for them."

"Even at your own expense?"

"Sometimes. It depends on how much it hurts you, I guess. Or what you have to give up. Telling your dad about Maddie didn't hurt me, and I didn't have to give up anything. It would've hurt him if he didn't know and something happened to her."

"So you encourage selflessness? Is this yoga talking?" I crack a smile at her.

Her serious demeanor breaks and she laughs. "Maybe. I encourage selflessness and selfishness. They're situational." She rises from her seat and walks to the door.

Propping the crutches properly beneath my arms, I follow. She turns to look at me when I catch up. Her face is close to mine. "Miranda seems to really care about you," she whispers.

"That's because I pay her to," I whisper back.

My mother makes a *tsk, tsk* sound with her tongue. I nudge her forward with my shoulder, and she laughs again, leading the way to the kitchen.

---

"Are you sure you don't want to stay for a few more days?" my dad asks.

The flames from the outdoor fire pit illuminate his hopeful face. He and my mom have each had a bottle of wine, and its effects are showing. She's cuddled up next to him, and his arm is wrapped casually across her. It's good to see them openly showing affection, but it's a little...weird. Good weird, I guess.

"Miranda has already set up my rehab in Atlanta." I glance at Miranda, who's sitting in the chair across from me. She nods. This afternoon, after I talked with my mom,

Miranda called the physical therapist I was referred to in Atlanta and set up my first appointment.

Entering an Atlanta-based appointment into my calendar hurt every part of me, but I didn't have a choice. It needed to happen.

"Starting rehab is priority one," I tell my parents.

"And then?" Mom asks.

I wind a hand around my neck, knead the tight muscles for a moment, and shrug. Before my injury a life without soccer seemed impossible, yet my foot hasn't touched a soccer ball in a month. "I don't know, Dad. I still need to rehab my knee for as long as it needs, even if I'm not playing anymore. After that, I'll start thinking about my future."

"I might retire in a few years," Dad says. "Maybe you could come back here and take your place at the helm of this ship." He gestures around us. Though we can't see them, the acres upon acres of grapes are out there.

"I don't know." Seeing Ember around town, seeing her with Matt. Then the sickening thought, *what if her stomach is swollen with his child*? "Don't count on me," I say tersely. "Ask Brody." I stare into the fire to escape the disappointment in his eyes.

"Too soon," I hear my mother say to him. "Miranda," she says, her voice falsely bright. "When do you and Noah take off tomorrow?"

"Tomorrow at noon." Miranda sounds relieved. Atlanta is her home. Shame fills me. I haven't thought of how she felt this whole time, not even once.

Miranda and my mom start a conversation about when she should come for a visit, and my dad and I stay quiet. I hate to upset him, but the wound is fresh. Right now, I can't imagine coming back here and living in the same town as Ember, without being with her. The way he has with

Maddie. Maybe he didn't love her the way I love Ember. Maybe they had fire, but no magic.

Maybe—

My phone vibrates against me. I pull it out, see who it is, and get up as quickly as my crippled ass lets me. Miranda stands to help me with the crutches, but I've got them already, and I'm hobbling away as fast as possible. I round the corner of the house and lean against it.

"Hello," I say, trying not to sound breathless. I'm in total darkness, but slowly my eyes adjust.

"Noah." Ember breathes my name.

The sound of her voice makes me want to ignore my resolve. Loud, incessant words pound through my head and I want to scream them. *Don't do it. He's not the one for you. We've been right since the beginning. We were kids but we knew. Even then, we knew.*

I hold it in, and at that moment I know it's the hardest thing I'll ever do. I want to give Ember everything she desires, and if Matt is who she wants, I have to back out. My broken heart is a small price to pay for making her happy.

"Noah, I—"

At the same time, I say, "I'm going back to Atlanta tomorrow. I'll rehab with the team and play again soon."

Lies. The words knife me. They are the wrong words. They leave a foul taste in my mouth, but it's a flavor I'll live with if it means Ember will be happy.

"I saw you with Matt today. I came by and saw you two in your back yard. Good luck with him, Ember," I choke out. "You deserve the best."

Her sniffles pierce my heart.

"Thank you," she murmurs.

"Goodbye, Ember." Two tears blaze trails down my cheeks.

"Goodbye, Noah."

She hangs up first, and I follow. My chin droops to my chest. My heart falls somewhere, maybe down to my feet. It may even be gone from my body. *So this is what it feels like to really sacrifice.* Ember said sacrifice feels good, but that's not true, because my chest is splintering and it feels a hell of a lot like agony.

Every ounce of me wants to call her back. Or better yet, go to her house and barge in, grab Matt by his ears and toss him out.

I hate this.

"Noah?" my mom calls.

Taking a deep breath, I push off the wall and rejoin my parents and Miranda. I fake my smile, I fake my laughter, I fake my jokes.

The pain in my heart?

Genuine.

# 32

# EMBER

When I was eighteen I remember waking up with this feeling in my chest. Hollow but somehow heavy. Pain is only painful until you get used to the feeling. Then it becomes your normal, until one day its absence is what you take notice of.

This morning, it's the return of the pain that is excruciating. I hoped to never feel like that again, but here I am, rolling over and clutching my sheet in a fist. I'm older now, but hardly any wiser.

*Noah leaves today.* I roll from bed, walk to the bathroom, and load toothpaste onto my toothbrush.

*Noah leaves today.* I stare into the bathroom mirror, my hands going through the motions, the scrubbing sounds secondary to the noise in my head.

*Noah leaves today.* Back to the bedroom, where I get dressed mechanically.

Today, it feels final. More final than college, more final than when he went to play professionally. We're real adults now. Our decisions carry more weight.

That's what I was thinking yesterday when I told Matt I

can't marry him. It wasn't just about Noah. I had to make that choice for me.

"Ember?" Sky pokes her head in my door. She's already dressed. Her voice is high-pitched, and her smile is so large it takes over her face. "Mom's doctor just called. She woke up during the night."

My hands freeze in my jewelry tray, my fingers on the metal cuff I was reaching for. Relief, joy, apprehension, and more joy fill me. Hot tears warm my eyes.

"Let's go," I say, slipping on the bracelet and jamming my feet into shoes.

Sky drives while I stare out the window and wonder if the plane I see up above is Noah's. It's heading north, and I know that's the wrong direction, but still. I pretend.

"You want to tell me what's going on?" Sky asks.

I sigh and look at her. She glances at me and then back to the road.

"Not really. I don't want to hear what you have to say right now." My tone is even, but I think I hurt her feelings anyway. I didn't mean to, but I can't listen to her tell me that Noah isn't worth this heartache. Because he is. He's worth all the minutes I've spent on him. There is no waste when it comes to Noah.

Sky doesn't say anything more, but on our way into the hospital she catches my hand and squeezes it.

I expected my mom to be *my mom*, but she's not. She's more like an awake infant. Her eyes are open, alert, but her arms randomly lift and flail, and she's not talking. Her lips move, but I can't tell if that's because she is trying to speak or if it's just twinges.

"Mom," I whisper, pulling a chair closer to her bed. My mom watches me, her cheeks lifting as she tries to smile. I sink down into the chair and Sky stands behind me, her hands on my shoulders. "We've been so scared for you, Mom—"

"Why didn't you wear your helmet?" Sky's anger and frustration comes out in her harsh tone.

Twisting around to look up at her, I shake my head. "Not now, Sky." She mashes her lips together and looks away.

I get it. I want to yell at our mom too, but right now, finger-pointing won't benefit anybody.

Turning back to my mom, I tell her what happened. "I don't know what you remember, but you were thrown from the motorcycle you were riding. You hit your head and were brought here. There is some brain swelling, and you're on medication to reduce that." I skip over telling her about the possibility of surgery. She might feel stress, and that would only make things worse. "You have a good doctor, and you're in good hands."

My mom's eyes widen as I talk. Her head tips to the side and she looks out her window.

"It's Wednesday," I tell her. "The accident was Sunday. Three days ago." I'm guessing what she wants to know, thinking of what I'd want to know if I woke up in a hospital this way. "The guy you were with broke both legs."

She looks back at me. I smile and take her hand. Her fingers move, like she's tapping piano keys.

Sky moves around so she's next to the bed, and leans down, kissing our mom's cheek. "You terrified us, Mom."

Mom looks up with an apology in her eyes, and tears fall down Sky's face. "I'm going to ask one of the nurses to send Mom's doctor in here," she says, clearing her throat. "I want to talk with him." She walks out, the door falling closed with a soft *thud.*

Rubbing a thumb over the top of my mom's hand, I open my mouth and words pour out of me. I intended to talk about nothing of importance, but when the words come out, they're about Noah.

"Noah came to see you. To be here for me. Dayton called him." I picture Noah on his crutches, swinging his braced leg around the waiting room, struggling to stay awake. My heart aches. "He's on his way back to Atlanta now. I didn't stop him from leaving. He said he's rehabbing with the team and he'll play again, and I couldn't say the words to stop him. I don't even know if I should have. I've never stopped him from pursuing his dream. How can anyone ask that of another person?"

I shake my head as I talk, feeling tears pricking my eyes. Mom watches intently, the corners of her eyes moving.

"I broke it off with Matt. I realized I was filling a Noah-shaped hole with someone who couldn't possibly fill it. Nobody can. I have to let Noah be a memory." I swipe at the tears. "Except, I don't want him to be memory, Mom. I don't." Shaking my head, I continue. "I've spent years loving him, but I have to admit it. It's over. I need to let him go. I can't keep doing this to myself."

Her fingers tap my hand, and I look down at them. They curl in, like she's trying to squeeze.

"Mom, I—" I'm halted when I look up and see her eyes. They are alarmed, like she's trying to tell me something.

"What, Mom?" I lean forward, as if that will help me decipher her thoughts.

"She doesn't agree with you." Sky says from behind me.

I turn around. Sky stands two feet inside the room. She walks closer and sits down in the chair opposite me, closer to the window.

"About what?" I ask.

"About Noah. She doesn't agree about letting him go."

"How do you know that?"

"Because she wishes she would've fought harder for poem guy. The one who wrote in that journal she keeps." She looks at our mom, then back to me. "Mom's a romantic, Ember. She wants you to go after Noah, maybe even fly to Atlanta, and tell him he needs to be with you."

I glance at Mom, and her eyes flicker with excitement. "And you know this for certain?" I ask, looking back at Sky.

"Yes," Sky chuckles, "but not because I'm a mind reader. Mom and I talked about it last month, after you and Matt saw Noah in the airport. She didn't think Matt was right for you, and she wanted you to call Noah and ask him to come home and be with you."

I look at my mom, astonished. She touches my hand, this time able to squeeze it harder.

"You should call Noah's mom, Ember," Sky says. "Figure out when he's leaving, or if he's already gone. Do something crazy and romantic and stop putting other people's happiness in front of your own. Go after what you want." She forms a fist and shakes it between us. "Take it. Make it yours."

"You should be a motivational speaker." I laugh, but excitement builds inside me.

My gaze swings to my mom. Her chin lifts and lowers, a micro movement, but it's enough. I see her agreement.

"Okay," I stand, releasing my grip on my mom's hand. "I'll call Johanna."

I step out of the room and pull my phone from my purse with shaky fingers. Weirdly enough, Johanna has been coming to my yoga classes for the past year. My shock over seeing her eventually faded and she became a welcome sight in my classes. One day, she hugged me when she said hello. Now that's how she always greets me. If it weren't for that, I wouldn't feel comfortable calling her.

The phone rings and rings, then goes to voiccmail. Defeated, I go back into my mom's room.

"She didn't answer." I chew my bottom lip and stare at the phone in my hand, willing it to light up with her return call.

"Why don't you go to her house?" Sky asks.

I narrow my eyes at her. "What's going on? You don't even *like* Noah."

She shakes her head. "Not true. I didn't like how broken-hearted you were, and I didn't like him coming back when his brother got married and breaking your heart all over again. But, I do like him for you. In your heart you've never been able to let him go, even though you do it physically." She stands up and comes to me, resting her hands on my shoulders. "I just want you to be happy, Ember. I want you to put yourself first."

From the hospital bed Mom makes a garbled sound and we both rush to her. She tries it again, and another sound comes out. Over and over she does it, until the sounds turn into pieces of words. Sky brings her a sip of water, and she keeps going. Eventually she manages a short, hushed sentence.

"I love you girls."

"Mom, we love you too," Sky says through her tears.

I laugh even though I'm crying. My despair over Noah is overshadowed, until my phone rings from the counter. I peer over, reading the name flashing across the screen.

"It's her." I gulp, looking at my mom. Mom points to the phone insistently. I answer and bring the phone to my ear. "Johanna, hi."

Her elegant, smooth voice comes through. "Ember? Is everything okay? How is your mother?"

"She woke up." I smile at my mom. "She's doing great."

Just then the doctor walks in. Sky greets him and gently pushes me out of the room. "I got this," she whispers. "You take care of you."

I nod and walk a few feet down the hall, away from the flurry of activity at the nurses station.

"Sorry, Johanna, I had to leave the room I was in." I pause to rub my forehead with my hand. "Listen, I know this might sound crazy, but I want to know when Noah is leaving today, if he already left, what airline he's on, or if I should even be asking. I know he's going back to Atlanta, and he's going to play again, but—"

"Ember, slow down."

I take a deep breath, nodding even though she can't see me.

"First off, Noah and Miranda's plane took off thirty minutes ago. They caught an earlier flight. Second, what do you mean he's going to play again? He quit."

I'm silent, staring at an indentation in the wall, trying to wrap my mind around Johanna's words. *He quit?*

"He told me he's rehabbing with the team, and he's going to play again."

"Oh, dear." Johanna lets out a heavy breath. "That's not true, Ember. I think," she pauses, the line is quiet, then she says, "I think maybe he was letting you think that, so you could be happy with Matt. We had a conversation about sacrifice and selflessness. It's his way of letting you go."

"No," I whisper. The indentation on the wall becomes watery, my vision swirls, and the tears flow quickly. He can't let me go. He can't. Not my Noah. Not the boy who pulled me from a lake and peered into my soul.

This crack in my heart is the worst of them all. I could patch the others, because I was letting him go to pursue a dream. But this... This is misery.

"I'm sorry," Johanna says.

"I need to go," I whisper, and hang up.

There is no place for me to hide. No place for me to break down. I want to rage. Wail. Scream. Pound my fists on the wall.

Squeezing my eyes and hands shut tight, I breathe in and out. In and out. My mind races even in my attempts to calm myself. Thoughts hurtle through my brain, colliding.

For years I've been holding on to the most precious parts of Noah. I always let him go chase his dream, but he never really left. He was in my heart. In my mind. He was softness at the end of my fingertips when I closed my eyes. A brush of lips against my temple when I let myself remember.

I've been the one letting him go. Not this time. That makes it so much worse. He quit the team. He's going back to Atlanta.

*He let me go.*

# 33

# NOAH

A MESS. THAT'S WHAT I AM.

Miranda might kill me. I think she has reached the end of her rope with me. Doesn't matter anyway. Soon she'll be free from my crutches and ineptness.

I'll have a life now. One that doesn't include soccer. I don't know what that looks like, or means, but I'll have it.

Miranda must be sick of driving me around. She didn't complain when she loaded my suitcase into the back of the car, or shoved my crutches alongside our bags. She's quiet on our drive now. I can't blame her. She's probably thinking about all the things she needs to do. She has a life too.

My good leg bounces anxiously as I check my watch. We should be somewhere over Texas by now, maybe even Louisiana.

"Thirty more minutes, Noah." Miranda has the tone of a parent talking to a child.

I laugh. I don't know if that's the correct response, but my insides are jumbled and I can't manage a sentence right now.

My heart was screaming at me long before the crackling

voice came on the airport intercom system and announced our delayed flight. While Miranda went to the restroom I walked up to the counter and canceled our flight.

My heart had it right all along. I had to go back to Northmount. Ember needed me to fight for us.

The drive is excruciatingly long. At least, it feels that way. LA traffic made me want to pull my hair out. I tipped my head back, closed my eyes, and once we were through it I spent the remainder of the drive picturing Ember's face. Finally, we make the turn onto Ember's street. Miranda slows to a stop and parks.

"Noah," she starts, but pauses.

"What?"

Her lips twist, like she wants to say something. She's probably going to tell me I'm crazy, that Matt is still in the picture, that none of this makes any sense. All things I already know.

"Nothing," she says, shaking her head slowly. "Good luck."

I nod to her and reach back, pulling my crutches with me as I get out. Miranda drives away, and I realize she didn't ask if she should stay or go. I make my way to the front door and knock. Nobody answers. There aren't any cars in the driveway either. I could call Ember, but I'd rather see her. I need to see her face when I talk, watch her eyes, touch her soft skin.

I wait. The afternoon sun pours onto the front porch, and soon my shirt is sticking to me. I get up, go around the front of the house, and reach over and unlatch the gate. I caught enough of a glimpse of the backyard to know there will be shade. I'm going to be here as long as it takes.

There's a bench in the backyard, but it's in the sun. It

takes some work, but I manage to get myself settled under a large tree in the corner of the yard.

I wait. And I wait. I tip my head back against the trunk and close my eyes.

Eventually I hear voices, but it's hard to know if they're coming from Ember's house or the neighbor's. Suddenly the back door opens and Sky walks out. She sees me, jumps, and throws a hand over her mouth.

"Ember?" she yells, her voice shaking. "Can you come out here please?"

There's a second voice from inside the house but I can't make out the words.

Sky keeps her eyes trained on me. She looks...happy? Not exactly the response I was expecting from her.

Ember appears on the porch beside her sister, but she doesn't see me. She's looking at Sky. "What?"

Sky points and Ember's gaze follows her finger. To me.

She gasps and hurries down the porch steps. I roll onto my side, reaching for my crutches.

"Don't," Ember yells, laughing.

I ignore her. This bum leg isn't going to stop me from getting up and holding her in my arms.

She's reached me by the time I make it up on my feet. Her lips part to speak, but I don't let her. My hands hold her cheeks and I silence her words with my mouth. She clings to my waist, pressing herself against me. Her scent surrounds me, engulfing my senses. I inhale every essence of Ember. My crutches fall to the ground with a thud, and I find I can stand if I keep most of my weight on my other foot.

Ember pulls away and looks to the ground, cupping her mouth. I stop her when she bends to pick them up.

"Don't worry about those. I have to tell you something."

"I know you quit," she blurts, then laughs. "I thought

you were supposed to be in Atlanta right now. Why did you come back?"

I tip my head and keep my gaze on hers. She is the most beautiful sight I've ever seen. "I'm not sacrificial like you. I can't bow out because Matt proposed and you've moved on. That's what I was trying to do, but I couldn't. I can't go back to Atlanta and let you marry him." I know I'm rambling, but the words keep coming. "I've never stopped loving you, Ember. Not at all. I'm grateful you encouraged me to pursue my dream, but it took me a long time to realize how easily a dream can become a delusion." My thumb grazes her jaw. She watches me through her thick eyelashes, her features soft. "Sometimes the heart knows better than the mind. My heart has never left you, Ember. We are good *and* right. Don't marry him. Marry me."

Shock widens her eyes, rearranging the softness of her features. Her lower lip drops, her mouth forming an *o*.

I tip my head back and laugh into the late afternoon air. I wasn't planning a proposal, but now that I've said it, I can't think of anything better.

If I've ever thought I've seen Ember happy, I was wrong. She's beaming, her eyes luminous, like her insides are aglow.

Leaning forward, she places both hands on my cheeks, and kisses me. Her lips on mine is a feeling I never want to be without. And I don't plan to.

She pulls away with a smile. "I broke up with him. That's what I was calling to tell you last night, but you said you were going back to Atlanta and I froze." She leans back in, rubbing the tip of her nose against mine. "We could've saved ourselves all this heartache."

Turning my head, I trail kisses from her cheek to her jaw. "True. But I would've missed the opportunity to sit in your backyard for hours and propose to you." My kisses move to the space under her ear. "You haven't answered me," I murmur. "Yes or no?"

Ember leans back slightly, bringing a finger to her chin and pretending to think. I wiggle the fingers I have wrapped around her waist and she laughs and squirms.

"Of course I'll marry you, Noah."

Her hair falls around her shoulders, and I can't believe she's mine. The girl who swam into my world and shook it to it's very core, is going to be mine forever.

"Come on," she says, reaching down for my crutches and handing them to me. Ember places a hand on my back as we walk across the yard, sneaking glances at one another and grinning like fools.

*This is it. This is where I belong.*

Ember pauses on the bottom step and wraps her arms around my waist, burying her face in my neck. "Welcome home."

# EPILOGUE

EMBER

*PRESENT DAY*

"ALMOST TIME, LOVE." DAYTON'S BLOND HEAD PEEKS AROUND the door. When he sees I'm dressed, he straightens and walks in. "I'm not even going to tell you you're beautiful. You already know it."

I laugh and shake my head.

"Sky did my make-up." I smile at my sister. She leans against the counter, looking into the mirror and finishing the last of her own make-up. She meets my eyes and winks at me.

I look back to Dayton. "Is he ready?" Nervously I pat my hair.

"Brody's checking on him. Honestly, how much time does the guy need to spend on his hair? Never mind, I took thirty minutes." He waves his hand around his head.

"And it looks amazing." I smile at him.

"Yes, well. I was blessed with a good head of hair. The nose however..." He pushes a pointer finger against the tip of his nose, making himself into a pig. "It's a tad bit upturned."

I laugh so hard I have to hold my stomach.

"Perfect," Dayton announces, letting go of his nose. "You needed a little color on your cheeks. No offense, Sky."

"Dayton," I say softly. I'm feeling emotional. "You always know what I need."

"Baby, a bat would know you needed some color. Your nerves are washing you out."

Playfully, I deliver a soft punch to his shoulder. "You know what I mean."

He takes me in his arms and I thank God I stepped foot into that thrift shop on a blustery January day.

"Am I really supposed to let you go today?" Dayton lays a cheek on top of my head. "Let's run away together. We could have one of those common law marriages and be anything but common."

I know I'm supposed to laugh, but instead a tear slips down my cheek. Then a couple more. I sniff and swipe at them. Dayton pulls back and frowns. "Don't ruin your make-up."

"Please don't ruin it," Sky says, depositing the lip color we're both wearing into her small purse.

"Water-proof. Long-wearing. Whatever." I wave my hand around. "Something like that."

"Let's not test it, okay?" Dayton cups my cheeks and grins. "Time to get you out there and married, so you can start adding to an already overpopulated earth."

"Dayton!" I yell, half in surprise and half in defense of any yet-to-be created child of mine. He tips back his head and laughs. I roll my eyes. "You're insane."

"Maybe," he says, dropping his hands, only to weave his fingers through my right hand. There's a quick knock on the door, and through it comes Brody's voice. "He's waiting for you."

I take a deep breath, nerves blossoming in my stomach. They are the best kind of nerves—excited, tense, bubbly. Like my core is effervescent.

Dayton tugs my hand gently, and I follow him to the door. "Time to give you away."

My entire life I never spent any time wondering who would give me away at my wedding, and I didn't spend any time thinking about it after Noah proposed.

The three of us leave the little dressing room at Sutton House. "How do you think mom's handling things out there?" I ask Sky, biting my lip and looking out one of the large windows facing the courtyard. From this vantage point, I can't see much.

"We're going to have some awkward Christmases, though I think her new beau will soften the blow." Sky rolls her eyes. A few months ago my mom met someone online. We're uncertain, but she's all in. I think her time in the hospital and recovering forced her to take her life more seriously, and finally get over poem guy.

Noah's dad... I never would've guessed. I haven't told Noah about their journal. It's too personal to be shared.

We stop before the double doors that lead outside. Dayton pulls one open a few inches and peeks. He straightens, smiling, and lets the door fall softly back into its place.

"I didn't know it was possible." He shakes his head, eyebrows raised.

"What?"

"Soccer stud even makes a monkey suit look good. Too bad he isn't gay." Dayton sighs dramatically and throws the back of his hand against his forehead.

"Mine." I point at my chest and pretend to growl.

"Yes, I know, and I'm about to give you to him. Then he's going to take you away for a year before he takes his rightful place as the grape heir." Dayton laughs at his own joke.

"Yep," I grin, trying not to jump up and down. One year abroad. We're starting in Costa Rica and working our way through South America. From there we'll head over to Africa, and then on to Greece and up through Europe.

"Postcards," Dayton reminds me with a wagging finger. "I want things done the old-fashioned way."

"Yes, yes." I agree quickly. I point between Sky and Dayton. "You two better take good care of the studio while I'm gone."

"We will," Sky says reassuringly.

"Everything will be *fine*," Dayton says. "I have a little bit of experience running a business, you know."

"Sorry, sorry." I hold up my palms.

Two Sutton House employees come around the corner carrying our bouquets. One of them reaches for the door handles while the other extends the flowers.

I turn to Sky, touching her shoulder. "You first."

A deep breath fills her chest and her smile wavers. She steps forward, taking the smaller of the two bouquets and nodding at the employee holding the door handles. He pulls them back and Sky steps into the opening. Music starts, she casts one more glance at me, then steps from view.

Dayton takes my veil and flips it to cover my eyes. "Are you ready?"

"Yes," I say, trying not to sound impatient. Now that I'm here, I am more ready than I've ever been for anything in the history of ever.

Dayton offers me his elbow. "Let's do this."

We step into the sun pouring through the open doors. It warms my skin instantly. Beyond the guests are grape vines as far as I can see. The Sutton vineyard. Noah has spent the past year learning everything he can about the family business. When we get back from our trip abroad, he will take over and his dad will finally retire.

Pausing, I look down the aisle and find him.

*Noah.*

I'm transported back to the day I felt rough arms pull me from beneath the water's surface. I was shocked, maybe a little indignant, until I saw his face. Intent, worried, confident. How long did it take him to get me back to the edge of the lake? A minute? That's all the time it took for magic to engulf us, as if Aphrodite herself looked down and cast a spell.

I'm supposed to wait for Dayton to lead me, but I start forward. I can't wait a moment longer.

Dayton falls into step and leans into my ear. "Behave," he says in a voice so soft it's barely a whisper.

"We'll see about that," I sass back, but my eyes are on Noah.

His body looks relaxed, but his eyes are the opposite. Emotions swim through and seep out on to his face. The sun illuminates slivers of moisture on his cheeks. I reach him, and he pulls me close.

"Okay, now I think I'm drowning," I whisper.

He leans his forehead against mine. "Me too."

*The End*

*Download The Lifetime of A Second, the third and final book in The Time Series.

## THE TIME SERIES CONTINUES...

**The Lifetime of A Second**
(The Time Series Book Three)

Escape. That was my sole focus. Forget the headlines, forget the threats. Forget what happened?

Never.

I fled the big city in the desert to hide in a small town amongst the pines. My plan was to blend in, work until I had enough money, then vanish.

There's just one problem: I didn't factor in having a boss like Connor Vale.
He's quick-witted, sexy as sin, and has a heart the size of Arizona.

The longer we work together, the more difficult it is to keep him at arms length.

I know better than to return his smile. I know better than to shudder at the feel of his hand on the small of my back. And I definitely know better than to lean in when we're working close together.

Even when I know he wants me to do all those things.

Falling for him would be easy, if it weren't for one inescapable truth: for every action there is an equal and opposite reaction, and nobody around me is safe.

*Turn the page for the entire first chapter of The Lifetime of A Second…*

# THE LIFETIME OF A SECOND

CHAPTER ONE

**Brynn**

I blinked, and they're gone.

The Saguaros, I mean.

The tall, multi-limbed cactus only grow in the Sonoran Desert. I only grew in the Sonoran Desert too, until it became clear Phoenix could no longer be my home.

All I had to do was climb into a car and point it north. Such a simple ending following a catastrophic journey.

Me and the Saguaros. We've disappeared.

The vehicle I'm in does a terrible job absorbing the black tar road. The road noise rushes in, whirling around us. It doesn't even matter. The air is already thick with awkward silence. What does a little road noise hurt?

We drive on, through a wide-open swath of nothingness, and the car climbs higher. A small sigh escapes my lips at the first pine tree. In less than a mile we lose the tall, scrubby bushes and there are only pine trees, some clustering together and others spaced far apart. I feel somber at the sight of some that are barren and blackened by previous fire. It seems unfair they're left standing, bearing the marks of how they were ravaged for all to see.

At least my marks hide on the inside.

My shoulder bumps the hard plastic door as the driver changes lanes and speeds up to pass a semi-truck. He sends the massive truck a couple beeps from his horn as we go by. Under his breath, he grumbles about the left lane versus the right.

I should've known someone who spells his name Geoff would be a bad driver. The moment I saw his name I wanted to call him *Gee-off* but resisted the urge.

Leaning forward, I open my mouth and say the first words spoken to one another in two and a half hours. "It should only be twenty more minutes." Looking down, I check the map on my phone again.

I look up, catch his gaze in the rearview mirror, and immediately avert my eyes.

"I've never been asked to drive this far before," he says.

He's fishing for information. And he's going to come up empty. The phrase 'Life or death' used to be said by my dad when I complained and he wanted me to see how inconsequential my complaint was. But this is not like that.

This is actually a matter of life or death.

And to make this all work, I have to trust a stranger who drives too fast and wants to know why he's taking me to a small town in the woods.

If he recognizes me, I'm screwed.

I pull the ball cap lower onto my forehead. Without thinking, I reach for my long hair, being held back in a ponytail. My fingers keep reaching, curling against the cloth interior of the seat instead of my hair.

I've done that so many times since I chopped off my

long, blonde hair two days ago. I wonder when that will end? The hair is gone.

Another sacrifice.

Or, perhaps, a penance.

If giving up my hair could atone for what I've done, I'd be bald in a heartbeat.

Nothing can change what happened.

The judicial system decided I wasn't guilty, but in my heart?

Guilty.

Guilty.

Guilty.

We're almost there.

"Number forty-seven," I tell the driver. He crawls down the street at the same time I'm filled with an overwhelming urge to arrive. *So now you go slow?*

My nails dig into my palms as I will myself to calm down. To distract me, I study the homes we pass. They are small, squat, and each one has a chimney. The front yards are tidy, some of them have flowers rising from terra-cotta pots. I lean in, focusing on the house on the corner. The tip of my nose pokes the window. The house is nondescript, no flowers or bushes in sight and the door is black. Shiny, midnight black.

That door screams its message loud and clear: *Stay away.*

I want that door.

Too bad my rental agreement won't allow me to paint. Or install an alarm system.

"Here you are," Geoff says, slowing to a stop.

By the time he makes his way to the rear of the car, I've pulled out my two bags and placed them on the ground.

This is the first time I've seen him standing. He never got out when he pulled up to pick me up from the gas station I gave him the address for.

Geoff's left leg is missing. In its place is a metal rod. Now I feel like an ass for disliking his name.

"Accident when I was a kid," he says, pointing down. He shrugs. "Sometimes I forget it even happened."

I nod because I don't know what to say and I still feel awful. I was a terrible companion for that long car ride. But that's the thing about disappearing. It comes with stipulations. Starting with: Don't be memorable. I can't tell a funny story or have a meaningful conversation. I can't be a vibrant color in someone's memory. No magenta, or teal. I am beige. Endless, insignificant beige.

I used to be the brightest shade of yellow. Happy, outgoing, ebullient.

One second of time turned me into a neutral shade.

And it will be my color forever.

I've come to accept that. It's one of the reasons I decided to run. Well, that and the other thing. The thing that will always have me looking over my shoulder.

"Good luck, Ms.—"

"Brynn," I say quickly, not wanting Geoff to say my last name again, in case one more passage of it through his lips prompts it to stay in his mind longer than necessary.

Already I regret not using a fake name. My middle name seemed like enough of a deviation, but I'm not so sure now. Last week, this was all just an idea in my head. I received his most recent hate mail, and after I placed it alongside his other letters, thought *You should skip town.* From that one tiny thought came big choices. I began searching for places to rent in northern Arizona, and when I found a place ready for immediate move-in, I snapped it up. Ginger, the owner of the eleven hundred square foot cabin, was chasing her dream of backpacking through Europe and would be gone for six months.

Perfect, I told her. What I didn't tell her was that I'll be long gone by the time she comes home. Three months of wages is all I need. Just enough to pad what my parents will give me when their season is finished. I arranged a property manager for my place, packed my bags, gathered all my important documents, and Elizabeth Brynn Montgomery dropped the Elizabeth. I did not pass Go, I did not collect two hundred dollars.

I ordered a car and had it pick me up two blocks from my condo.

Now that car is driving away.

And I'm here in Brighton. A town dwarfed by sprawling, sunny Phoenix. Standing on the sidewalk and staring at the small home in front of me.

The yard is neat, the grass a deep green and trimmed.

Three stairs connect the front walkway to the porch, and each step is buffered by a small pot of geraniums. On either side of the front door hang two rustic lights that resemble lanterns.

"Here we go," I mutter, and *bump bump bump* my rolling suitcase along the cracks in the short driveway. Ginger said the house key would be under a pot of flowers. I lift one after the other until on my fourth try I find one gold key on a silver key ring.

The inside of the home looks much like the outside. Tidy, modest, and sparsely decorated. Ginger must have a thing for apples. The curtains are blue and white gingham with red apples lining the bottom and top. A large, framed picture of apples hangs on the wall in the living room. Fake apples are piled in a basket on top of the fridge.

It takes only a few minutes to walk through the place. In the hallway, I find a locked closet and realize Ginger must've put some personal items in there. There are no photographs in the place, no books, or anything that tells me anything about Ginger as a person. They all must be in that closet, and it strikes me as sad that these things can mean enough to take up space in our homes but can so easily be locked away. Is that the way it is for everything? Are things only as important as we make them?

The thought depresses me, but the feeling isn't new.

I won't take those pills the therapist gave me. At the request of my parents, I went to see someone. She kept calling what happened *the accident*. But it wasn't an accident. The therapist said she understood that, but for my sake, they would call it an accident because from my standpoint it was one.

I rub my eyes, an attempt at banishing the thoughts. Thinking them won't help anything. What's done is done. And it can never be undone.

Instead, I search the place. Open every cabinet, sift through every drawer, until I'm certain I know every inch. After that, I dump my suitcase on the bed and put everything in its proper place. The master bedroom is large, Ginger said, because she'd knocked out the wall between the two bedrooms. "When you're single, one large is better than two small," she'd said, then asked me if I was single.

I answered her quickly, saying, "Yes, and I plan to keep it that way."

Besides, nobody will want me now.

Not after what I've done.

\*\*\*

I don't remember falling asleep. Or what woke me up.

I roll over, place a hand over my eyes, and take a deep breath. I know what I will see when I open my eyes, but I'm not ready to see it. The unfamiliar walls, the furniture that isn't mine.

*Tap, tap, tap tap tap.* I sit up, my heart banging in my chest. Instinctively I know it's not him. He wouldn't knock.

I stand, glance in the mirror above the dresser, and swipe my fingers under my eyes. The mascara streaks don't budge.

A second knock drifts to me, this one soft and out of cadence. Turning away from my reflection, I hurry to the door and peer through the peephole.

*A woman.*

My lips twist, thoughts rushing through my head. Meeting people is unavoidable, but so soon? I planned to hide out as long as possible, living off the protein bars I brought until I was ready to venture out. Grocery shopping and finding a job have to happen soon, but I wanted a couple days to hole up and absorb what I've left behind.

I gulp in a breath of air and open the door.

The young woman smiles. She lifts a hand, waving. "Hi. I'm Cassidy Anders. I live next door." She points to my left. Looking down, she says, "This is Brooklyn."

*A child.* I hadn't noticed a child. She stands only three feet tall, her head barely reaching her mother's mid-thigh. Gripping the door handle, I try not to slam the door closed. I want to be away from these people.

My therapist taught me what to do in these situations when panic grips me and I feel like my world has tilted off its axis. Breathe in *one, two, three, four* and out *one, two, three, four.*

"Are you okay?" Cassidy asks, eyes squinting with concern.

"Yes," I bark, wincing at the harshness in my voice.

Brooklyn hides behind her mother's leg, and shame fills me. Like the depressed feeling from earlier, shame is not new to me either.

"Yeah, okay. Well, I, uh…" Cassidy holds out a silver tin with a clear plastic lid.

I don't want what she's offering, but my hands reach for it anyway, a reflexive response.

I look down at what is in my hands, then back up to the woman. She is young, very young, maybe my age. She has smile lines that I don't have. A swipe of flour dusts her forearm.

"You made me a pie?" The astonishment in my voice is embarrassing. Baking a pie is not a new concept. Someone being kind to me? That hasn't happened in a while.

Innocent until proven guilty are words we use to remind us not to judge too quickly. But let's be honest. It's really guilty until proven innocent, and even then, the guilt leaves behind traces, like smudges of ash following a fire or particulates floating in the atmosphere after an explosion. The slate is never fully wiped clean.

"You're our new neighbor, right?" Cassidy offers a friendly smile, but I can't seem to reciprocate.

"Uh-huh."

"And your name is?" She cocks her head to the side, her eyes tentative. Her smile has faltered. Maybe she has that sixth sense that mothers develop. My own mother claimed to have one.

"Brynn," I answer finally, balancing the pie in the crook of my left arm and offering her my right hand.

She seems relieved by this customary display of

normalcy. We had a rocky start, but perhaps I've passed her test after all.

"Mommy, can I go play now?" Brooklyn's little voice floats up from her hiding spot behind Cassidy. Her head is stuck out and she looks up at her mother, eyes big and wide, waiting.

"Sure, sweetie, but not for too long. Taylor will be here soon."

Brooklyn yells with excitement and jumps down each stair, landing on each step with two feet and a solid *thud*. When she hits the grass, she bolts for her own front yard.

Cassidy turns back to me. "She loves her babysitter. I, on the other hand, do not like needing a babysitter."

"Oh," I say. I could make conversation. Ask Cassidy why she needs the babysitter. Ask her about Brooklyn. *How old is she? Is she in school? What's her favorite color?* Hell, I could even ask Cassidy what flavor the flipping pie is.

But, no.

I'm not in Brighton to make friends.

I'm here to blend in, make money, and run.

*Go here to Download The Lifetime of A Second*

# ALSO BY JENNIFER MILLIKIN

## Hayden Family Series

The Patriot

The Maverick

The Outlaw

The Calamity

## Standalone

Return To You

One Good Thing

Beyond The Pale

Good On Paper

The Day He Went Away

Full of Fire

## The Time Series

Our Finest Hour

Magic Minutes

The Lifetime of A Second

Visit Jennifer at jennifermillikinwrites.com to join her mailing list and receive Full of Fury: A Full of Fire novella, for free. She is @jenmillwrites on all social platforms and would love to connect.

# ACKNOWLEDGMENTS

Writing a novel is a one-man show, but getting it from my brain and into readers' hearts takes a team.

A hundred thank you's to Julia, the very first person to read this book and set me straight on Northern California weather. Without you it might be snowing in wine country.

My BFF Kristan. You called me at night when you finished reading to tell me you needed Noah and Ember to fight harder for their love. A friend who will tell you what you want to hear? That's easy to find. A friend who will tell you the truth because she wants to make you better? Priceless.

Murphy Rae at Indie Solutions, thank you for making my beautiful, eye-catching covers. Before someone reads my blurb or my words, they see your cover. It's possible your job is the most important one.

# ABOUT THE AUTHOR

Jennifer Millikin is a best-selling author of contemporary romance and women's fiction. She lives in the Arizona desert with her husband, two children, and Liberty, her Lab who thinks she's human. Jennifer loves to cook, practice yoga, and believes chips and salsa should be a food group.

facebook.com/JenniferMillikinwrites

instagram.com/jenmillwrites

bookbub.com/profile/jennifer-millikin

Printed in Great Britain
by Amazon